Y0-CBH-669

Temptation's Warrior

Temptation's Warrior

Gabriella Anderson

Five Star • Waterville, Maine

This novel is a work of fiction. Names, characters, places and incidents are either the product of the author's imagination, or, if real, used fictitiously.

First Edition
First Printing: November 2005

Published in 2005 in conjunction with Tekno Books.

Set in 11 pt. Plantin by Liana M. Walker.

Printed in the United States on permanent paper.

Library of Congress Cataloging-in-Publication Data

Anderson, Gabriella.
Temptation's warrior / by Gabriella Anderson.—1st ed.
p. cm.
ISBN 1-59414-418-4 (hc : alk. paper)
1. Knights and knighthood—Fiction. 2. Mistaken identity—Fiction. 3. Abduction—Fiction. 4. Revenge—Fiction. 5. England—Fiction. I. Title.
PS3601.N54345T46 2005
813′.6—dc22 2005019068

Anyu,

Még akkor is ha nincs fantáziád, ezt neked ajánlom. I love you. Thanks for the cooking, the cleaning, the laundry, the sleepless nights while I was at boarding school, making me check in with you whenever I went and still go on vacation, regaling me with the stories of *Apu* and your adventures escaping from Hungary, teaching me a love of language and languages, and above all showing me what a great mother does. Even your son-in-law loves you (and truly likes you, too).

Prologue

Lincolnshire, 1347

No moon helped light the woods. The forest was dark at best, but on a moonless night such as tonight, shadow blended into shadow until the world seemed shrouded in a black cloak.

"Sally, yer getting fanciful in yer old age." The old woman cackled, but kept her gaze on the small oil lamp that glowed like a beacon in the darkness.

A few more minutes and she'd go home. An owl hooted in the trees, and Sally's gaze searched for the bird even knowing she'd never see it in the inkiness.

She looked back at the small flame and started. A figure bedecked in black sat on a horse just inside the weak circle of light. "Heavens, sir, ye frightened me."

The knight nodded his head once, but didn't speak.

"Sneaking up on a person like that, me hearin' so poor and all. And dressed in black. A body would think ye were Satan himself, if ye weren't such an angel."

Sally chuckled and held up the lamp. She leaned heavily on the gnarled stick in her other hand and peered into the eyeholes cut in the woolen cloth that covered the knight's face. "I keep thinking one of these nights ye'll appear without the mask, so I can see yer face." She held the light higher. "I can't even make out the color of yer eyes."

The mask fluttered ever so slightly, as if the knight had laughed under his breath. He shook his head.

"Ye keep yer secret then. Perhaps if ye feel guilty enough about keeping me out of me bed these past four nights . . ."

Shrugging his shoulders, the knight spread his hands open in a gesture of apology.

Sally cackled. "Didn't expect it to work, but ye can't blame me for trying. And I don't mind the wait. I need little sleep anymore. But sometimes I wish ye'd have picked a better spot to meet than the woods at night."

The horseman raised his hand, but Sally interrupted. "Nay, ye've been kind to us. I was but making a jest. What do ye have tonight?"

Removing a knife from its sheath at his waist, the knight sliced through the ropes on either side of the saddle. Two loud thumps followed. The mare lifted her head and pricked up her ears, but didn't move.

Sally placed the lamp on a stump and limped to the first bundle. Despite her dependence on the walking stick, she dragged the sack away from the horse with surprising agility. She peered into the coarse bag. "A ham. Bless you, sir."

She left the sack where it lay and waddled to the other, larger bundle. She pulled this one with greater effort and peered inside. "Venison," she panted. "I'll get me sons to fetch these. The villagers shall enjoy them."

The figure in black reached to his waist and removed a small pouch. This he handed to Sally. The jangle of coins brought a grin to her face.

"Ye always know how to help us best." She opened the small bag. "There should be enough here for taxes and more besides."

Stirring in the saddle, the knight clasped his hands over his elbows and rocked his arms.

"A baby? Ah, yes, ye're asking about Mary's baby."

He nodded in response.

" 'Twere born dead. The babe never drew a breath. But Mary's a fine strong woman. She'll have others."

The knight's shoulders drooped as if the weight of her answer pressed them down. His hand fumbled in his tunic and tugged. He gazed at his fist, then handed an object to Sally.

Black silk strings hung from the end of a wooden cross. Ivory and onyx decorated the simple object. Sally gazed at the gift. "For Mary?"

Another nod.

"She'll be sending her thanks, I'm sure."

The flame flickered, then grew steady again. "I suppose I should be getting back to me bed now." Sally straightened herself with a groan. "These old bones complain more often these days. Shall I come again in two weeks?"

Lifting his gloved hand, the knight raised three fingers.

"Three weeks then. I suppose there is a lot of doin's at the castle, what with the wedding."

Sally tucked the pouch into her waist and turned to memorize the location of the meat. She would wake her sons right away, before the wolves could get at the sacks. She looked up again. The knight had melted back into the blackness.

"God bless you, Black Knight," whispered Sally.

Chapter One

The tread of his foot was no louder than a whisper of wind against a cheek. Nevertheless, Payne glanced around. Except for the odd servant performing his mysterious errand of the night, the castle slept. Payne scratched his neck as he looked up in disgust. This task didn't sit well with him. Neither did the coarse wool he wore, but if anyone encountered him, his simple tunic and hose bore out his story of being a servant. Even if the wretched clothes itched.

With every step, Payne climbed higher into the keep. The full moon was a blessing. Enough light shone through the narrow windows that he didn't have to struggle with a lamp. The tapestry he carried proved awkward enough.

Past the third door, fourth—here was the fifth. Payne paused for a moment. He wished he had a swig of ale to remove the taste of loathing from his mouth. To think he wasted his abilities on an errand such as this. The promise of Coxesbury's gold had enticed him, but Payne wondered if the money was worth this dishonor.

The sooner he had enough money, the sooner he could refuse to peddle his services.

He inched the door open, his ears straining to catch any squeak. When the gap was wide enough, he slipped inside, then closed the door. His gaze surveyed the room. And stopped in disbelief on the bed.

Two bodies? There were two people in this bed. Satan's teeth. Payne swallowed the groan of irritation that rose in his throat. He should have known. Guests filled the castle for the wedding. Every free spot now housed a pallet and a sleeping body. He should have realized the bride would share her bed with a relative. At least no servant occupied the room.

Two bodies didn't change his plan. He placed the tapestry on the floor and rolled it open. From a pouch at his side, he pulled out a wad of wool and three cloth strips of varying lengths. These he placed on a table by the bed. Now he was ready. He faced the bed.

Holding his breath, he reached over and glided the covers down from the sleeping figures.

Although the night was warm, the two sleeping women stirred as the air hit their skin. Payne watched, ready to spring if one awoke. Thankfully, neither did. His glance shot from one to the other. Which one did he take?

One woman lay with her arm flung over her head. A loose plait draped along her side like a silver snake. Her thin lips were open and she emitted a soft snore with every breath. Her cheek rested on her other hand. She was comely enough, Payne supposed.

Then he turned his gaze to the other woman.

Payne's stomach tightened at the sight of her. His own breath came harder, and for a moment, he forgot his purpose for being in the chamber.

She slept with one knee crooked, which lifted her night-dress almost to her hips. The slender limb that extended from the hem reached the end of the bed. Her hair, unbound, rioted around her in sleep's fury. The moonlight glistened off its burnished gold lengths. His hand ached to bury itself in the thick tresses. Her lips parted as she stretched in her sleep. A sigh filled his ears with its melody. What did she dream, he wondered.

His hand was halfway to her hair before he shook himself from his reverie. What had come over him? One woman was much like another. He had neither the time nor the inclination for an entanglement. If he continued to save his money, he would have time for a woman in a few years, but now he had business to take care of.

What had Coxesbury said? Lady Agnes was pretty. Both these women were pretty, even if his own tastes preferred the one with the unbound hair.

Forget her, Payne. Remember your task.

What else had the Baron said? She was tall with golden hair. Payne felt his stomach turn. It was she. Regret twisted in his gut as he recalled the distasteful task still ahead of him.

Maybe Coxesbury spoke of the other woman. Hoping against hope, Payne examined the two women again.

Tall, golden hair, comely. Damn. The other woman was pretty, but her hair was more silver than gold. Perhaps he could blame the color on the moonlight, but he couldn't explain away her height. No, he knew which one he had to take.

Before he could change his mind, Payne clamped his hand over her mouth. Her eyes flew open—bright green eyes, glittering with fright.

"Forgive me, my lady," Payne whispered by her ear. "I mean you no harm, but I'm afraid you won't make it to your wedding."

He shifted his position so that he pinned her body between his free arm and his hips. She was strong enough to put up a fight, yet strangely she didn't. But the fear in her eyes didn't disappear. "Lady Agnes, I will release you if you promise not to cause a stir."

She nodded.

As soon as he lifted his hand, she opened her mouth. Just as he thought she might. *Clever girl.* He grabbed the wad of wool and stuffed it between her lips. The fear disappeared, replaced by fury. He trapped her arms by her side.

"Again, I apologize, but if you wake your companion, I shall silence her as well. Surely you don't wish me to hurt her."

Her shoulders drooped in defeat. She shook her head.

"I thought not. If you cooperate, your discomfort will be minimal, and no one need suffer from your actions. I'm afraid I shall have to tie your arms and legs now, but only until we are out of the castle."

She glared at him and spit the wool out of her mouth.

Holding both her hands in one of his, he poked the wool back. "I must curb your desire to speak. We can't have you scream an alert."

He reached for a length of cloth. Wrapping the strip over her mouth, he secured the wool in place. A second length bound her arms in front of her. The third he wrapped around her ankles.

"Your companion is a sound sleeper. Someday you will tell her how lucky she was."

He lifted her from the bed. For all her height, she was surprisingly light. And she fit into the curve of his arms as if they existed solely for her use. Her gaze met his, stealing his breath.

She was not his. She was not his.

Of course, she was not his. He had no desire for any woman to be his. He had more important concerns.

Payne placed her on the tapestry a little harder than he had planned. She gave out a muffled grunt.

"Forgive me."

She sat on the woven material and glared at him.

He almost laughed at her expression. "I suppose forgiveness is a bit much to ask for, but I assure you your comfort means much to me. Now if you would lie back . . ."

Fear returned to those green eyes.

"Nay. I just wish to roll you up in this tapestry. It's how I'll get you out of here."

Shaking her head, she began to squirm.

"You don't wish to rouse your companion, now do you, Lady Agnes?"

She stilled at once. Throwing him a last hate-filled look, she laid back.

"Thank you." Payne tucked up the edges around her and rolled her into the fabric.

Hoisting her onto his shoulder, he stood. With no reason to delay any longer, he stole out the door and descended the circular stairs.

The bundle on his shoulder began to stir. "Hold still, Lady Agnes. You wouldn't want me to fall down these steps." He was in no danger of falling, but she didn't have to know.

Her head hung in front, her legs in back. Even if she was able to move in the tapestry, his arms pinned her to him. Now all he had to do was get her to—

"What are you doing there, man?"

A guard stepped up to him. The man was big, but Payne was bigger. Payne could overpower him, but he had already planned for just such an occurrence. He tightened his grip on the roll.

"The lord wants this tapestry in the hall for the wedding." Payne bowed his head as befitting a servant.

"I knew nothing of this."

"You can wake the lord and ask him." Payne saw the uncertainty in the man's eyes.

"Nay. You'd best finish your work. But be quiet. The house teems with guests, and you don't want to disturb them."

"Oh, no, sir, thank you, sir." The subservient tone tasted bitter on Payne's tongue, but better this play-acting than raising alarm.

"Move along." The guard waved his hand.

Payne continued through the castle. The hordes of guests occupied nearly every clear spot on the floor. Pallet after pallet lined the wooden boards. An odor of warm bodies permeated his nostrils. Careful not to step on anyone, Payne picked his way through the sleepers. Those who stirred would think nothing of a servant carrying a large bundle. Until later. For an instant, a smile lit upon Payne's lips. He was disappointing many people by stealing the bride. The wedding they had come for would not take place.

The cool air of the night stroked his face as he stepped outside. Although his burden was not particularly heavy, his excursion had warmed him, and he welcomed the relief. He had but one more obstacle to overcome. A change of story, planned in advance, should suffice.

He walked through the courtyard toward the portcullis. Here would be the real test of his abilities.

"Here, now. What are you doing about in the middle of the night?" Arms crossed, the sentry stepped forward to block Payne.

" 'Tis nearly dawn, sir."

"Aye, that it is." The sentry looked at him, his gloved fingers rapping out his impatience against the mail on his own forearm.

"The lord promised the abbey a gift of this tapestry, and

amidst the preparations, he forgot to send it. He bade me do so before the wedding. If I don't leave now, I shan't get back in time."

"True enough. You may pass." The sentry opened the gate. "Be wary of thieves, although a man of your size should hardly have trouble."

"Thank you, sir."

Payne stepped across the footbridge, leaving the castle behind.

As soon as he was sure the castle gate was out of sight, he turned off the road and plunged into the darkness of the woods. "Don't fear, Lady Agnes. We have but a little ways to go."

He tapped her back through the tapestry. Her muffled response brought a laugh to his lips, but as he opened his mouth, a twig at just the right height filled his mouth with leaves. He spat out the foliage.

He kept a straight path for a mile, avoiding the occasional tree and bush, then turned north. Another mile, and he saw the faint glow of a light. He smiled. His keen sense of direction had served him well yet again.

The sky turned a deep lavender, heralding the approaching dawn. Payne hurried to cover this last distance. As he leapt over fallen tress and exposed roots, he heard the stifled grunts of his captive. Branches covered the way, but he pushed through them as if they were cobwebs until he reached the small clearing.

"Douse the light, Nigel. I have returned."

A small man stretched his arm overhead as he squinted up at Payne. His eyelids were heavy with sleep, but he rolled over on his pallet and threw sand over the small fire. "You have her then?" he croaked.

"Aye." Payne patted the roll.

"She won't be happy when you release her." Nigel slipped his tunic over his shirt.

"I don't expect she will be. Make some room. Let's get her out."

Nigel rolled up his pallet and stashed it into the back of a small wooden cart. He kicked some larger stones out of the way, before he turned back to Payne. "Do you think you want to put your own clothes back on before you let her see you? You're not very impressive in that coarse wool."

Payne arched an eyebrow. "You don't think this suits me?"

"They make you look like the village ox."

"In deference to your age, I'll let that remark pass."

"Don't let this touch of gray fool you, boy. I have more than one trick that will still surprise you. Do you change your clothes, or no?"

"She's already seen me such as I am." The tapestry squirmed on his shoulder. "Besides, I think she is anxious to come out of her confinement."

Payne knelt to lower the bundle to the ground. Nigel stood back as Payne unveiled the weaving. With a final flip of the cloth, she was free. Of the tapestry at least.

For a moment, the woman lay there, blinking into the semi-darkness. Her nightdress had twisted around her, exposing the long slim legs once again to his gaze. Her hair had wrapped around her neck and face. She shook her head to free herself of it, and Payne found himself staring once again into those sparkling green eyes.

He knelt beside her and removed a knife from his boot. Her eyes flashed wide for an instant, but relaxed as he bent to cut the binding from her ankles and wrists. She sat up and rubbed the skin where the cloth had chafed her.

"I'm going to free your mouth next, Lady Agnes. Even if

you scream, no one will hear you. We are far from the village and the castle. Screaming will serve no purpose now but to irritate. I have no desire to bind your mouth again, but I will if I have to."

She nodded.

He slid the knife under the strip, and with a quick slash, he freed her mouth. She spit out the wad of wool and stretched out her tongue as if in distaste. Payne couldn't help but notice how pink it was. Even though she contorted her mouth, stretching it as though she wanted to remove the feel of the gag, he still felt the urge to taste those full lips.

"I trust you are not hurt, milady." Nigel stepped to her with a gown in his hands. "Lord Gilbert Fitzhugh, Baron Coxesbury, sends these clothes with his wish for your forgiveness." Nigel bowed and offered the gown to her.

She stared at the short man, then back at Payne.

Payne shrugged. "Coxesbury knew you would need clothes."

"Aye, milady. He wishes you no further discomfort than that which you have already suffered. And when we arrive at Pellingham, you'll see he is well prepared for your stay."

"But I can't go to Pellingham."

Her voice, soft and husky, resonated through Payne with the warmth of good mead. He shook off the thought. "Your pardon, Lady Agnes, but you do not have a choice. Coxesbury hired me to deliver you to his castle where he will wed you."

"Yes, I understand that, but you see . . ." She paused and looked Payne straight in the eyes. "I am not she."

Chapter Two

"What?"

Lady Elfreda of Renfrey looked at the man called Nigel. Her mouth was dry, her wrists throbbed, and her feet still tingled from being bound, but, with some satisfaction, she watched the older man's frustration. He ran his hand through his gray hair as if he looked ready to rip it out. Nigel's uneasiness was well deserved.

"Don't worry, Nigel. Of course she's Lady Agnes."

"I'm not." Elfreda met the giant's angry gaze with a calm she didn't feel. He was formidable, this one. And huge. The simple peasant's garb didn't hide the broad shoulders or the expanse of chest. No wonder her journey had felt as if she traveled on rocks. Solid. That was the word she'd use for him—solid.

But even more daunting was the glow of his golden eyes. Black hair framed his face, but those eyes . . . the hazy light of the advancing day was enough to show her how they hardened in anger at her response.

Nigel bunched the gown in his tightened fists. "Did you bring the wrong woman?"

"Think a moment, Nigel. Coxesbury said she was tall, pretty, with golden hair. Yes, there were two in the bed, but look at her."

Tall. Elfreda cringed inwardly. Her height had always been her bane. She had towered over so many of her suitors, her uncle finally declared she should join a convent, and she had agreed. She would make an imposing nun. And she would never have to suffer from the foolish pride of men again.

"Yes, but—"

"If you were Lady Agnes, wouldn't you lie?"

The shorter man examined her, then released a deep breath. "You're right, of course. Good thing Coxesbury described her to you."

Elfreda threw her hands in the air. "Fine. Don't believe me."

The big man gave her a controlled grin. "Baron Coxesbury also said was that Lady Agnes was very clever." He took the clothes from Nigel. "Now if you would kindly get dressed . . ." He shoved the clothes at her.

"Where?" Elfreda crossed her arms.

"Behind the cart."

"But—"

"Lady Agnes, we have the luxury of neither time nor space. Either you take these garments and slip behind the cart to dress, or I will do it for you."

Elfreda glared at the man and knew his threat wasn't in jest. Giving a grunt of disgust, she snatched the clothes from him and stepped behind the small wagon. She glanced at the sky. The lavender tint of the pre-dawn would soon give way to full light. Darkness would no longer hide her. Unfastening the tie at her neck, she let her nightdress slip to the forest floor. She grabbed the chemise and yanked it over her head.

There. That brute couldn't have seen more than a bit of shoulder.

She pulled on the undergown. The garment was soft and settled over her like a breeze. The overgown was dark green embroidered with gold. Clearly Baron Coxesbury was trying to meliorate her anger with the quality of clothing. Elfreda shook her head. As she put it on, she noticed the gown hung short, but fit her as if the tailor knew her every measurement. So much for trying to convince the brute she wasn't Lady Agnes.

At least her cousin Agnes could marry in peace, while she dealt with Baron Coxesbury. Ugh, what a thought. Still, the idea calmed her. She enjoyed the concept of foiling the Baron's plans, and soon she would find an opportunity to escape back to the castle and warn her uncle of the Baron's perfidy.

After tightening the laces, she stepped out from behind the cart. "I'm ready." She looked at the big man. His face was set as if chiseled from stone.

Elfreda pressed her fists against her hips. "Don't you think this journey might pass faster if you tried to be friendlier?"

The big man scowled at her. She could imagine the sternness of that face would scare a lot of men. Then again, she wasn't a man.

"I don't even know your name." Elfreda gazed at him without flinching.

The scowl disappeared as surprise flitted across his features. Elfreda nearly flinched then. That deep golden gaze touched her, warming her skin. She didn't enjoy the sensation. "You know, you look almost human when you're not frowning," she said.

He threw his head back and laughed. "You are a brave one, Lady Agnes. Many a man wouldn't dare talk to me as you do." He gave her a short bow. "I am Payne Dunbyer of Castlereigh."

Her eyes widened. "Payne, the Bear?"

"Golden Bear, if you will. I can't imagine where I got such a ridiculous appellative."

"Hmph. I can," muttered Nigel.

"Now, my lady, you will wait with Nigel while I get out of these itchy things." Without a backward glance, Payne grabbed a bundle from the cart and stepped into the trees.

Elfreda marveled that the trees hid the great man with such ease. "He's not a man of wasted action, is he?"

"I wouldn't know, milady," Nigel mumbled as he packed the cart.

"Yes, you would. In fact, I wager you know a lot more than you're willing to tell me. Why is he called 'the Golden Bear'?"

"It's his eyes, milady. The 'Bear' is easy to understand, especially after you see him in his accustomed garb, but his eyes . . . his opponents swear they flash at them, blinding them in battle."

"I can believe that," she muttered to herself. Straightening her shoulders, she faced the smaller man. "I'm telling the truth when I say I am not Lady Agnes. Lady Agnes is my cousin. I am Lady Elfreda. My friends call me Elf."

Nigel gazed up at her with a crooked grin. "Elf. Aye, that's a proper name for a woman of your size. No, Lady Agnes. You won't get me to turn against him. If he believes you're Lady Agnes, then you are. He's not known for making mistakes."

He did this time. Frustration roiled in her.

"Here, milady. The Baron sent you this girdle as well."

"Thank you." Elfreda took the bejeweled belt and examined it. The Baron had spared no expense to impress Lady Agnes. Jewels glittered in the growing light, and the fine silver links tinkled as she lifted it. Elf however noticed only how heavy and cold the girdle appeared. She fastened it around her waist, letting the chain rest on her hips.

"Good, you're ready."

Elf jumped at the words. She whirled to face Payne and froze. Gone was the simple peasant garb. He stood dressed in a black leather tunic. His hose, black as well, disappeared into high black boots. A wide belt girded his torso. The only other color was the white of his shirt, which gleamed in a great "V" at the neck of his tunic.

Elf remembered to breathe. She wanted to believe his appearance had frightened her, that the expanse of black startled her, but she couldn't delude herself. Golden eyes peered out from that sharp visage. The cap that covered his head had vanished, leaving his thick, black hair to tumble to his shoulders. A thin scar ran down his left cheek from the corner of his eye nearly to his mouth. She thought it gave him an air of danger—as if he needed more of that.

How silly was she? His appearance hadn't changed that much. What was wrong with her? Elf turned away from him.

Payne stuffed the peasant garb into the cart. "Remind me to give these to some deserving soul."

"Ha. As if they would fit anyone else." Nigel tied a rope over the cart to hold the belongings.

"We are later than I hoped. The sun has already greeted the sky," said Payne.

Elf glanced at the cart. "I have no desire to be bounced on the road in that thing."

"You won't. You'll ride."

Three horses stood hobbled not a hundred feet away. Nigel was bringing the stoutest one forward. Elf let out a puff of air in disgust. She hadn't noticed the animals. The Golden Bear had blinded her as well.

Nigel made short work of hitching the horse to the cart. He climbed onto the narrow plank that served as a seat, while Payne led her to the other two horses.

She eyed the two palfreys. "I'd have thought you'd ride a destrier."

Payne lifted her onto the leather and wooden saddle with little effort and cocked his eyebrow. "I do, but only in battle. I wouldn't waste Caesar's talents on this errand. Merlin is more than equal to this task." He rubbed the star on the brown horse's nose. The horse nudged him back.

"Merlin? Can he perform magic?"

"Let's just say he's a clever animal." Payne moved to the other mount.

Elf waited until his foot was in the stirrup, then she kicked the side of her horse. Payne couldn't know she was an accomplished horsewoman. She would disappear before he or Nigel could stop her. She held the reins as Merlin sprang forward.

A shrill whistle pierced the glade. Merlin stopped short, jerking her for an instant into the air. She landed in the saddle with a thump that knocked the breath out of her. A less skilled rider would have landed on the ground. Payne rode up beside her. His eyes shone in merriment as she righted herself.

"As I said, Merlin is a clever animal."

She glared at him and opened her mouth to retort, but Payne turned his mount and rode to Nigel. Payne ignored her. She stared after him, dumbfounded. Heat rushed into her cheeks.

"Are you ready?" said Payne to Nigel.

"Aye, lad. The sooner we finish this task, the happier I'll be."

"I, too, old friend."

As the trio started off, Elf enjoyed the anger that roiled within her. Confident they wouldn't harm her, she gave the

Bear a look of haughty disdain as her horse fell in line. He ignored her this time as well.

Elf let out a sigh. If traveling with this brute and his henchman assured Agnes a peaceful ceremony, she would do it. Not that it would matter. Her cousin would probably be upset that Elf had managed to outdo the bride on her wedding day. If they noticed she had disappeared at all.

The morning passed with excruciating slowness. No one spoke during the journey. Elf thought she had ignored Payne with admirable success, until she noticed he had little interest in speaking to her either. After that she sulked. Pausing for a brief meal at noontime, they continued the journey in silence through the afternoon. By evening Elf was ready to scream, if only to relieve the quiet. Furthermore, her rump hurt.

"Here." Payne's sudden shout startled her.

The sun shone red in the sky as she looked around. They had stopped in a small clearing not too far from the road, but far enough to avoid unwanted attention. Nigel jumped from his perch and unhitched the cart. Elf waited until Payne dismounted and tied up his horse. She would have liked to escape, but knew he would just stop her. Or rather her horse.

Payne stepped up to her. Without asking, he spanned her waist with his hands and lifted her off Merlin. Her eyes widened. He lifted her as if she weighed no more than a feather. Her gaze flew to his face. She had never felt small or dainty in her life, yet beside this bear of a man, she *was* small and dainty.

His hands released her, but his fingers lingered, drawing a line around her waist that embraced her like a belt. Their warmth lingered on her waist. Confusion reigned within her. She should hate this man.

He turned from her, and she found herself watching his retreat. Heat rushed into her cheeks as she spun away in mortification. She had been staring at him. Her gaze met that of Nigel, and the discomfort grew. Nigel had seen her fascination with Payne. The older man's grin relayed his amusement. She wanted to crawl under a rock.

Why was she thinking of a man anyway? She was entering a convent soon. Her uncle had promised. As soon as Agnes was married, Elf could enter the abbey. She didn't have to look at any man ever again.

"Nigel, get the tent. I'll see to the horses." Payne led Merlin away to the other two mounts and hobbled him near some grass. Nigel grabbed a large bundle from the cart and threw it onto the ground with a loud thud.

Elf glanced around. The two men paid her no heed. Here was her opportunity to flee. She took a cautious step backward, then turned. Two more steps. No shout or attempt to stop her followed. Another step. A rush of exhilaration flowed through her blood.

Then she stopped short.

Where would running get her? She could find the road again, but to what end? Night would soon cloak the land and shield all manner of thieves, robbers, or worse. A lone woman upon the road at night begged for trouble. Better to stay with the Bear. Tomorrow, when Baron Coxesbury saw the error, he would send her home. Elf returned from her short flight of freedom.

"I see you've realized you've nowhere to go." Payne's voice rang with humor.

Elf tossed back her head. "I am no fool. Besides, I've decided I want to enjoy the look on the Baron's face when he discovers your mistake."

"Don't start again, Lady Agnes." Payne shook his head. "Your tent is almost ready and we'll have our supper soon enough. Tomorrow should see you safely at Pellingham."

He unhooked a bow and quiver from his saddle. "Watch her, Nigel. I'll be back with our food in a bit." He stepped through the trees, sending a slight ripple through the bushes he grazed.

Elf marveled again at the ease with which the great man slipped into the woods and disappeared.

Tying up the last rope to a tree, Nigel stepped away from the small tent. "Best get a fire going. There should be plenty of wood here." He bent to pick up a piece about the thickness of his arm.

"You might want to wait to see if he returns with anything. No use doing all that work for nothing."

Nigel eyed her with a look of patience. "You don't know Payne. He'll bring us food, never you fear. We need the fire in any case. If you find waiting dull, you might want to help."

"Aren't you afraid I might hit you over the head with a hefty log?"

"Not particularly. I believe we've already established you aren't going anywhere without us." Nigel chuckled as he picked up another piece.

"Arrogant men," muttered Elf as she bent to collect wood.

Soon a fire crackled and flames licked the air. Elf sat on a stone Nigel had rolled near the fire for her. She placed her elbows on her knees and cupped her chin in her hands. Her stomach growled. If she were at home, she would be enjoying the wedding feast now, not waiting for an errant knight to hunt down some meager fare.

"Good. The fire is just right to roast these."

Elf sat up with a start. Payne had returned as quietly as he had left. The flames lit his face and the scar on his cheek danced in the uneven glow. He held two hares by the ears. Elf shivered, though not from the cold.

She watched as he removed a knife from his boot and with

an ease of motion, skinned and skewered their fare on a pike. The shadows around them lengthened and darkness fully claimed the land when their meal was ready.

The smell of the roasted meat wafted under her nose. Her stomach growled again, loud enough that Payne glanced at her. She sat back and clasped her hands together in her lap.

When Elf made no move to eat, Payne turned to her with a frown. "Are you not hungry?"

She gave him a look of impatience. "I have no knife. In my haste to depart, I failed to bring it along."

"Forgive me, I had forgotten. Coxesbury sent one for you." Payne retreated to the cart and poked among the supplies until he found what he sought. He returned to the fire and handed her a tooled sheath.

She pulled out a slim blade with an ornate handle. Amid the swirls and whorls, a single ruby cabochon decorated the hilt. Another elaborate gift to pacify an unwilling bride.

Elf eyed the knife, turning it over in her hand. "I could use this on you."

"What? And ruin it for eating this delicious meal? In any case, I've suffered worse wounds than that blade could possibly inflict."

That he thought her so harmless rankled her. If he knew what she was capable of, if he knew . . . Elf sighed and cut herself a piece of rabbit. The meat was still warm. She took a bite and chewed. Her stomach welcomed the food. She finished and reached for more in little time.

"You were hungry." Payne watched her, his eyes crinkling in amusement. "You should have said something."

"I am not one to complain."

"That's good to know. I'm glad you enjoyed your food."

"It would have been better with spices." Elf bit off another chunk of meat.

"I thought you weren't one to complain."

"That's not a complaint, merely a statement of fact."

"Next time I'll remember the spices." Payne grinned.

Elf eyed him with distrust. "I doubt you'll have the need to abduct me again."

"Probably not, but I'll remember just the same."

His words confused her. She wiped her fingers on a leaf and stared at him across the fire.

"That's all there is of the meal, milady," Nigel interjected. He followed her lead and wiped his fingers as well. "Tomorrow you'll have a banquet as befits your station. Baron Coxesbury will see to it."

I doubt it. She suppressed a yawn. With her stomach satisfied, the rest of her let her know just what a long and difficult day it had been. She didn't think she could walk to her bed.

Her bed. She saw only the one tent. She narrowed her gaze at Payne. "Where are you sleeping?"

"Right here." He patted the ground. "The tent is for you. Nigel and I will guard you out here. You have enough sense not to try and slip out in the back and run away."

"I've already told you, I am no fool." She lifted her chin a notch.

Nigel hurried to the cart and returned with a thick bundle under his arms. He placed it in the tent and slipped out again. "It isn't a proper bed, but you'll be warm. Your sleeping gown is there as well."

"Thank you, Nigel."

"Do I get no thanks for the supper?" Payne raised an eyebrow in a mocking challenge.

"You forgot the spices." Elf turned and retreated into the tent.

Chapter Three

Payne watched until she disappeared into the tent. Then he let out a deep breath.

"She isn't afraid of you." Nigel scratched his head.

"No, she isn't." Payne turned back to the fire and stared at the flames.

"I think you enjoyed that."

"What's to enjoy? She's Coxesbury's bride. I have no interest in her except to deliver her and to collect my fee for her."

"Aye. That's why you couldn't keep your eyes from her this entire day." Nigel poked at the fire. The shower of sparks lit his grin with a red glow.

Payne growled. "I don't care what you think, old man." He rose and pulled out the rolled up bedding from the cart. He spread it on the ground in front of the tent.

"Running away from me, are you?"

"Not in the least. You got sleep last night. I didn't." Payne brushed a leaf off the bed with an angry flick of his hand.

"I don't suppose I need to tell you to have pleasant dreams."

"Shut up, Nigel." Payne stretched out on the pallet. The ground was hard, but he'd slept in worse places. He was tired. He hadn't slept for two days because of this errand. He closed his eyes.

The fire crackled and popped. Payne rolled over to his side to block out the flashes of light. He heard Nigel retrieve his bedding. Payne listened as his companion settled on the other side of the fire. Quiet, at last. Nigel was wrong. That chit meant nothing to him.

Then why couldn't he sleep?

Maybe if he tried his other side. Rolling over, Payne stretched into another comfortable position. He *was* tired. Sleep should come any minute.

Instead, the image of burnished gold hair and green eyes flashing in anger rose to his mind. He *had* watched her all day, but he would never admit that to Nigel. And this morning, when she had changed her clothes . . . the glimpse of her breast had rocked him, then haunted him for hours. It wasn't even the whole breast, just the creamy side, pale and smooth, looking like silk—

He groaned. Heat pooled in his loins. What was the matter with him? He had seen more comely women, yet he had never felt his control slip as it had time and again today.

Tomorrow he would be rid of her, and he would have added a hefty sum to his savings. There was a pleasant thought. In fact, after Coxesbury paid him, he'd have enough to stop for a while. He could go back and visit the brothers at the monastery. Nigel would enjoy that. They hadn't visited Castlereigh for five years. Yes, that was exactly what he would do as soon as he got his money from Coxesbury.

The castle came into view just after midday. Relief coursed through Payne. His task was nearly at an end, thank heaven. Once Coxesbury paid him, he could forget about Lady Agnes. And if dreams of her continued to plague him as they had last night, they would cease over time.

"We'll leave as soon as Coxesbury settles with us."

Nigel raised his eyebrows. "Don't you think we're entitled to enjoy the wedding feast?"

"Perhaps, but I don't want to wait that long." He turned to her. "You'll forgive us, Lady Agnes."

"There is nothing to forgive, for there won't be a wedding," she responded in a mocking tone.

"As you say." Payne didn't trouble to hide the disbelief in his voice.

The guards waved them through the castle gate. In the courtyard, a flock of servants scurried to unload the cart.

"Just leave my things," ordered Payne. "Take only the lady's belongings. Nigel, see that the rest of our possessions make it onto the cart."

Payne turned to Lady Agnes. He lifted her from her horse. His hands wrapped her waist. Through sheer force of will, he released his grip when she stood on the ground. "I'm sure your bridegroom has been informed of your arrival."

She lifted her head. "Let's not keep him waiting. I'm eager to see how he greets me."

Payne gave a curt nod. He swept his arm forward and fell in beside her as she moved toward the keep. Coxesbury was sure to be in the great hall. Payne ignored the knot in the pit of his stomach. He was happy to relinquish her to Coxesbury. Better the Baron wear the chains of a woman than he.

Gilbert Fitzhugh, Baron Coxesbury, sat at the head table surrounded by his men. He quaffed something from a bejeweled goblet, then wiped his mouth with his sleeve. Payne eyed the man with distaste. Coxesbury roared with laughter, elbowing the man beside him. His guffaws reminded Payne of a donkey.

The Baron looked up and stood his goblet on the table. "Payne, my friend. Good to see you've returned. Come share a drink with us."

"No, thank you." He felt Lady Agnes hide behind him.

"But where is she? Where's my bride?"

"Right here." Payne stepped to the side.

For an instant silence filled the hall. Then Coxesbury's face broke into a grin. "I never knew you to jest, Payne. Where is Lady Agnes?"

Elf turned to watch Payne. For the first time since her abduction, he looked less than certain.

"She stands before you."

"This is not she. My God, man, what have you done?" Coxesbury's face grew mottled. "This is Lady Elfreda."

Elf couldn't prevent the smug smile that slipped onto her lips. "I told you."

"What kind of fool are you?" roared Coxesbury.

Holding her breath, Elf expected Payne to kill the Baron. Instead she watched his scar grow white and his eyes narrow.

"A fool who depended on your description." The words were spoken with calm, but Elf could see the hint of danger in his eyes.

"My description? I told you Lady Agnes had hair of gold, not rust."

Payne shot a glance at her hair. "Her hair is more golden than the pale silver of her companion's."

"I also said Lady Agnes was comely."

"You also said she was tall."

"Yes, tall, not a monster."

Elf winced at that comment. *You'd think you'd be used to it by now.*

"By the saints, she is old, too. Who would want her as a

bride?" Coxesbury curled his lip in disgust.

Elf lifted her gaze until she peered into the Baron's eyes. " 'Tis clear women feel the same about you. Agnes is already a bride, and not yours."

Payne coughed beside her. She shot him a glance, but Coxesbury's sputtering reclaimed her attention. The man opened and closed his mouth like a fish.

Coxesbury turned away from her and faced Payne again. "I needed Agnes's dower lands to enlarge my holdings. I wanted an alliance to Matthew."

The Baron paced back and forth for a minute, then stopped with a jerk. He stared at Elf. "Then again, maybe I can make use of your blunder."

Elf didn't like the way he looked at her. Coxesbury stood in front of her and tilted his gaze up to see into her eyes. A shiver slunk down her spine. Whatever the Baron said next, she knew it wouldn't hold good tidings for her.

"I'll marry the Lady Elfreda instead."

"What?" Elf swallowed the panic that threatened to engulf her. "You can't."

"Of course I can."

"I'm going to the convent soon. I'll be no man's bride."

From the corner of her eye, she saw Payne's gaze dart to her, but she didn't turn from Coxesbury.

The Baron shrugged. "Plans change, Lady Elfreda."

"I won't marry you."

"Tomorrow in our chapel, you shall become my wife and Baroness Coxesbury." Coxesbury reached his hand to stroke her cheek.

Jerking her head to one side, Elf heard Coxesbury laugh. He stretched farther and slid his fingers down her cheek.

"Yes, the more I think on it, the more I realize what a suitable bride you are. I wanted a tie to the Meredith family. You can provide me with that." Coxesbury sighed. "There is the matter of Agnes's dowry. Her lands would have given me riches to equal the king's, which was why he broke off our betrothal. He never considered marriage to you a threat, because everyone knew you would never marry. Your dowry will suffice. I won't be as rich, but it will suffice."

"I won't say the words."

"That doesn't matter. My priest knows who keeps him fat and well fed. He doesn't need to hear the words." Coxesbury gave her a sneering grin.

She stared at the man. His jowls were starting to hang loose from his jaw. Gray sprinkled his hair. She couldn't possibly wed him. For once she was grateful she hadn't eaten. The contents of her stomach would have graced the room. "I can't . . . I won't—"

"You will. Tomorrow. Now you may go to your chambers and prepare yourself for your wedding day. I'll have food sent up in a while. You'll find everything you need in your room. The gowns might be a little short, but they will have to do. I had ordered them for Lady Agnes, after all, and you can't expect me to order new ones."

Coxesbury snapped his fingers and waved two of his men forward. "Show your future mistress her room. Make sure she has plenty of time to grow accustomed to her new home. In fact, I don't think she needs to come out again until the wedding."

The two men nodded, then flanked her.

"Until tomorrow, Lady Elfreda. Since I won't see you until the wedding, I'll wish you a good night."

"And I'll wish you to the devil." Elf followed her escorts out of the hall.

"That woman has spirit," said Coxesbury, nodding his

head. "She'll bear me fine sons, even if she is difficult to abide."

Payne eyed the man with contempt. "She doesn't want to marry you."

"She is only a woman. What she wants is unimportant. You'll stay for the wedding, of course."

"I would prefer not to."

"Come now. Where do you have to hurry to?"

A humorless smile twisted Payne's lips. The truth in Coxesbury's statement irritated him less than the disgust he felt for the man. And himself. "I'd like my fee, then I'll be gone."

"No business now. Wait until after the wedding. You and your man must stay and celebrate with me."

"After such an invitation, how can I refuse?"

"Excellent. Go find yourself a tankard and have some ale."

"After I tell Nigel of the change in plans." Payne turned and strode from the hall. As soon as he passed the doorway, he released the scowl he had suppressed. He didn't know whom he despised more—the Baron or himself.

For the first time, he questioned his chosen life. How could he profit from someone's misery? It was different when he won a tournament. There he just left bodies. Here he was afraid he was leaving a soul.

He found Nigel in the courtyard, packing the final items.

"We're off, then?" Nigel tied a last knot to secure the load in the cart.

"Not just yet. The Baron hasn't paid me yet."

"Why not?"

"He wants us to stay for the wedding."

Nigel raised his eyebrows. "Lady Agnes agreed?"

"She isn't Lady Agnes."

"What?"

"It seems I brought the wrong woman."

Nigel stared at him. "She was telling the truth?"

"Yes. We delivered the Lady Elfreda." Payne rubbed his forehead.

"And she agreed to marry Coxesbury?"

"No, but Coxesbury weds her on the morrow anyway."

"Great heavens, boy. What have you done?"

"Don't start, Nigel. You can't say anything I haven't already told myself."

"I guess there's nothing for it. Wasn't the Baron angry?"

"At first. Then he seemed to accept the change. I couldn't make any sense of it."

"And Elf?"

"Elf?"

"Sorry. The Lady Elfreda. She told me her friends call her Elf."

"I don't suppose we count among her friends. Especially after this farce."

"This task has turned into a comedy of errors." Nigel shook his head.

"But Lady Elfreda isn't laughing." Payne wanted to smash his fist through the castle's stone walls.

"Isn't Lady Elfreda happy with her impending wedding?"

"Hardly. She was to join a convent soon." Payne remembered how sick she looked at the Baron's pronouncements. She looked like a prisoner being led to her death. "No, she isn't happy."

"What a shame. She demonstrated such high spirits. I'd hate to see them quashed. Still, there are worse things than being Baroness of Coxesbury."

"Such as?" Payne scowled.

"Don't snap at me, boy. I didn't make the error." Nigel reached out to untie the knot he had just tied.

"Are all our belongings here?"

"Yes. And since we're staying a few days longer, we'll be needing some of these things. The sooner the Baron gives you your money, the happier I'll be." Nigel's fingers busied themselves on the knot. "If I have to pack and unpack one more time—"

Payne's hand shot out and stopped Nigel's work. "Leave it."

Chapter Four

The situation was eerily familiar.

Payne climbed the stairs of the tower. The moonlight wasn't as bright tonight, but he knew this castle. He knew which room held Lady Elfreda, and he also knew she'd have two guards in front of her door.

This time he wouldn't have to use a tapestry. Lady Elfreda would be happy to help abduct herself.

The two guards played a dice game on the landing. They looked up when they heard him, but didn't jump to a position of wariness. Just as he had hoped. Payne smiled to himself. His face was now as common in the castle as one of their own.

"Care to wager with us, Payne?" one guard said. "We'd love to relieve you of some of your earnings."

Payne squatted beside the two men. "I've heard of your luck with dice."

Laughing, the guard scooped up the dice. He rolled them again. The two men leaned forward to view the results.

With a quickness that belied his size, Payne knocked the two heads together. One man sprawled onto the ground; the other looked up in a daze at him.

"Sorry." Payne pulled his arm back and let his fist fly into the man's jaw. The guard joined his companion on the floor. The door was unlocked. Payne pushed it open.

Lady Elfreda lay across the bed fast asleep, but fully clothed. He could see the tracks of tears on her cheeks. Payne cursed himself once again. He had never meant to bring the lady such sorrow.

He lowered himself to the bed. She didn't stir. When he leaned over, the faint smell of roses tantalized his nose. He brushed her hair from her face. Her head turned toward his palm. For a moment he allowed himself to hold the silken cheek that rested against his skin. But they could tarry no longer.

Clamping his hand over her mouth, he watched her eyelids fly open, just as they had two nights ago. Fear flashed in those green orbs, until recognition came. He removed his hand.

"This grows tedious. You've interrupted my sleep twice now." Elfreda sat up and moved away from him.

Payne hid his smile. "Tedious indeed, but I believe you'll be happier to see me tonight. Let's go."

"Where? Have you forgotten my betrothed's friends outside the door?" The venom in her voice didn't surprise him.

"By no means. They won't trouble us for a while."

She peered up at him with a suspicious glint in her eyes. "Are you abducting me again?"

"Yes, but I expect you'll be eager to join me in my efforts this time. Unless you wish to stay and become the Baron's bride."

Elfreda rolled off the bed. "Let's go."

"You must remain quiet until we leave the castle."

"You don't have to worry. This time you won't need to

bind my mouth." She grabbed his hand and pulled him toward the door.

The touch startled him for an instant. He stopped. Her hand was so soft in his.

"Are you coming?"

"Absolutely." Payne pushed her behind him and cracked open the door. The two guards still kissed the floor, although one stirred. Payne signaled her to remain where she was. A quick blow and both guards slept on.

Stepping over the bodies, Payne moved to the stairs. Elf looked at the two prone men, raised her eyebrows, and shot her gaze to Payne. He shrugged in return. She grinned and followed him.

When she stood beside him, he whispered, "If we run into someone, don't say a word."

She nodded.

As he started down the steps, Elf tracked him like a shadow. In the silence, her heartbeat thundered in her ears, yet she felt no fear. Payne's back concealed her. The dark obscured the angles and twists of the stairs, but she kept her gaze on Payne and didn't miss a step.

Just before they reached the bottom, the voices of two men reached her ears. Payne pushed her into a corner.

"Trust me." He pressed his lips against hers.

For an instant, Elf couldn't imagine what he was doing. The tug of his mouth on hers sent little bursts of excitement down her spine. He tasted of wine, and she wanted to drink her fill. Then the reality of his action struck her. He shouldn't kiss her. She pushed against him. He didn't budge. Her squirming had no effect on him. And all the while he kissed her.

And she enjoyed it.

"Ah ha. I see you've found yourself a bit of entertainment for the night, Payne."

Dear God, it was Coxesbury and one of his minions. Elf's heart raced in her chest.

Payne lifted his head. His expression held a stern warning. After a moment, he turned his head to the men. "I am skilled in many ways, my friends."

The men's response was raucous laughter.

"Perhaps we should let the maid decide who is the most skillful," Coxesbury said.

"No, I shouldn't want her to end the night in disappointment."

More laughter followed that retort.

"Let us at least see her face so that we may know whom to ask when you leave." Coxesbury tried to peer around Payne.

Elf buried her face against Payne's chest. His arms tightened around her.

"I think not. Should I turn around now, the sight that would greet you would only make you feel . . . small."

"Bragging again, are you Payne? You might be called the Bear, but I've heard other parts called a cold fish." Coxesbury clapped his companion on the back as they roared with laughter.

"This wench seems to enjoy fish." Payne's voice held humor as he spoke. "But I digress. You've interrupted me for long enough. I have business to finish, and I prefer to finish without an audience."

The men chuckled again. Coxesbury spoke again. "We'll leave you to it. Our turn will come soon enough. Then we'll see who has the bragging rights."

The men moved on. Payne felt Elf tremble against him. "Shh. It's over."

She turned her face up to him. "Are all men so crude?"

"Most."

"Then I'm glad I shall be in a convent soon and never have

to deal with such creatures again."

Her words cut him. He knew the jesting was lewd, but in this instance it had been necessary. That she thought him on a level with Coxesbury bothered him. But he could not defend himself to her. "Come along before we run into someone else."

They continued through the darkened castle until they reached the courtyard. Nigel waited near the door. Merlin stood ready for his rider. A stout workhorse pulled the cart, and behind the cart a huge horse pawed the ground. Elf stopped and stared at the beast for a moment, then walked toward Merlin.

"I'm afraid not, milady." Payne's hand stopped her. He pointed her toward the cart.

With a shrug, Nigel lifted a bundle and revealed a long, narrow space.

Elf regarded it with a frown. "I suppose I should be used to your traveling arrangements by now." She climbed into the space without another word. She could lie only on her side, and something jabbed her in the back, but discomfort was better than a wedding.

Payne mounted Merlin. "Ready, Nigel?"

Nigel's answer was to climb onto the seat and click his tongue. The horse moved forward and the cart rolled behind him.

Payne rode in front of the cart. They still had to pass the sentry at the gatehouse. He made no attempt to hide their departure. Lady Elfreda knew to keep quiet, and the guard had no reason to alert the castle of his departure.

Payne stopped at the sentry's signal.

"Leaving us so soon? Why aren't you staying for the wedding? I heard the Baron's planning a bountiful feast." The guard grinned, revealing blackened teeth and a large gap.

"I have no stomach for such celebrating. If I delay any longer, I'll miss the tournament at Reading."

"Planning to win again?" The man winked at him.

"Do you doubt it?"

"Never. But why depart in the middle of the night?"

"It's hardly the middle of the night. Dawn is but an hour away."

"True. I suppose it's been a long night." The guard sighed and leaned against the wall.

"Reading is three days journey from here, but if I leave now I may pare half a day from my travels." Payne leaned closer to the man as if taking him into his confidence. "Besides, if I stay until morning, the Baron would just try to keep me here. You know how he loves to get his own way. I didn't wish to cause trouble."

"A man like you would indeed stir up trouble. Pass then, and good luck at Reading."

"Thank you."

Nigel drove through the gate. Payne followed him. They rode in silence until Payne was sure the sentry couldn't hear him. He spoke to the cart. "We must put as much distance between us and Coxesbury as possible. When the castle is out of sight, you may come out, Lady Elfreda."

Muffled words responded.

Payne grinned. Lady Elfreda must hate traveling like baggage, but it was safer—for her and for him.

The memory of the kiss sprang into his mind. His heart began to race, his blood to rush, as if he prepared for battle. She was as dangerous as any combat. He could still taste the plump softness of her lips. His body remembered as well. The warmth he felt had naught to do with the weather.

Oh, yes. She was dangerous.

She could cause a man to forget his dreams, to abandon

his duty, to lose his soul. And now he was stuck with her because of his mistake. The last time he had made such an error was . . . he couldn't remember ever making such an error. Honor demanded he rectify this one.

"Payne, are you deaf?" Nigel yelled.

"What?"

"I've tried to get your attention three times now."

Yes, she was dangerous. "What is it, Nigel?"

"Where do we stand?"

"Without Coxesbury's wages, too far to think on it. I'll make up some of the losses at Northstoke, but it won't be enough. Three years, maybe four until I can offer for the property."

"Can't be helped, I suppose." Nigel stroked his chin, then pointed to the back of the cart. "Can she come out now? It can't be very comfortable in there."

Payne looked over his shoulder. He saw only the crenellations of the castle. "Yes, she can come out." *Though I'd prefer she stay hidden.*

Nigel patted the tarp that covered the cart. "Did you hear, milady? You can come out now."

Elfreda pushed aside the bundle and tarp and sat up. She stretched her arms. "Where am I to sit?"

"You may ride next to Nigel." Payne pointed to the plank on the front of the cart. "Be careful not to fall off as you climb. I don't wish to stop."

"Of course not. You wouldn't deign to make it easy for me." Elf grumbled as she left the narrow space. Climbing over the load wasn't difficult, but she bumped her shins twice on the uneven lumps before reaching the hard plank.

"I'm sure my uncle will reward you when I am returned." She smoothed the front of her gown as she settled herself on the seat.

"Not likely, since I'm the one who abducted you the first time." Payne didn't spare her a glance.

"Nevertheless, he shall reward you. You didn't have to rescue me from Coxesbury. Besides, they shall hardly have missed me at home."

"They will by the time we return there."

"What do you mean?" A sense of foreboding rose in her.

"We are going to Northstoke first."

"You can't be serious."

"I am most serious, Lady Elfreda. There is a tournament I wish to participate in. I cannot take you home and arrive in Northstoke in time, so you will accompany us. After the tournament, I will bring you home." Payne clicked his tongue and Merlin sprang forward.

"Why?" she yelled after him, but he didn't turn around.

"Because this little incident has cost him money," answered Nigel. He tapped the horse with the reins. The horse's gait quickened.

"Money? He doesn't seem the type to care about money." Elf stared at the large figure moving ahead of them in the predawn.

"It isn't the money itself. He wants to buy a holding. Coxesbury owes him a lot of money."

"And the Baron wouldn't pay him because he brought me instead of Agnes?"

"Not exactly. The Baron didn't want to pay him until after the wedding. Payne wouldn't wait."

"Whyever not?"

"Because the one thing he prizes more than money is honor. He couldn't let you become Coxesbury's bride when it was his error that made you so."

"That doesn't make sense. He was willing to sacrifice Agnes to Coxesbury."

"But there had been a betrothal between the Baron and your cousin until the king called it off."

Elf fell silent. Agnes would have married Coxesbury if not for the king's intervention. The two families had agreed to the match.

She stared into the darkness not pretending to understand the man who rode ahead of them.

"He hadn't planned on attending the tournament in Northstoke," continued Nigel. "The abduction was the last in a series of tasks the Baron had for him. He fought in France, you know. Coxesbury sent him in his stead."

"I heard stories of the Bear in France." Her voice sounded small to her own ears.

"Now he has nothing to show for two years of service to the Baron."

She understood the death of a dream. Her own had died with the death of her father. She tried again to peer at the man in front. A wave of guilt washed over her.

Guilt? What was she thinking? He had abducted her. If he suffered for it, well, that wasn't her problem. She refused to feel sorry for something he had done. She crossed her arms over her chest. "I've already said my uncle will reward him. Perhaps it won't be as much as what the Baron owes him, but that's his own fault."

"He knows that, milady." Nigel clicked his tongue again, and the cart lurched under Elf.

She grabbed onto the plank. "If he's so honorable, why can't he take me home first?"

Nigel remained quiet for a minute. Elf started to believe he wouldn't answer, when he sighed. "You don't understand the lad."

Lad? "Perhaps if you'd tell me—"

"He is the third son of the Earl of Thornheath. His youth

was spent at his father's castle. His two older half brothers were sent to squire at their father's friend. Payne remained at home. His mother wanted him to join a monastery."

"The Bear at a monastery?" Elf couldn't keep the disbelief from her voice.

Nigel grinned. "Exactly. But his mother brought tutors and scholars to teach him. When he arrived at the abbey, his mind was prepared, but his body . . . well, let's just say he didn't fit in very well. He and the monks soon realized he was incompatible with monastic life."

"I'd say."

"His mother forfeited a small fortune to get him out of the order. All her dower lands. Then his father died. His eldest brother became lord and treated Payne's mother with contempt. She no longer had her dower lands to escape to, and William never let her forget she was there at his charity. Payne could do little against his half brother. When he learned how much she suffered, he vowed to take her far away from Castlereigh. She died before he had a chance." Nigel paused. "He still blames himself for her death."

"And so he became a mercenary." Elf had difficulty imagining anyone defeating the Bear.

"It was logical. He was strong, smart, willing to fight hard. He wants nothing more than to earn enough money to purchase a holding for himself and remove himself completely from his half brother's influence."

"And if he dies?" Elf swallowed at the discomfort of the thought.

Nigel shrugged. "He has no family."

"What of you?"

"Ah, I am free to go whenever I wish. Payne's father requested I stay with him for as long as he needs me. As of yet, I've felt no desire to leave."

Elf stared at the shorter man. Gray streaked his hair, and age had left lines on his face, but his bearing showed the strength of past years. “You don’t seem worried about his safety much.”

Nigel grinned. “Why should I be? Who do you think trained him?”

Chapter Five

Elf eyed the partridge leg she held between her fingers. She wasn't sure she enjoyed meals in the fresh air, but it was hot and she was hungry. With a hint of resignation, she bit into the meat. The fresh game fowl erupted into a riot of flavor on her tongue. She glanced up in surprise to find Payne's gaze upon her.

He shrugged. "I remembered the spices."

For some reason, his words warmed her more than the fire that crackled in front of her. Why was he making it difficult to hate him? She frowned at her thoughts and tore off another bite with her teeth. Despite her best intentions, she had to admit the meat was delicious.

Perched on a fallen log, she watched him through the tongues of flame that shot from the fire. Although darkness hadn't fully claimed the land, the fire was cheerful and comforting. Payne sat on a boulder. Although he ate heartily, he seemed more intent on their surroundings than his meal. Nigel, too, ate with a distracted air.

In the next instant, Payne sprang to his feet. His dinner rolled onto the dirt. Fixing his gaze upon the bushes outside the circle of firelight, he grabbed the hilt of his sword.

Nigel set his food aside and rose, likewise gripping his sword. "What is it?"

Before Payne could answer, a voice cried out from the darkness. "Hail, travelers."

Payne relaxed his stance, but didn't sit. As Elf watched him, the initial panic that twisted her stomach subsided.

Nigel sat upon the log and picked up his food. Before he took another bite, Elf heard him mutter, "Tedric. Not the most pleasant end to a fine meal."

A tall, lanky man stepped through the bushes. With a broad grin, he held up a jug. "If I provide the wine, may I share in your repast?"

"Have I any hope you are just passing through, Tedric?" Payne eyed the man with look of mild annoyance.

"You know me better than that, Payne." He turned to Elf and bowed. "You must be the Lady Elfreda. Tedric of Almstone, my lady. If I may be so bold, I can see why Coxesbury wants your return."

Elf recognized flattery and didn't respond.

Without waiting for further permission, Tedric took Payne's seat on the rock, placed the jug on the ground, and pulled his knife from his belt. He sliced a chunk of meat from the bird on the spit.

"Won't you join us?" murmured Nigel under his breath.

Payne glanced at the man, then cut himself another portion of food from a second partridge. He moved to another spot around the fire and stood as he ate.

"You've created quite a fuss," said Tedric as he chewed. He chuckled. "The Baron was livid to discover you'd left."

A twinge of fear snaked through her. "Are you here to take me back?" asked Elf.

"No. Although the Baron has offered a large reward for

your return." Tedric unstopped the jug and hefted it to his shoulder. He tilted the vessel on his arm so that a stream of red liquid spilled into his mouth. He wiped his mouth on his sleeve. "I have no desire to fight Payne at the moment, which, I imagine, is the only way I could convince him to let you come back with me. Wine?" said Tedric and offered the jug to Payne.

Payne shook his head.

"Go ahead. I've already said I'm not here to take Lady Elfreda back."

"Then why are you here?" asked Payne.

"As I said, the Baron has offered a generous reward to the man who brings him Lady Elfreda. I'm willing to wait until you decide to relinquish her of your own free will. I'm not in a hurry." He took another swig.

"What of the others who would claim the reward?"

"Most of them are headed toward the tournament at Reading. Nice feint that. They don't know you as well as I. I knew if you were headed for Reading, you'd never have told anyone your destination." Tedric nodded in apparent satisfaction at his mental prowess as he placed the jug on the ground.

"I'm returning her to her uncle," said Payne.

"That's fine. I'm sure her uncle will give me permission to return her to Coxesbury. He always wanted an alliance with the Baron."

"Will you stop discussing what you will do with me as if I weren't present?" Elf scowled at the two knights. "I won't return to Pellingham."

Payne nodded his head, but Tedric glanced at her in surprise. "But, my lady, these matters are no concern of yours. It is for your uncle to decide."

"My uncle has decided to send me to an abbey, and I quite

agree with his decision." Elf sniffed in triumph. "I'm all too happy to disappoint the Baron."

Tedric shrugged. "It doesn't matter to me, but the Baron is quite adamant about your return. As long as I get my reward, I don't care if you do end up at the abbey." He bit off another chunk of meat.

Elf furrowed her brow and glared at Payne. She had no difficulty summoning distaste for Payne as long as the man made no effort to contradict Tedric. Apparently, once Payne returned her to her uncle, Payne's conscience would no longer trouble him.

"Where are we off?" Tedric threw the denuded bone into the fire.

"Northstoke," Nigel answered as he, too, tossed a bone into the fire.

"Excellent. I had hoped to compete in that tournament, but my duties to Coxesbury prevented me. This is a well-met chance." Tedric stood and bowed to Elf. "Something else for which I must thank you."

Nigel's gaze narrowed. "Payne competes as well."

"Indeed? How wonderful. A chance to change my luck against you. That is, if we meet in the final."

"We'll meet," Payne said.

"Such was my intention as well. How shall we celebrate this fortunate meeting? I know. A song. Perhaps you've heard this one, Lady Elfreda." Tedric cleared his throat.

"Oh, hell," muttered Payne.

Tedric sang:

In far off France a battle waged.
King Edward was at war.
And by his side as the mêlée raged,
Fought a warrior of lore.

Payne buried his head in his hands.

The Bear stood firm when the Frogs came on.
He did not bend his head.
With one great roar, he frightened Dawn
Into crawling back to her bed.

"Overblown foolishness," said Payne to Elf without lifting his head.

In the darkness, the French felt fear.
Who was this terrible beast?
One glance at him, and death was near,
And then the battle ceased.

From his eyes shot golden light,
The field a bloody brine,
He slew a legion on that night,
Then stayed to drink their wine.

"That much is true," whispered Payne. "We recovered many casks that night. 'Twould have been a sin to waste them."

Oh, the town of Castlereigh rejoices,
For this warrior hails from there,
And calls his name with gladdened voices
Payne Dunbyer, the Golden Bear.

"If I ever find that loathsome minstrel . . ." muttered Payne.

"I have indeed heard this song, Sir Tedric. But never so sweetly. Perhaps you should consider plying your talents as a troubadour rather than a knight," said Elf in dulcet tones.

Payne roared with laughter.

"No, my lady. I'm afraid I enjoy battle too much. Besides, I can earn more with the Baron than singing for my wages. But we aren't fighting tonight. Come. Have a drink with me." Tedric lifted the jug and passed it to Payne, who uncorked it and sniffed it with caution. Tedric laughed. " 'Tis good wine, I assure you. From the Baron's own cellars."

Payne took a swallow, then passed it to Nigel. Nigel drank as well then passed it back to Tedric.

Elf rose in a huff. "I'm so happy you've made your peace. It matters to none of you that I don't wish to go to this tournament or to return to the Baron, does it?"

"But Lady Elfreda, has no one told you that I am one of the Bear's oldest friends?" Tedric grinned at her. "If he wishes to return you to your uncle, I shall help him. We merely want a bit of play first."

"A tournament hardly qualifies as play, sir." Elf grabbed her skirts and stormed into the tent without saying a word of good night.

"She has a fiery temper, doesn't she?" said Tedric with a chuckle.

"She tends to make her departures memorable." Payne heard her emit a muffled cry of irritation from the tent and smiled. He knew she couldn't help but overhear.

"Why did you take her, Payne?"

Payne paused for a moment. "I made an error. She shouldn't have to pay for it."

"Yes, but the Baron was furious. He nearly put a reward on your head as well."

Payne raised an eyebrow. "What stopped him?"

"I pointed out that you were a hard man to catch, and if caught, even harder to kill."

"This is true." Payne chuckled. "So I owe you my life?"

"Hardly. I wouldn't want to face you in mortal combat, Payne. At least not until I know I can beat you. Perhaps after this tournament . . . ?"

"Not if you want to keep that pretty head of yours to please the ladies."

"There is that. However, I'm sure the weight of the winning purse will persuade many a wench to overlook a scar or two."

"It does." Payne stretched his arms overhead and yawned. "How do you plan to compete without your armor?"

"I have it. Once I found your trail, I sent word to my man to follow me. As your pace wasn't brisk, we caught up with ease. I have left him with my horse in a glade not far from here."

"So *you* were the stomping I heard behind us. Stealth was never your strongest skill."

"You heard me?"

"Why do you think I greeted you with sword drawn? I knew someone was following us. But if it makes you feel any better, you made less noise this time."

"Good to know." Tedric slapped his knee in merriment. "Better watch your back, Payne. I just might surprise you one day."

"Perhaps when I'm drunk." Payne let a slow smile curve his lips. "Even then, I'm not sure. So, will you share the fire?"

Tedric rose. "I'd be happy to. I'll go fetch my man." He disappeared through the bushes from whence he came.

"Did you really need to invite him to our fire?" asked Nigel. He rose and brushed the crumbs from his tunic.

"Certainly. He can't harm us and he provides amusement at times. And the best way to keep him under control is to have him with us. Besides, he left us the jug of wine." Payne lifted the jug.

"I knew there was a reason for your hospitality." Nigel grinned and took the jug from Payne. "The Baron does have good wine."

Throughout the next hour, Elf heard the sounds of wheels rolling closer to their camp, the whinnies of horses, and the low mutterings of several men. Warring against her curiosity, she refused to poke her head out to see how their party had grown. She had heard the conversation through the canvas, and couldn't believe Payne would be so reckless as to invite the man who declared he would return her to the Baron into their midst. So much for his supposed honor.

The fire died down. The shadows on the tent grew more distorted and grotesque. But for the sounds of the nighttime wood, silence descended over the clearing. Elf tried to rest on the furs and rugs that served as her bed, but sleep eluded her. Her hair and clothes smelled of the smoke of the fire, not an unpleasant scent, but one that did not ease her into sleep. She flopped to her stomach and stared at the flickering light as it played on the canvas. The fur beneath her tickled her nose and she sneezed.

She knew what would calm her, but she didn't dare take such a risk tonight. Still the urge was too much. She rose from her bed and slipped her head through the opening of the tent.

Four men lay around the fire, varying volumes of snores rising with the smoke from the flames. She stepped into the night air and took a deep breath.

Easing her way from the circle of light, she tiptoed from the tent, over Nigel, then nearly stumbled as a hand grasped her ankle. "Oh," she gasped.

"Where do you think you're going?"

She stared down into golden eyes. "Do you never sleep?" she whispered.

"You didn't answer my question." Payne released her ankle and pushed himself from the ground.

"I couldn't sleep. I thought a stroll might help."

"Alone?"

"Of course alone," she hissed in an angry whisper. "You don't see anyone with me, do you?"

"And did you also think you might slip off into the night and return to your uncle's by yourself?"

The fire glinted in his eyes. Elf saw the anger shining there, but also something else she couldn't name. "No. As I have told you, I am no fool. I know a woman cannot travel alone."

"You want me to believe you?"

"I don't care what you believe, but it's the truth."

Payne released a deep breath. "Very well. We stroll."

"We?" Elf stared at him.

"You don't expect me to let you walk alone through the wood?"

"But I . . ." Elf fell silent. She couldn't tell him how often she went out by herself at her uncle's home. He'd never believe that. "Very well."

They walked without speaking for several minutes until they could no longer see the small flames of their fire.

"Are you troubled?" Payne's question broke the silence.

Elf longed to give her tongue free rein with her answer, but chose instead to ignore the question.

Payne chuckled beside her. "Never mind, I know the answer. What I should have asked was why can't you sleep?"

"I just wondered at the wisdom of inviting yet another knight, one who is still in the Baron's pay, to join us."

"Tedric? He poses no threat."

"No threat to you perhaps, but forgive me if I feel differently about the man."

Payne chuckled again, the deep sound enveloping her in its timbre. "He won't harm you, either. I give you my word."

"And after you return me to my uncle?"

"He won't touch you."

Elf tried to read his expression in the dark, but failed. She gave vent to her frustration. Doubt colored her words. "Thank you. I feel so much safer now."

Beside her, Payne stopped and pulled her to face him. "I gave you my word."

By the dim light of the stars, she could just make out his features. Anger marked his brow and his mouth was no more than a thin line. The scar twitched slightly as his teeth clenched together. Strange that she felt no fear staring at his hard visage. Instead, shame filled her.

"Forgive me." She hung her head. "I had no right to scorn your word."

Payne expelled a loud breath. He released her. "I ask your forgiveness as well. It was my error that brought you here, but I swear to you I shall return you to your uncle."

"I know that now." She gave him a half-smile.

She didn't move for a moment. The darkness of the wood covered them as surely as a blanket. As they stood together, far from the others, she felt an unfamiliar comfort steal over her. She lifted her face toward him, felt his warmth as he leaned toward her, and then both she and Payne stepped away from each other.

"I think I might sleep now," she said.

"Perhaps we should return," he said at the same time.

A few minutes found them by the glow of the fire. Elf looked at Payne, then ducked into her tent without another word. Inside, she stopped and tried to slow her breathing.

She heard him settle onto his pallet, but the snores of the other men drowned out any other sound. Her heart still raced and she pressed her hand to her chest. She knew it wasn't their quick return that caused her discomfort, but she didn't want to think about what had.

Chapter Six

Payne stood over Elf. In sleep she looked so peaceful, so serene. Who would have guessed that, awake, she wielded her sharp tongue with nearly as much power as a sword? The thought made him smile. He had never met a woman with such grace and strength. And with so little fear.

She stirred, letting out a soft puff of air. He envied her sleeping. He hated the summer nights. The sun occupied the sky for far too long for him to rest well, and he needed his rest if he was to win the tournament. Thoughts of Lady Elf were no tonic for sleep, either. Hadn't she plagued his mind this entire night past?

With a muttered curse, he bent over her sleeping form and prodded her with his finger. "Arise, my lady."

Elf jerked away from his touch, then turned her head to squint at him through puffy eyes. "What do you want?"

Sleep altered her voice into a husky purr. Her words brushed over him like a light caress, even if they were less than polite. He shook off the effect, exhaling in anger at himself. He didn't have time for foolish fancy. " 'Tis morning. Time to wake."

Elf rose to her elbows. "Surely not yet. I just fell asleep."

"Nevertheless, you must rise. We need to pack the tent."

She gazed at him with suspicion. "You're trying to be horrible to me, aren't you?"

"We must be on our way if we're to reach Northstoke in time for the tournament. While I apologize for your discomfort, your needs are not topmost in my mind."

"I didn't think they would be." Elf stretched her arm overhead. "Very well. Leave me to dress. I shall be ready in a few minutes."

He nodded and left the tent. Just before the flap closed he heard her mutter, "How much worse can this be than rising for Matins?"

Payne stopped for a moment. While standing above her, he'd forgotten she was meant for a convent. Good. If she were in a convent, he wouldn't have to think of her anymore.

So why did he still picture her in his bed with that glorious red hair as her only gown?

Clenching his fists, he strode to the cart to help Nigel load the bedding.

As Elf pushed the canvas flap aside and stepped into the young day, she stretched her arms overhead. The green gown she wore rose above her ankles then swished back into position when she dropped her arms. She was tired of this dress—hated it, in fact. It was a gift from Coxesbury, and she would just as happily burn it, but she had no other and no coin to purchase new garments. She doubted she could persuade Payne to part with his money. Didn't Nigel tell her Payne wanted wealth?

"Good morrow, Lady Elfreda." Tedric bowed low to her.

"Good morrow." Elf nodded.

"You look lovely today." Tedric raised her hand to his lips and kissed it.

From the corner of her eye, Elf saw Payne frown. With an exaggerated smile, she focused on Tedric. "Your words are kind, but I cannot believe you. I have worn this gown for three days, I have no comb or brush to untangle the unruly mess I must call my hair, and I've had no chance to clean myself properly."

"Nevertheless, you are a vision. When we reach Northstoke, I hope you shall allow me to remedy some of your ailments."

"That would be most welcome."

Payne strode to the pair. "She's my responsibility, Tedric. If she needs something, I'll get it for her."

"You'd deny me the pleasure of giving the lady a gift?" Tedric grinned.

"I don't want her to be in your debt," said Payne with a shrug.

Elf glanced around the camp. Nigel had already moved to the tent and popped inside. She could hear the snap of the bedding as he shook it out. He must be packing her meager belongings. Nothing remained on the ground in front of the tent except the now cold fire. The flattened plants and grass gave evidence to the bodies that had occupied those spots during the night.

Payne crossed to the tent, waited until Nigel reappeared with the bundles from inside, and then pulled up the ropes that fastened the tent to the ground. The canvas collapsed with a *whoosh*.

"You are eager to leave." Elf sat on a log.

"I don't intend to miss this tournament."

Tedric took a seat next to her. "You haven't seen the Bear when he's decided on a course of action. Woe unto anyone who tries to get in his way."

"You're not helping, Tedric," muttered Payne.

"Of course not. I've already packed my things. I'm traveling without a fair lady."

"That's not what I meant."

"I know."

Their bickering reminded Elf of two small boys trying to provoke each other. Their banter wouldn't end until they came to blows. Or their mothers stood between them. Elf stood. "Would it be too much to ask for something to eat?"

The men stared at her.

"Break my fast?" she continued. "I don't suppose you've left anything for me?"

"We haven't eaten," said Payne. "I hadn't planned to delay long enough to eat."

"Oh." Elf sat, then rose again. "Can you delay long enough for me to . . ." She gestured toward the bushes.

Payne swept his arm, granting her leave. She walked a short distance from the camp, then washed in a nearby stream. When she returned a few minutes later, Nigel held half a loaf of bread and a bit of cheese toward her.

"Perhaps this might soothe your hunger?"

"Thank you, Nigel." She took the meager fare and sat on the log to eat.

"Perhaps you might also consider eating as we travel?"

Elf saw Payne already mounted on Merlin, and Tedric and his man waiting at the edge of the clearing. With a sigh she rose. "Very well."

She climbed into the cart and clutched her meal to her as the cart rocked under Nigel's climbing. She waited until Nigel set the cart in motion before she risked a bite. As they continued along the road, Tedric whistled or hummed. Elf begrudged the man his good humor. Goodness knew she hadn't had much to sing about in the past few days.

As they traveled through the day, they passed small villages, an abbey, and saw a castle in the distance. Payne made no move to stop at any of these. Indeed, the sun was low in the sky as they left yet another village behind them. Elf looked back at the houses with longing. Dwellings meant lodging, lodging meant beds, and beds meant a good night's sleep rather than suffer the hardness of the ground. Her stomach craved food, and she believed if she never sat on a cart again, she would say a prayer of thanksgiving daily for the rest of her life.

As she expected, Payne found a clearing that met his liking in what seemed like hours later. He pulled off the road and started setting up the tent with Nigel. Tedric and his man did little more than watch.

"Don't you have a tent, Sir Tedric?" she asked.

"Yes, but I can sleep just as well under the stars. I have no need of the tent until we reach Northstoke." Tedric leaned back and smiled at Nigel and Payne's work. "I'm sure Payne wouldn't bother with one either, were he traveling alone."

"If you think to rouse my compassion for him, I would remind you that he wouldn't need to provide a tent for me had he left me with my uncle."

Tedric laughed. "I have no desire to rouse your compassion for the man. The more you hate him, the more easily I can coax you from his side."

"I hold no fondness for you either, Sir Tedric."

His laugh grew merrier. "I can but hope."

"Hope is for fools who do not command their own destiny." Payne stood behind her.

His sudden appearance startled her, but his choice of words angered her. "Like women?" Elf glared at him.

He looked surprised. "What do you mean?"

"Women have no control over their destiny. We must either marry a man not of our own choosing or enter a convent.

And I won't even speak of peasant women and their lot in life."

Tedric crossed his arms and gave Payne a look of amusement. "And what say you to that?"

Payne shrugged. "She speaks the truth."

Elf stared at him.

"Shall you help obtain our dinner tonight, Tedric, or do you filch your meal from my skills again?" asked Payne.

"Ah." Tedric rose and stretched. "I suppose I would like to impress Lady Elfreda with my hunting prowess."

"Good luck with that," muttered Elf under her breath.

The incessant call of a lark woke Elf the following morning. She stretched and winced. Despite Nigel's effort to preserve her comfort, her nightly encounters with the ground stiffened her joints. It was too early to rise, but now that she was awake, she wouldn't fall back to sleep. She peeked out of the tent. Nigel, Tedric, and his man slept around the banked fire. Of Payne she saw nothing.

He must be hunting our morning meal.

She pulled her head back into the tent, only to pause. Here was a chance to bathe. The brook ran just beyond the small clearing. With no men to worry about, she could give herself a proper scrubbing.

Lifting the canvas once again, she slipped past the sleeping men and hurried to the water. Without pausing at the bank, she threw off her overgown and lifted the skirt of her undergown. Ready to fling it from her as she stepped into the cool brook.

"If I had known you wanted to bathe with me, I would have waited."

Elf screeched and whirled to face the voice. Payne stood in a small pool. His waist stood above the water, and above his waist she saw a bare expanse of chest. Although the swirling water veiled his lower region, she could tell he wore naught beneath the water either.

"Lady Elf, fear not," shouted Nigel as, sword drawn, he burst through the brush to the banks of the creek. When he saw the two in the water, he nearly stumbled as he stopped short.

Tedric followed behind him. His eyebrows shot high as he took in the scene in front of him. His sword, too, flashed in the air until he lowered it.

"Don't fret, Nigel. Lady Elfreda sought to join me in my bath." Payne splashed the water around his waist.

Heat flamed in her cheeks. "I did not."

"I don't think Coxesbury would approve of you bathing with his wife, Payne," Tedric said. He re-sheathed his sword.

Elf gripped the edge of her skirt until her knuckles turned white. "I was not bathing with him. I sought to bathe alone."

"Perhaps next time you should look before you plunge." Payne made no attempt to move.

Nigel shook his head. "Come along, Tedric. We'll leave them to sort this out."

"I don't know. It isn't often I witness a lady's bath. Why should Payne have all the pleasure?" Tedric shuffled some leaves aside as if to make himself a seat.

"No," said Elf. "I won't be staying."

"Such a pity," said Tedric with a loud sigh.

Clenching her fists, Elf said, "If you would leave now, I will get dressed and join you presently."

"As the lady wishes." Tedric bowed to her, then turned to Nigel. "It seems we are not wanted."

"Speak for yourself," said Nigel, but he returned through the bushes. Tedric followed him.

Payne still had not moved. "The water doesn't grow any warmer."

Elf glanced at him, then blushed anew. "I'm going." She stepped from the water and grabbed her overgown, which dangled from a branch where she had flung it. Slipping it over her head, she chanced a peek back at Payne. He had turned his back to her, and for an instant the water dipped low enough that she saw the slight rounding of his backside. She saw the tracks of scars across his broad shoulders, but noticed the taper to his waist and the strength of his muscles even more. Heat revisited her cheeks, and she fled the brook.

A few minutes later, Payne stood fully clothed by the fire. She couldn't bring her gaze to meet his.

"If you wish, you may now bathe without intrusion while we strike the tent, Lady Elfreda."

She nodded and made her way back to the brook. Not daring to tarry long, she doffed her dress and slid into the pool. The cold water took her breath away, but did little to quench the burning image of Payne in her mind. Washing herself as best she could, she willed herself not to think about the former occupant of this water.

She failed.

Two days later, the small company pulled into a vast green expanse on the outskirts of Northstoke. A myriad of colorful banners flew from the tops of a sea of tents, like birds swooping over the crests of waves. Elf took in the spectacle with wide eyes. Although she had heard of tournaments, her uncle had never taken her to one, preferring instead to leave her behind to run his castle while he entertained his wife and child.

As the cart moved through the throng, she twisted her head to view the passing tents and people. The noise was near deafening—horses whinnied, men shouted, dogs barked, and everywhere was the clank of metal upon metal. The acrid smell of too many bodies and too many animals assailed her nostrils. She wrinkled her nose.

"Is something amiss?" asked Nigel.

"No. The crowd surprised me, and I suppose I am unaccustomed to the smells and sounds."

"Aye. I've forgotten how it stirs the blood. Makes me wish I were a young man again. I'd teach these pups a thing or two."

Elf hid a smile. Stirring her *stomach* described her reaction better. Only men could find such pleasure in sweat and noise. "Why are we moving so far from the center?"

"Payne prefers his privacy. He wants to give Caesar as much peace as possible before the tournament."

As if to illustrate Nigel's words, a horse near them reared, pawing the air with his forelegs. The men holding the reins cursed and jumped away from the frantic animal. Caesar lifted his head. His ears flicked forward and his gaze turned from one side to the other. Words from Payne soothed the steed, but Caesar still lifted his hooves and struck the ground with more force than their pace warranted. Elf could sense the unspent excitement rampant in the horse.

Tedric and his man stopped at an open spot. "This is where I'll set my tent, Payne. Unlike you, I want to be closer to the action."

"Suit yourself," said Payne.

Tedric bowed to Elf. "Lady Elfreda, we shall meet again. Dare I hope you'll cheer for me?"

Elf smiled at the exaggerated hope on his face. "I do wish you luck, Sir Tedric."

Payne shot her a glance, but she merely arched her eyebrows.

"I can ask for nothing else. See you on the field, Payne. Or better said, see you on the ground." Tedric roared with laughter.

"Only if you've fallen there first and I must help you rise," retorted Payne. He urged Merlin forward without another glance at his opponent.

At the farthest edge of the field, Payne dismounted and threw Merlin's reins over the low hanging branch of a nearby tree. Nigel pulled up into the spot. The cart jerked to a stop. Without any exchange of words, the two men sprang to work. Payne led Caesar to a different tree and tethered him. Nigel pulled the largest bundle from the rear of the cart and let it fall to the ground with a loud thump. Together, the two men erected the tent in little time.

Elf watched from the side. She might have helped, except she felt her help might actually be more of a hindrance. Nigel unloaded Payne's armor. The metal clanked as he carried it into the tent.

Elf opened her mouth to protest, but Payne spoke first. "Don't worry. We need to keep the armor from any rain, but I won't use the tent until I make sure you're not there. Nigel and I will sleep outside as we have these past few nights."

"Oh." Elf pursed her lips. She hadn't meant to act like a shrew, but apparently Payne thought her one if he had to respond to her complaints before she even voiced them. "I'm sorry to have inconvenienced you so."

"You haven't. Any inconvenience I brought upon myself."

Elf fell silent. His acceptance of his guilt troubled her, though she didn't understand why. *He* abducted *her.* She never asked that he take her. This show of chivalry wouldn't change her opinion of him. Nevertheless, she feared a twinge of guilt niggled at her.

"Nigel. Can you handle the rest of the unpacking?" Payne called out.

"Yes. Go ahead." Nigel bent over the bedding.

"Come along then, Lady Elfreda." Payne held out his arm.

"Where are we going?"

"You needed to make purchases. We should find all you need here."

He remembered. A shot of warmth melted through her at his thoughtfulness. Elf took his arm. "When we return to my uncle, I'll see you get repaid for my things."

"That isn't necessary." He led her through the vast labyrinth of tents.

"But . . ." Elf didn't finish her sentence. She knew he was saving his money, but he probably would spend his money just to spite her.

Payne wondered what she was about to say, but he didn't press her. She was too independent by half. A woman like that belonged in a convent. She would either learn to restrain her impulses or become the abbess.

"May I ask you a favor?" she asked.

A retort had already risen to his lips, but she continued without waiting for his response.

"I've never much liked my name. Would it be too much trouble to call me Elf?"

"Elf?"

"I know it's a silly name for a woman as tall as I, but Elfreda is such a mouthful. And under the circumstances . . ." She shrugged. "We'll be spending a lot of time together, and you have to call me something."

"Very well, Lady Elf." He couldn't very well tell her he'd been thinking of her as Elf since he learned her real name.

"Lady Elf? I suppose that will do, if you cannot be less formal with me."

Was that a hint of sadness he heard in her voice? And why did it matter to him in any case? He needed to concentrate on the tournament, then return her to her uncle and get her out of his life.

They passed a sweetmeat vendor. Elf's gaze lingered on the honey-covered delicacies. On an impulse, Payne stopped and bought several. Elf lifted a sweetened almond to her mouth. Her pink lips parted, and she dropped the treat into her mouth. She chewed with deliberation before she turned to him with a grin.

"Delicious."

A tiny drop of honey remained on the corner of her mouth. Before he could think, he lifted his finger, wiped it off, and tasted the sweetness himself. "Indeed."

A blush stole into her cheeks, bringing a smile to his lips. She looked enchanting, very much like the Elf of her name.

"Here, you must try more than a drop." She pinched another almond between her fingers and lifted it to his mouth. He closed his lips around her fingers as he took the treat with his tongue. As she snatched her finger from his mouth, her blush grew deeper.

"Delicious, indeed," he said.

They continued through the maze of tents, stopping here and there to buy her a brush and comb, a length of cloth, and a few other items. Then they stopped at the tailor's with the cloth. The tailor measured her, then promised to have an overgown ready by the next day. It would be simple, but it would be clean. Payne asked the man to make two, and as they left the tent, the man was already cutting the fabric and shouting for his assistants to prepare the needles.

As they wandered back toward their own tent, his arms full

of their purchases, Payne caught sight of colorful ribbons. He stopped and bought two lengths—one dark green, the other white. He presented them to her with a bow. "For your hair."

Elf took the ribbons and ran them through her fingers. "You've bought me enough already."

" 'Tis my money. I may spend it as I wish."

"What of the holding you wish to buy?"

Payne paused. "You know of that?"

"Nigel said you've been saving every penny."

"A length of ribbon won't deplete my pockets."

"Yes, but what of all the other things you bought me today?"

"They are gifts."

"I don't want you to spend your money on me."

Payne's gaze narrowed. "I thought you enjoyed your purchases."

"I did, but I shall have my uncle repay you. You don't need to buy my gowns. He and I can well afford today's expenses."

"Whereas I cannot?" Anger rose in him.

Elf raised her hand. "I mean no offense."

"Yet offend you do by refusing my gifts. I owe you at least this much for my error."

"You intend to buy my forgiveness?" Elf's eyebrows arched. "Much as Baron Coxesbury would have bought his bride's with the extravagant things he purchased?"

"That's different."

"How?" She placed her fists on her hips.

"I am not he."

"No, I thought you had more sense."

"Very well, you may repay me. You're right, of course. The money means more to me than bringing you a little joy." He turned from her. "Bring the ribbons. I mustn't forget those when I give your uncle my accounting."

He didn't wait for her to say anything, but started back toward the edge of the field. "Don't tarry. I wouldn't want to waste more time searching for you in this crowd."

Payne listened for her footsteps, but didn't turn to her when she caught up. Neither spoke, even after they returned to Nigel. Nigel glanced between the two of them, but Payne had no desire to enlighten his old friend either.

Despite the noises that surrounded them, their day had turned quiet.

Chapter Seven

"Six jousts? Are you mad?" Nigel placed his fists on his hips.

"Three are but pups. The others . . ." Payne shrugged his shoulders. "Caesar is strong enough."

" 'Tisn't that daft beast I'm worried about," muttered Nigel.

Payne grinned. "Which daft beast are you worried about?"

"You haven't fought six in a day in two years." Nigel shook out the horse's blanket, then folded the black cloth and set it to the side. "You aren't as young as you once were."

The grin never left Payne's face. "Watch your words, old man. You'll frighten the lady. I promised to return her to her uncle, and she might think I won't live to carry out my promise." He turned to look at Elf, who sat to the side of the small fire watching the two men.

Elf saw his attention and turned her head. Payne almost sighed. They hadn't exchanged more than polite words since their afternoon of shopping, but even she couldn't dampen his spirits this morning. This was the third day at the tournament site, the second day of the tournament, but the first day Payne would participate in the contests. His blood raced through him in anticipation of the coming events. He had missed this excitement while serving the Baron.

With his sleeve, Payne wiped a non-existent spot on the shaffron. The horse's armor gleamed like the sun off a mirror. As if the animal knew Payne thought of him, Caesar pawed the ground.

"He senses your excitement," said Nigel. He carried the black cloth to the destrier and tossed it over the animal's back. The golden bear emblazoned on the cloth leaped into view as the material draped over Caesar's withers. "I'll wager he's missed this as much as you."

Payne's eyes widened. "I never mentioned I missed fighting in the tournaments."

"You didn't have to. Your grin speaks words." Nigel adjusted the saddle's cinch around Caesar's girth.

Payne carried the shaffron and crinet to the destrier and placed them over the horse's head and neck, while Nigel placed the peytrel across Caesar's chest. Caesar's muscles jumped and quivered under Payne's touch. "Easy, boy. We'll be in the lists soon."

The horse whinnied as if in response.

Nigel turned to Payne. "Now you." Nigel ducked into the tent.

Payne bowed before Elf. "With your permission, I would use the tent to ready myself for the joust."

Elf waved her hand. "By all means."

He bowed again and brushed the canvas flap aside.

Elf sighed as the flap fluttered shut. She far preferred the rudeness they had shared in the past to this cold politeness. At least their verbal jousts had entertained her.

The hollow thud of Caesar's hooves caught her attention. The horse lifted and dropped its foreleg as if beating out a rhythm. The creature was dressed for war, and he looked magnificent. The gleaming silver of his armor and the glint of a golden bear from the black of the horse's covering filled her with a fearsome awe. A shiver snaked down Elf's spine. She would hate to face such a sight riding against her. How much worse would the vision seem when Payne sat atop his mount?

She didn't have to wait long to find out. Payne emerged from the tent clad in mail and armor. He held his helmet under his right arm and his shield on his left. The helmet had no crest or other adornment. The face of the shield was black, and a golden bear rising on its hind legs slashing the air graced the center. He looked formidable.

"Will you watch from the stands?" he asked.

"I haven't decided yet."

" 'Tis a worthy spectacle even if you choose to cheer for my opponents."

"I don't wish you unwell."

"I didn't think you did, but neither do I deceive myself into thinking you wish me well."

Elf didn't answer.

"If you choose not to attend, stay near the camp. You'll be safer here." He lowered his helmet over his head.

From the narrow slit in the helm, Elf could see his golden eyes flashing at her like a light from a lantern. His black hose and tunic gave the impression of a bodiless spirit inhabiting the armor. She shivered again.

With practiced ease, Payne vaulted onto the saddle. "Are you ready, Nigel?"

"I come anon." Nigel crossed to the cart and removed four long poles tapered to blunt ends. "Lady Elf, I can take you to the stands if you wish."

"No, thank you, Nigel. I have not yet decided if I care to watch the joust."

Nigel shrugged. "As you will." He stood beside Payne.

Payne lifted his gauntlet in a stiff salute. "Until later, Lady Elf."

She nodded her head.

The pair left the site, one on Caesar's massive back, the other running alongside.

Elf stared after them. She would have liked to see the jousting. After all, she never had, but stubbornness kept her from running after the pair. Instead, she lifted the flap of the tent and went inside. If she wasn't going to see the jousts, she might as well sleep. Goodness knew sleep had eluded her these past few nights.

As she lay upon the pallet, she tried not to think of Payne in combat. He was a mighty warrior, well-versed in battle and jousting. No harm would come to him. But the cheers and shouts from the field didn't ease her concerns. An hour later, she gave up on the illusive quest for sleep and rose. Perhaps a short walk would help soothe her.

As she made her way through the labyrinth of tents and stalls, she noticed little custom. *Everyone must be at the tournament,* she thought. As she passed the sweetmeat vendor, the image of Payne feeding her a honey-covered almond rose unbidden to her mind. Gritting her teeth, she walked on, turning her head neither left nor right.

Like a ripple in a pond, a buzz traveled through the collection of tents. Merchants dashed from one stall to the next, raising their voices in excitement. Elf wondered what news could bring forth such a response. She leaned forward to catch the words at the next stall.

"I do hope they don't cancel the tournament. 'Twould cost me much if they canceled," said the baker. "I haven't earned nearly enough yet."

"I heard he wasn't an important knight, belonged to no house he did," answered the weaver. "Nay, he weren't important enough to cancel the tournament for. Now if he were the king's man . . ."

"Pardon me, my good men, but what are you talking about?" interrupted Elf.

The men bowed to her. "Forgive us, my lady," answered the baker. "It seems a knight has been killed in the lists."

Cold seeped into her blood, and Elf knew the color drained from her face. "A knight?"

"Yes, my lady. But doan ye fret. He was a mercenary. I'm sure you couldna have known him."

For an instant, Elf couldn't breathe. Then she grabbed her skirts and ran toward the field.

It couldn't be Payne. Payne couldn't be dead. She repeated the words to herself as she dashed through the narrow paths between tents and stalls. When she saw the lists, she ran faster still.

At the edge of the field she spotted Tedric's coat of arms. She ran to the only other knight she knew. Tedric sat on a stump with a mug in his hands while his man cleaned the length of his lance. Tedric stood. "Lady Elf. What brings you to me? Dare I hope for a favor from you?"

"Payne," she managed to say as she panted. "Where is he?"

A look of comic disappointment covered Tedric's face. "I should have known you weren't looking for me. Such a pity."

Elf grabbed his arm, ignoring the pain that shot through her hand as the hard metal cut her palm. "Please tell me where I can find Payne. I heard a knight was killed . . ."

"Ah. I understand now. You needn't fear, Lady Elf. Payne still lives. I believe he and Nigel are holding themselves to the other side of the field."

"Thank you." Elf released Tedric's arm and ran to the opposite side of the lists. She scanned the rippling banners until she spied the golden bear on the field of black. Only when she saw Caesar, and then Payne beside him, did she sense relief coursing through her.

Payne looked at her in surprise. "Lady Elf. What are you doing here?"

She couldn't prevent the rush of tears that stung her eyes. "I heard a knight had been killed, and I—" She hiccuped on a sob.

For a moment, Payne examined her; then he gave her a gentle smile. "I am uninjured, Lady Elf." He took a step toward her.

Elf averted her gaze. She didn't want him to see how frightened she had been. "The knight who died . . ."

"He was careless. He shouldn't have challenged any of these knights." Payne shook his head. "I would never have answered him."

Elf nodded, her throat too constricted to give words to her relief.

"Lady Elf, you're hurt." Payne took her hand and turned it over. A scrape across her palm oozed blood. He reached for a clean cloth and dabbed the blood away. "How did this happen?"

"I'm not quite sure. I think I must have cut it on Sir Tedric's armor."

Payne stiffened. "Tedric did this to you?"

"No, I think I did it to myself. I grabbed his arm when I saw him. I must have cut it then."

"Tedric's armor is sharp for a tournament," said Nigel.

"I was thinking the same myself," said Payne with a nod. He wrapped the cloth around her hand and tied it. "This should stop the bleeding."

"Thank you," she whispered. "I didn't mean to cause you concern before your jousts."

"I have already won three challenges, my lady."

Elf arched her eyebrows. "Three?"

"Yes, but two took only one pass." Payne grinned at her. "Will you stay and watch the others, Lady Elf?"

Now that she could once again breathe, Elf nodded. "I may as well. I've never seen jousting before, and I've heard it's very exciting. Although I don't suppose the family of that poor knight thinks so now."

"He had no family."

Elf stared at him. "Was he a friend of yours?"

"No, I wouldn't call him a friend, but I knew of him. I suppose he was trying to garner the attention of some nobleman, perhaps hoping to become part of a household and train squires for someone. The man was too old to fight much longer."

"How sad."

"At least he no longer has worries, and he died in a manner that brought no shame upon him."

Elf wondered how much of Payne's words reflected the truth of his own life.

Nigel approached her. "May I take you to the stands, my lady?"

"Yes—no, wait." Elf reached up and untied the ribbon in her hair. As she unraveled her braid, the ribbon grew longer and her hair more unkempt. When she finished, she offered the ribbon to Payne. "I've heard ladies sometimes give tokens to the knights they favor."

"They do."

"Will you accept this from me?"

For a long second, Payne didn't move. Then he knelt before her and held out his helmet. "I would be honored."

The ribbon still in her hand, Elf looked at Payne.

"Tie it to his helm, my lady," whispered Nigel with encouragement. She couldn't help but notice the grin on the older man's face.

Heat rushed to her face as a blush crept into her cheeks. She threaded the ribbon through an opening in the helmet.

"Make sure it isn't too long. You don't want to block his vision," said Nigel.

She nodded and looped it around again. Then tying it in a bow, she stepped back. "Is that right?"

"Perfect," answered Nigel.

Payne rose. He touched his gauntlet to her chin and raised her gaze to his. "Thank you, my lady."

Elf couldn't turn her eyes from him. She knew her cheeks glowed in a fiery blush, but she didn't care. His gaze made her feel like the most beautiful woman in the world.

"I'd best take you to the stands now, my lady," said Nigel.

"What?" said Elf, still staring at Payne. Then she shook herself. "Yes, the stands, of course."

"Farewell, my lady," said Payne.

"Good luck, Payne," she answered. *And be careful,* she thought to herself as she followed Nigel away from the field.

The morning sped by as Elf watched the jousts. She held her breath as Payne raced to unseat a knight, and cheered when the dust settled and he remained atop Caesar. Payne won the next one as well, although a lance broke on him during one pass. At last he faced the final challenge of the day. With a gasp, Elf realized the knight he jousted against was Tedric.

A woman beside her spoke. "The Golden Bear wears someone's favor. Whose do you suppose it is?"

Elf turned to answer when she realized the woman wasn't speaking to her.

"I don't know," answered the second woman. "He's never worn a favor before."

Elf couldn't remain silent. "Do you know the Golden Bear?"

The women looked at her. The first one answered, "No, but I've seen him at tournaments in the past."

"He's a mysterious one," added the second woman. "He keeps to himself, and I've heard he never comes to any of the celebrations. But he is a marvelous warrior. I've heard he's never lost a joust."

"Some say he uses magic to give him strength," continued the first.

"That's ridiculous." Elf frowned at the two women. "Payne is just an ordinary man."

"I don't know. Most of us are frightened of him," said the second.

"Just because you are silly little geese, doesn't mean he uses unnatural powers. Magic indeed. Hah. And I'll thank you not to spread such rumors any further." Elf sniffed in derision.

The two women looked offended and turned away from Elf. She didn't care. Payne and Tedric had taken their places at the opposite ends of the lists.

Chapter Eight

Caesar shifted beneath him.

"Steady, boy. This is the last one." Payne peered through the slits in his helmet to the other end of the field. Tedric sat on a dappled gray steed. Payne knew Tedric would pay well to recover his horse after the joust, but he also knew Tedric wouldn't be as easy to defeat as the others had been.

The trumpets sounded, the flag waved, and Payne lowered his lance. Tightening his knees around Caesar, he rolled with the horse's initial jump onto the field and aimed for Tedric's shield. The thunder of the two horses' hooves drowned out the cheer of the crowd. In fact, Payne heard his own breathing and the beat of his heart over any other noise.

His lance shattered as he landed a solid blow against Tedric's shield just as he deflected Tedric's strike on his own. He reached the end of the lists and turned Caesar with a quick squeeze of his knees. Nigel handed him a new lance.

The flag waved again. Caesar leaped into the row with a powerful stride. Payne eyed his on-coming opponent. He aimed his lance.

From the corner of his eye, he saw a flash of white fluttering by his head. For an instant, he wondered what it was, and then he remembered. The ribbon must have come loose from its bow. Elf's favor. He couldn't prevent the contentment that flowed through him at the thought.

Too late he realized his concentration had wavered. An angry snarl roared through him as he realized he hadn't prepared himself for Tedric's next attack. His own lance missed the knight, but Tedric's landed in the middle of his shield. The sound of splintering wood echoed through Payne's helmet. A searing pain ripped through his arm as he nearly lost his seat. Gripping Caesar with his thighs, he gritted his teeth and tried to keep his balance on his horse. He pulled himself upright, then cursed his foolishness. At the end of the lists, he whirled Caesar around, ready to attack anew. Tedric had scored two points off him. He had to unseat Tedric on this pass.

"Payne, your arm," Nigel shouted to him.

"Not now, Nigel." Payne gripped his lance and waited for the signal. He heard a collective gasp rise from the crowd, but he didn't permit the noise to concern him. His shield arm burned, but he focused on the knight at the other end of the field.

The flag fell, and he lowered his lance as he started down his side of the lists. Anger at himself, at Tedric, and at Elf fueled his concentration. Tedric's new lance aimed for his chest, but Payne deflected it with ease, planting the tip of his own lance squarely against the armor on Tedric's chest. The resounding clunk and bits of flying wood told Payne of his hit, but only after he turned did he see Tedric prone on the ground, his man rushing to help him rise.

Payne reined in Caesar. The great horse reared, but Payne remained in his seat. He waited for Tedric's man to give him the signal that the joust was at end. When a second man arrived to help Tedric stagger from the field, Payne knew he was the victor. He handed off the remnant shaft of his lance to Nigel. Doffing his helm, he rode to the viewing stands to pay homage to the nobleman hosting the tournament.

Only then did he notice the silence of the crowd. He looked back and saw Tedric walking, albeit on unsteady legs. Tedric was not dead. What held the spectators' attention?

Nigel grabbed Caesar's reins as they approached the stands. "Payne, your arm."

Payne looked at his shield arm. In the meaty flesh between his elbow and his shoulder, a long, thin sliver of wood protruded from between the joints of his armor. The wood still bore evidence of the paint of Tedric's lance. Blood trickled down his arm into his gauntlet. This explained the pain in his arm.

Ignoring his injury for the moment, Payne bowed to the nobleman and the ladies at his side. The earl rose and applauded Payne. As he did so, the remaining spectators leaped to their feet and roared their appreciation of the knight's bravery. One of the earl's daughters leaned out of the stands to present him a small box. Payne bowed to her, then rode off the field.

As he passed the stands, he searched for Elf but didn't see her. He dismounted at the end of the lists and waited for Nigel to reach him.

Nigel took his helmet and Caesar's reins. "How do you fare?"

"It will hurt more when I remove it." His arm sent shots of white-hot pain flashing through him with every movement. Payne tried to make a fist, but the effort only caused more intense throbbing. "We'll see to it at the tent."

When he arrived at the tent, he knew why he hadn't

spotted Elf in the stands. She was here, waiting for him—scowling at him.

"You needn't look so fierce. I won." He set aside the box. "Nigel, would you water Caesar for me?"

Nigel led Caesar to the stream to let the horse drink.

"Do you not care that you look like a hedgehog?" As Elf crossed to him, she stared at the spike that stuck out of his arm.

Payne ignored her and sat on a rock. "Nigel, help me with my boots."

"I'll do it." Elf straddled his legs and pulled without much success on one boot. Payne grinned at the sight of her shapely backside wriggling with the effort. Before the first boot came off, she turned back to him. "That thing will have to come out before you can remove your armor."

"I know."

The first boot came off, then the second. Payne gritted his teeth as he lifted his hands so she could remove his gauntlets. He winced as she tugged on his injured arm. Blood dripped from his fingertips and from the inside of the gauntlet.

Elf gasped.

Nigel returned and examined Payne's arm. "Do you want me to do it?"

"No."

Nigel nodded and took the gauntlets from Elf's hands. "I'll clean these."

Payne turned to Elf. "You shouldn't see this, my lady."

Elf clenched her teeth together and shook her head. "No, I've cared for wounds before, and I will again. My duties as a nun will include caring for the sick. After I take my vows—"

Payne didn't want to hear her finish. He reached up with his right hand, grabbed the sliver and yanked it from his arm, letting out a shout as he did. Elf's face lost its color as she watched open-mouthed. At least she no longer spoke.

The long piece of wood lay on the ground in front of him. He let his head fall back and closed his eyes. Blood flowed freely from the wound.

"Let me help you, boy." Nigel unhooked the armor from the hauberk, then lifted the mail itself from Payne's shoulders.

Blood seeped through his tunic. Nigel took one look at the wound and said, "I'll get the needle." He disappeared into the tent.

Payne removed his tunic, gritting his teeth with the effort. The tunic seemed to fly over his head. He looked up to see Elf with the garment in her hands. Her frown no longer held disapproval, only worry. He lifted his right hand and stroked her cheek. "I've had worse wounds than this."

"Not when I've been present," she answered. Tears shimmered in her eyes.

"Don't cry, Elf."

"I'm not."

Nigel emerged from the tent with a ewer. "I'll need water."

Elf ran to him. "I'll fetch some. She took the jug from his hand and ran to the brook. After filling the vessel with cool, clear water, she hurried back to the men, managing to keep more than half the water in the crockery. Nigel was mopping the blood from Payne's arm.

"Here." Elf thrust the ewer toward Payne. The water sloshed over the side and splashed onto his groin, seeping into the fabric of his trousers.

Payne sucked in his breath. "That water is cold."

Elf let out a puff of air. "I would think your arm should be of greater concern to you."

Nigel dipped a cloth into the remaining water, then

handed the cloth to Elf. "You clean him. I'll fetch more water." Nigel took the container and ran toward the stream.

Elf pulled her bottom lip between her teeth and dabbed at Payne's arm with a feather-light touch.

"You couldn't clean a spider's web that way." Payne shook his head.

"I didn't want to hurt you."

"I won't break."

But as Elf wiped the blood from his arm, she saw the little pearls of sweat on his brow. "You *are* hurting."

He nodded. "Aye, but the needle shall hurt more."

Elf swiped at the wound. For an instant, the gash stayed clean, then welled anew with his blood. Dear God, what if it never stopped?

Nigel returned with the water. She poured more water on the cloth and wiped Payne's wound again. Payne closed his eyes. Nigel pressed a clean cloth to the injury. "Lady Elf, please hold this against the wound. Press hard. I must ready the needle."

Elf bit her bottom lip again and tried not to look at the grimace on Payne's face. She had tended injuries before, although never one as deep. Why should this man's blood bother her so?

"Ready." Nigel lifted the needle from which trailed a long thread.

Payne didn't flinch as Nigel brought the needle to his arm. Elf did. Then again, her eyes were open. She removed the cloth from the wound and grimaced as Nigel sewed the edges of the gash together. Payne clenched his teeth, but held his arm straight. Perspiration dripped from his forehead, but he never even whimpered. Elf whimpered for him.

"Done," said Nigel after a few minutes. He bit off the end of the thread. From a small crock, Nigel spread some salve on the stitched gash. Elf thought it smelled of camphor, but before she could be sure, Nigel pressed a fresh cloth to the wound. Ripping another piece of fabric into strips, he tied the cloth to the injury. "Don't move it."

Payne nodded, but didn't rise. Elf tipped the ewer, moistened a fresh cloth, and wiped his brow. Payne opened his eyes to a slit.

She shrugged. "I thought it might feel good."

"It did." He shut his eyes again.

"Go lie down, boy. I'll bring you some wine to strengthen your blood," said Nigel.

"I'll take the wine, but I won't lie down."

"Suit yourself." Nigel moved off to the cart. Elf followed him.

"Nigel," began Elf.

Grasping a vessel of wine, he turned to her. "Yes, my lady?"

"Will he recover?"

"If the wound doesn't fester." Nigel took the wine back to Payne.

A shudder ran through Elf. If Payne were to fall ill . . . no, she wouldn't think of it. He had promised to take her home.

She watched Payne throughout the rest of the day. He regained his strength, but Elf looked for any sign of weakening or fever. When he moved, he carried his arm with care, holding it away from his body and trying not to jar it. At the presentation of the prizes, Payne held himself straight. No hint of his wrap showing beneath his tunic. As the tournament champion, he received his award, a small golden likeness of a shield and lance. When he returned to the tent, he opened a small casket and placed his prize inside. Elf caught a glimpse of gold and jewels before he closed it. He grabbed the small box and went to add it to his hoard.

"What is in the box?"

"I haven't looked yet." Payne opened the lid. On a bed of red velvet sat a small emerald.

A rush of anger stirred within her. "You must have pleased her mightily to receive such a gift."

Payne shot her a surprised glance. "I think she rewarded me for my bravery as a hedgehog."

"Was that all?" Some part of her knew she acted foolish, but the anger blocked most of her reason.

"You sound jealous."

"Jealous? Why would I be jealous?" She was afraid he was right.

Payne didn't speak for a moment. "Sometimes, when a nobleman backs a tournament, he will give his wife and daughters trinkets to present to any knight who pleases them. Apparently the earl's daughter enjoyed my joust."

"I'm sure it doesn't matter to me. You must be pleased to have earned so much at this tournament." Elf turned her back to him and sat on a rock.

"Aye. Now you can wear your ribbons without guilt."

At nightfall Nigel prepared the pallets, as Payne couldn't help, and Elf retired with some reluctance to her soft pallet.

She must have slept, for when her eyes opened, the night was silent save the chirruping of the crickets and the occasional hoot of an owl. She rolled to her side, then froze. The firelight showed the clear silhouette of someone standing outside her tent.

Her heart pounding, she crept to the opening and peeked out.

Payne stood by the fire drinking from the jug of wine.

"Are you ill?" asked Elf.

Payne whirled to face her. "You should be sleeping."

"As should you." Elf left the tent and crossed to him. "Is your arm troubling you?"

"Aye." Payne looked at his offending limb. "I find myself rolling on top of it and waking myself."

A loud snort came from Nigel. Elf glanced at the older man sleeping on the ground.

Payne chuckled. "Perhaps we should lower our voices." He returned to his bedding and sat, propping his back upon the stone behind him. Lifting the rim of the vessel to his lips, he took another long swallow of the wine.

"Does the wine help?"

"It dulls the senses. If I can feel numb, then I can sleep on my arm."

Elf thought for a moment. "You need your rest. Why don't you take my bed?"

"Ha. And where will you sleep?" His voice roused Nigel to another snort.

"Hush." She pointed at Nigel and knelt beside Payne. "I'll sleep out here by the fire."

"Nay. You'll not be safe out here. It's best if I continue to woo the wine." He raised the jug to his lips.

"Don't be foolish. You can sleep on my pallet. I'll . . ." She glanced around.

"You could join me." Payne grinned at her.

A fiery blush rose from her neck. Before she could answer, he continued. "No, I forgot. You're promised to the abbey. Fear not, fair maid, you are safe from my advances."

She didn't know whether to kick him or cry. She chose neither. "Go to bed, Payne, before the wine makes you regret the morning."

His demeanor serious, he said, "I cannot leave you unprotected, milady."

"Very well. We'll sleep inside." She grabbed his bedding

and pulled it into the tent. Payne followed her.

As she spread the blankets on the ground by the edge of the canvas, she felt his gaze. He sat on the soft furs of her bed, and sighed. " 'Tis heaven. You are truly an angel of mercy to accommodate me so."

She didn't answer, dismissing his words as wine-induced flattery. She patted her new, hard pallet. "There. I shall be quite comfortable here."

She turned to face him and sighed. Payne lay face forward on the furs, his eyes closed and his mouth open slightly. He was asleep. She gave in to her desire to touch him and brushed a lock of hair from his face.

"Good night, good knight."

Chapter Nine

The following morning, Payne stumbled out from the tent. Nigel raised a single eyebrow.

"Don't start, Nigel."

"I didn't say anything." Nigel rolled up the bedding. "We are leaving today, right?"

"As soon as we can. Have you collected the ransom for the armor and horses?"

"Aye, all save Tedric, but I'm sure the braggart will come by soon." Nigel tossed the roll into the cart, then paused. He pointed to the tent. "Do you want to get her out?"

Payne glanced at the tent, then shook his head. "I think I'll let you."

"What did you do, boy?" Nigel scowled.

"Nothing. At least I don't think so. She offered me her bed, because of my injury. I fell asleep. I think." He ran his hand down his face.

"I'm only afraid that you weren't thinking." Nigel ducked into the tent, still frowning.

In a few minutes, Elf appeared. She stretched her arms overhead, yawned, then smiled at him. "Good morrow. How are you feeling this morning? How does your arm fare?"

Payne eyed her with suspicion. "I am well, thank you."

" 'Tis a fine morning. Did you sleep well?"

"Aye." He paused. "I thank you for your . . . uh, my . . . the bed." To his surprise and dismay, he felt heat creeping into his cheeks.

She waved her hand. "You were injured. I couldn't let you suffer. Besides, the ground wasn't too hard." She rubbed her hand over her hip and frowned.

"Is something amiss?"

"Nay," she answered, her hand still rubbing the spot on her hip. "It seems there was a small pebble that plagued me all night, but don't fret on it. I'm sure I shall heal sooner than you."

Payne raised his injured arm and steeled his face against the wince that wanted to cross his features. "I fare better, my lady. You should have woken me if you were uncomfortable."

"And you, sir, are stubborn beyond fault. A small pebble is hardly reason to steal a bed from an injured man."

Ire stirred within him. She was treating him as if he were an invalid. "My wound is hardly grave."

"But you'll heal faster if you rest. You weren't resting last night until you came to my bed."

Her words sent more heat through him, but not to his face. His groin tightened at the thought of sharing her bed. Payne gazed at her face. Clearly she had no idea what she had just said for she continued without a pause.

"In fact, I'm thinking we should delay leaving until you are stronger. My uncle will never know if we are three or four days later than we already are."

What was she saying? Spend an additional three or four days alone with her? "We are leaving today." Payne stood and crossed to the tent. "Nigel, are you finished in there?"

"Almost."

"Good. Then we can leave as soon as I get my gold from Tedric." He frowned at her. Think him weak, did she? If it were possible to drive the horses that fast, he'd get her back to her uncle tomorrow.

Elf sighed. "Very well. If you'll excuse me, I wish to wash before our departure." She headed for the stream and soon disappeared from his view.

Payne stared after her. What was it about this woman that caused her every word to stick him like a thorn? In three days, four at the most, he would return her to her uncle and be well rid of her.

Curious how the thought brought him little relief.

From the corner of his eye, Payne saw Tedric approach. Payne turned a little too swiftly and his injured arm swung out too far. He bit back a curse.

"Payne, you're looking well this morning. A little too hearty for my liking, but I never was a good loser." Tedric grinned. He held out a pouch. " 'Tis a good thing I won my other jousts, else I couldn't afford to pay you for my loss."

Payne took the pouch. A hefty weight. He enjoyed the feel of it in his hand, most especially since it was from Tedric. "Seems to me you're still leaving here with more money than you came."

" 'Tis true, 'tis true, but as I said, I don't enjoy losing. Even to you." Tedric laughed and clapped Payne on the back. "So where are we off to this morning?"

"We?"

"Of course. I've already told you my plans for the Lady Elfreda. Coxesbury won't pay me if I don't have her."

"We leave as soon as we load our cart. I hope that won't inconvenience you."

"That soon? I'd better get back and tell my man to lower the tent. I had hoped to stay another day or two to enjoy the local hospitality, but I can see you're eager to be off. Ah well, perhaps we can persuade Lady Elfreda's uncle to feed and provide us with entertainment."

Payne glared at Tedric, but the man had already turned and was walking away. Payne had hoped Tedric wouldn't be willing to leave so quickly. He had *hoped,* but he hadn't deemed it probable. Elf would hate the additional company, especially since that company intended to return her to Coxesbury.

Nigel tossed several rolls through the tent flap, then came out himself. "You've got your money then?"

"Aye. You heard?"

"How could I not? The man's voice carries further than the blast of a horn. The lady won't be pleased to see Tedric again."

"Nay, that she won't." Payne fell silent. He watched Nigel hoist the rolled up pallets, one over each shoulder, and carry them to the cart. He rose and grabbed a third roll.

"Watch yourself, boy. I don't want to see my sewing be undone."

The movement did hurt, but not enough to make Payne stop. He dropped his load into the cart and returned to the tent. With his good arm, he yanked up a corner of the canvas.

"Stubborn," muttered Nigel, as he moved to the opposite corner of the tent. Together they toppled the shelter, folded it, and packed it onto the cart.

The journey to her uncle's castle took four days. Elf couldn't say she enjoyed the journey, but it passed without incident. She wasn't particularly worried about Tedric's boast to return her to Baron Coxesbury. Payne had promised her he wouldn't let him, and somehow she trusted him. The sooner she returned home, the sooner she could enter the convent. She had one or two more things to take care of, then she could enter the abbey and begin her life free of the constraints of men.

So why did the sight of her uncle's castle bring so little comfort?

Elf's presence guaranteed their easy entry through the barbican. Their small band stopped in the courtyard. Elf climbed down from the cart. The knights dismounted and handed the care of their horses to the stable lads who flocked around them. Payne sent Nigel with Caesar.

Word of her return flew through the bailey and keep, until at last her uncle appeared in the courtyard. He strode to her, brushing past the servants to see his niece.

"Where have you been?" Her uncle's voice held little surprise at her return, and more than a little annoyance.

"Yes, I am well, thank you, Uncle Matthew," muttered Elf under her breath. She saw Payne raise his eyebrows and realized he had heard her words. She faced her uncle. "I trust Agnes is safely married?"

"Of course she is. What did you mean disappearing on her wedding day?"

"I didn't disappear, I was abducted." Elf brushed a speck of dirt from the front of her dress.

"Abducted? Don't be absurd."

"Baron Coxesbury decided he didn't intend to honor the dissolution of the betrothal. He thought to have Agnes carried off. He got me instead." Elf gave her uncle a disinterested stare.

"You aren't jesting. Good heavens, girl, we thought you had disappeared again. You were captured?"

With a mischievous grin, she turned to Payne. She read

the chagrin in his face and her grin grew wider. She knew what he expected her to say. "Yes, Uncle. May I introduce the man who . . . rescued me? This is Payne Dunbyer of Castlereigh—"

"Dear God, the Golden Bear?" Her uncle stepped around her to the tall man behind her. "You are welcome here, Sir Knight. How can I ever thank you enough for saving my niece?"

Elf enjoyed the consternation on Payne's face.

"And this other knight?" asked Matthew.

"Tedric of Almstone." Tedric stepped forward and bowed to Elf's uncle. "I am in the service of Baron Coxesbury."

"Baron Coxes—"

"Aye, but you have nothing to fear from me. I ask for but a few nights' lodging and perhaps a bit of your hospitality. Payne knows me well. He can vouch for me."

Elf's uncle glanced at Payne.

Payne said, "Aye, I can guarantee you have nothing to fear from him."

Was Elf the only one to read the warning in his words? She smiled at Payne.

"Welcome, good knights. I am honored to have you share my home. Let us move inside where I can offer you food and drink." Uncle Matthew led the two men into the keep.

Elf stared after them. Then she sighed. Leave it to her uncle to welcome the two men who posed the greatest threat to her while ignoring her. She grabbed her meager belongings from the cart and retreated to her room.

Within half an hour, she joined the men in the great hall of the keep. She passed Nigel at one of the tables. He looked to be enjoying his ale. Looking up at the dais, she saw Payne, Tedric and Uncle Matthew at the head table. The three men each had a goblet in front of them. Her uncle and Tedric laughed with each other. Payne, too, smiled, but Elf noticed he drank from his vessel less often than the other two men. And he didn't laugh with such abandon. She crossed to the table and took a place near her uncle.

"Elf, Tedric was just regaling us with the results of the tournament. Is it true you were present?" asked her uncle.

"Yes, Uncle Matthew."

"I never thought you might be interested in such things."

You never asked. She nodded to her uncle.

"Did you enjoy yourself?"

"I found it interesting, not that I had much choice in attending."

Her uncle roared at that. "I don't suppose you did. Tedric tells me you gave Payne your favor."

Elf felt the heat of a blush creep into her cheeks. "I did."

"Ha. Perhaps there is hope for you yet, girl." Her uncle quaffed his drink, then poured more ale into his goblet. "You haven't changed your mind about the abbey, have you?"

Payne's gaze focused on her. Her cheeks grew warmer. "No, Uncle."

"Well, I suppose it will be good to have some pull with the church." Her uncle guffawed again. He leaned close to Tedric. "Never could find a man who wasn't afraid of her."

Tedric laughed with her uncle. "If I found someone for her, would you agree to the match?"

Uncle Matthew seemed to think about this for a moment. Elf's blood ran cold with dread. Suppose her uncle agreed to the match between Coxesbury and herself? Suppose she found herself bound to that vulgar boor for life?

Uncle Matthew let out a blast of laughter. "I doubt you'd find anyone willing to marry her. No, I gave her my word she could enter the abbey. Here, allow me to refill your cup."

As Uncle Matthew poured more ale into Tedric's goblet,

Elf looked to the floor. Her throat tightened and burned with tears of mortification. She should be used to her uncle's disregard, but somehow with these witnesses present, her embarrassment seemed keener than before.

She glanced up and saw Payne's gaze fixed upon her. His expression read of understanding and something more. She didn't want his pity, or any man's pity. She would relish the days in the convent, and the time away from men.

"If you will excuse me, I will go to the kitchen. I find I am hungry." She rose from the table, and headed from the room.

"An excellent thought. Send some food back for me and my guests," her uncle called to her.

Payne saw her retreating back stiffen at her uncle's words. Elf continued without turning around. Truth was he understood the position of an unwanted relative in a household. Compassion for her stirred within him, but he felt something more than pity. He wanted to rescue her yet again, to take her away to her own home, to—

"Payne, I have a proposition for you." Lord Meredith raised his goblet into the air. "In whose service are you?"

"At the moment, I serve no man."

"Excellent. Tedric here is still pledged to Coxesbury, but I should like to hire you."

"Hire me?" The quirk of fate amused Payne. Hired by the uncle of the woman he had abducted. "Why?"

"I have a problem in my county that no one has been able to solve for me. Perhaps you might be successful."

Payne raised an eyebrow. "A problem?"

"Yes." Meredith slammed his goblet on the table. The ale sloshed over the sides, but he gave it no regard. "A thief has been plaguing my castle."

"A thief?" Payne shook his head. "I am no constable."

"Hear me out. They call him the Black Knight."

"Interesting." Payne took a swallow of his ale.

"He steals my food and my money. There is little pattern to his pilfering, but I know he must be privy to the workings of my house, else how could he know exactly when to strike? He never takes much, but it's enough to garner the attention of my steward." With each word, Lord Meredith's face grew ruddier and ruddier. He pounded on the table. "Just three weeks ago, he stole a venison shank and a ham, as well as a small pouch of gold. The peasants speak of him in glowing terms because he gives his booty to them. However, no one has seen his face."

"How am I to know when this Black Knight will strike again?"

"Ah, there's the rub. I don't know when or if he will, but perhaps if he learns you are now seeking him, he will think twice about robbing me again."

Tedric leaned back. "Payne, you get the most exciting tasks. I almost wish I didn't have the obligation to Coxesbury."

Payne refrained from comment. He turned to Meredith. "You haven't given me much information."

"I know, blast it. The knave leaves no trace of his activities until after the peasants have devoured the evidence."

"It sounds like a challenge worthy of my skills." Payne raised his glass.

Lord Meredith raised his in return. "To the quick and successful capture of the Black Knight."

"To the capture of the Black Knight," repeated Payne, and he drank.

Chapter Ten

Payne watched the castle for the third night in a row. He had discovered no sign of the Black Knight since Lord Meredith had asked for his help four days ago, but he had learned the Black Knight had last struck three weeks earlier. Logic told him the knight would wander out again soon. All he had to do was wait for him. Nights of waiting in the dark. In vain.

It didn't matter. The baron was paying him enough to wait.

Shadows blanketed the woods. Few lights burned in the keep or along the walls of the castle. Payne preferred the inky blackness. It hid him well. And Payne knew if the knight were to make an appearance tonight, he would have to come soon, for there weren't many hours of darkness left. Summer nights were short.

Payne glanced toward the woods and stifled a yawn. Nigel would be sleeping by now. They had set up the tent not far from here, realizing it would be simpler for them to stay outside the castle while hunting the Black Knight. Nigel had preferred to stay with him in the tent than remain at the castle. He claimed he slept better on the ground than in a bed anyway. Payne smiled at the thought of the older man's loyalty.

The moon did little to cut the dark. Payne yawned again. Another half-hour, perhaps a little longer, and he would finish this night's vigil. Then he could return to his pallet and sleep until morning.

Payne jerked upright in the saddle. There. Movement at the castle. He watched as a hidden door in the wall swung outward and a tall figure stepped out. Dressed from head to heel in black, including a black scarf to hide his face and a cloak to cover his form, the knight hefted two bags over his shoulders and stumbled slightly under their weight. Although the shadows blended into the knight's clothing, Payne had no trouble spotting the man as he headed along a path through the woods. Payne let out a soft chuckle. Black was his own choice of attire.

Payne's horse shifted beneath him.

"Easy, Merlin. Quiet, now." Payne clicked his tongue, and the horse stepped forward.

He didn't press his pace. He wanted to see where the Black Knight would lead him. The man walked with a confidence Payne knew was born of his past success. The knight neither looked left nor right, but stayed on his course without so much as a backward glance.

Within a few minutes, the knight strode toward a hovel. In a small pen in front of the hut stood a mare. Without hesitating, the knight dropped the bags to the ground and scratched the animal on the nose. The horse, too, was black, save for the star on its forehead. The knight murmured something to the animal as he stroked its flanks. Payne was too far to hear any words, but the animal tossed its head as if responding. Stepping to the bags, the knight lifted each one and tied them to the horn of the saddle.

Payne could have stopped the man then, but he was more curious about where the figure might lead him.

The knight mounted in a graceful arc. The horse didn't stir as its rider settled himself into the saddle. With a flick to the reins, the man rode out of the pen and into the woods.

With a soft jab of his heel, Payne set Merlin into motion again. He followed far enough behind that the knight wouldn't see him easily if he happened to turn, but close enough that the fellow couldn't slip into the darkness of the forest.

A few yards farther, Payne blinked. He didn't trust his vision. A light flickered ahead of him through the dark trunks of the trees. He pulled on the reins. Merlin stopped without a sound.

The Black Knight rode into a hidden glade and into the dim light of a small lantern. At this distance, the knight looked more a green youth than a seasoned fighter. The light from the flickering flame made the knight seem slimmer. Payne slipped even closer until he stood just outside the arc of light.

"Ah, so ye made it this ev'en." An ancient hag stepped forward clutching a gnarled walking stick in her hand.

The knight didn't reply; he simply nodded his head.

"And did ye enjoy yerself at the wedding?"

The knight still didn't speak.

"Can't trick you 'tall, can I?" The old woman cackled. "One of these nights, I'll get ye to talk to me. Ye ken yer secret's safe with me."

Payne wasn't sure, but he imagined he saw the knight's shoulders shaking in silent laughter.

"Ye're kind to think on us, Sir Knight. The baron, Lord Meredith, was generous with us for his daughter's wedding, but the village has long since run out of good meat."

Removing a knife from his belt, the knight slashed the ropes that held the bags to his saddle. With muted thuds, they landed in the dirt beside the horse.

Payne knew he should move now, but he was loath to deprive the crone and her village of the gifts the knight brought her.

The old woman grinned up at the knight, showing off the many gaps in her smile. "Thank ye. Me sons sleep not so far off. I'll wake them once ye've left and they'll fetch these home."

Again the knight nodded, then he held up a gloved hand, extending two fingers.

"Aye, two weeks. I'll come again and wait for ye."

Payne wanted to tell the woman that the Black Knight wouldn't come again in two weeks. In two weeks, the knave most likely would still be sitting in the dungeons for theft.

"Are you sure I can't convince you to stay and share a story with me?" The teasing lilt to the crone's voice amused Payne.

Shaking his head, the knight shook a finger in warning at the woman.

She laughed. "I didn't think so. God bless you, Black Knight. Ye're a good soul."

The knight bowed from atop his horse and pulled his rein to the left. The horse turned and disappeared into the woods.

Payne pulled left on his rein as well. At the click of his tongue, Merlin turned into the thicker shadows. Payne knew what his course of action must be. He had allowed the hag to take the knight's gifts, but he couldn't let the fellow escape. He urged Merlin to a greater speed than the knight. Branches of the trees scratched at him, but he wouldn't return to the path. He needed to get in front of the knight.

Excitement pounded in his blood. The thrill of the chase,

the nearness of his quarry, and the sureness of the end of his task quickened his heartbeat. Atop Merlin, he plunged through the trees just in front of his target.

The knight cried out in surprise. Payne thought the man's voice didn't match his build, but he didn't have time to ponder further.

"I am Payne of Castlereigh. At the baron's request, I was to find and capture you. This I have done. Will you come peacefully?"

The knight grasped the reins tighter in his hands. Payne couldn't read the man's expression through the woolen cover on his face, but he had no doubt the knight was searching for a path of escape. Payne shook his head. He had hoped the man would come without a fight.

A quick twitch of the knight's wrist was all Payne needed to see. The knight tried to turn his horse into the woods, but Payne had been waiting for just such an action. Before the horse could complete the move, Payne launched himself from his saddle. He flew across the short span between the two animals and grabbed the knight around the middle. In the space of a few seconds, Payne heard the grunt of pain from the man's mouth, then felt the rush of air as he fell to the ground. Still grasping the other man, Payne landed on top of the knight, who lay still beneath him.

Payne pushed himself onto his hands. He stared down at the man on the ground and cursed. This was no seasoned fighter. Payne had learned that at the first touch. At most the knight was a youth, too young to have developed strength, but old enough to have grown tall. What game had the boy been playing? Stealing from his lord was a crime. Did the child think he was some sort of hero to the peasants?

The boy still had not moved. Payne cursed again. He had injured the boy. Glancing down to reassure himself the child still breathed, Payne grabbed the woolen mask from the Black Knight's face.

Hellfire and damnation.

This was no youth at all.

Elf lay unmoving on the ground beneath him.

For a moment his heart stopped, then it started pounding harder than he had ever felt it before. He lifted her hand. "Elf?"

No answer came.

Panic rose in him and threatened to engulf him. Never in the many battles he had fought, never in the many tournaments he had jousted in, never in the many times he had faced death had such helplessness overwhelmed him. He had seen, treated, and suffered injuries in the past, but he didn't know what to do for this woman. He reached out to stroke her cheek and was surprised to see his hand shaking.

He drew in a deep breath. He would be of no use to her if he couldn't control himself. With care he reached forward again and removed the hood of her cloak. As he brushed the material from her hair, his fingers touched a large bump on the back of her head. This must be the cause of her unnatural sleep. When he pulled his hand away, terror gripped him. Blood stained the white of his palm.

Ignoring propriety, Payne ran his hand over each arm and then over her long legs. Her attire made his examination for broken bones much easier. Somehow he didn't feel as awkward as he might have had she been wearing a dress.

Her limbs seemed intact. If only she would awaken. Cradling her head in his palms, he turned her head. The bump was as large as a goose egg.

He slid his arms under her and lifted her. He had been correct in assuming the Black Knight didn't have much bulk. Her weight felt as nothing in his arms. He turned to Merlin.

His well-trained horse stood unperturbed nearby, munching on some leaves as he waited for his master. The other horse had fled.

He couldn't place her on Merlin's back without causing her more harm. Carrying her would be best. He started back up the path, then stopped. Where was he going? He couldn't leave her here, but how could he take her back to her uncle?

Payne nearly groaned with indecision. He had captured the Black Knight, but now what?

A horse whinnied from somewhere in the woods. Of course. The tent. He could take her there. He let out a long low whistle. Merlin stepped toward him.

"Follow me, lad." With purpose in his stride, Payne carried her toward the tent with Merlin keeping pace behind.

With every second that passed, Payne chafed at his slow progress. His burden didn't trouble him, but he didn't dare move faster for fear of harming Elf further. He cursed his rash action with each step.

When at last the tent came into view, he felt little relief. The canvas flap to the hut was shut tight against the night. He kicked at it with his boot. "Nigel, open the door. I need help. Nigel, wake up!"

From within he heard a grumbling voice. "Isn't it enough you drag me into the woods at my age? Can't you let an old man sleep?"

"Nigel open the flap. I need help!" he yelled through the closed portal.

The door flipped open as Nigel stumbled out. All traces of sleep fled the man's face at the sight of the woman in Payne's arms. "Bloody hell. It's Elf." He held the flap open as Payne ducked inside.

Two pallets covered the floor, but only one had been slept in. "Put these on top of each other. She needs a softer bed."

Nigel pulled his bedding on top of the other. Payne placed Elf on it, then sat beside her. The bed still felt hard as rock. She couldn't be comfortable on this thing. He needed to fetch some furs, or ticking, or—

"What happened?" Nigel stared at him as if he were accusing him of causing Elf's injury.

Payne grimaced. He had. "I knocked her from her horse. She must have hit her head when we fell."

"Of course she hit her head." Nigel brushed him aside and covered Elf with a blanket. His fingers probed her hair. "What in the blazes was she doing out in the woods at night?"

"She is the Black Knight."

"Bloody hell," repeated Nigel. "I knew she weren't no ordinary woman."

Payne dropped his head into his hands. "But you couldn't have imagined this."

"Nay, lad, I couldn't." Nigel looked at him.

"I didn't know who the Black Knight was until after I knocked her from her horse. I would never hurt Elf." Payne ran his hand through his hair.

Nigel patted Payne's shoulder. "You're not to blame, you know."

Payne didn't spare him a glance. "I attacked an unarmed woman."

"The Baron hired you to capture and stop the Black Knight. How were you to know *he* was *she?*"

Payne let out a puff of air in annoyance.

Nigel shook his head. Fetching a ewer and cloth, he bent to wash Elf's face.

"I'll do that." Payne took the cloth from Nigel and dipped it into the water. He wiped her brow. She made no movement.

"So what do you plan to do?"

"I intend to care for her until she awakens. And for as long as she needs me after." Payne knelt by the bed. As he gazed into Elf's pale face, he willed her eyes to open, her mouth to rail at him in anger, her eyes to flash at him. She did none of these.

Fighting back the fear that rose in him, he turned to Nigel. "There is a horse in the woods, black with a star on its nose. Find it and bring it here."

"A horse?"

"Elf's horse," snapped Payne with impatience. "Then fetch some things to make her more comfortable. A feather tick, more blankets, food."

"What shall I tell her uncle?"

"I don't know. Nothing. I haven't decided what to tell the man yet."

"He's bound to notice she's gone."

"Not likely. She was gone for weeks before, and he did little more than scold her. I'll worry about her uncle later. Just do as I ask this once, Nigel. Find her horse, then get those things. And some clothes. She can't stay dressed as a man." Payne returned his attention to the pale face on the bed. He heard the swish of the flap as Nigel left, but didn't move his gaze from Elf. He wiped the cloth on her forehead again as he whispered an urgent plea.

"Wake up, Elf."

Chapter Eleven

Elf was aware of the sounds around her before she opened her eyes. She didn't recognize the speakers' voices although she strained to listen. Their hushed tones made their words difficult to hear. She opened her eyes to a slit.

"Her uncle wanted to know how close you are to catching the thief."

"Tell him I've discovered . . . no, tell him . . . damnation, I don't know what to tell the man. Has he asked for Elf at all?"

Asked for her? And where was she? She wasn't in her own bed, this much was for certain. Elf turned her head slightly. Her eyes flew open.

Payne? Here?

In the next instant, the memory of the attack returned to her. She sat upright and promptly vomited onto the floor.

"Be still, Lady Elf," said Payne. He laid her back onto the feather tick and wiped a cool cloth over her face.

Elf didn't want to rise again. Her head pounded, and her stomach roiled. But her curiosity plagued her as well. "What are you doing here?"

"Hush. We have time for questions later. How are you feeling?"

She groaned. Just thinking made her head ache. "About as well as anyone hurled to the ground from a horse should feel."

"You must be feeling better. You're tongue is as sharp as ever."

Sharp? She lifted her head to retort, but dropped it as the hammering behind her eyes started again.

"Hush. I told you to lie still. You aren't well enough to move around."

She gritted her teeth against the pain in her head. "What are you doing here? And where am I?"

"You're in my tent, and I'm taking care of you." He wiped the cloth over her face again.

"Why? You caused this."

"I know." Payne said nothing else.

Elf closed her eyes.

"Elf, Elf! Are you awake? Elf!"

The panic in Payne's voice surprised Elf. She lifted her gaze to him. "Yes. I'm awake, but it hurts less when I close my eyes."

"Thank the heavens." Payne sat back.

"Why are you so worried?"

"You don't remember?"

"If I did, would I ask?" Elf shot him a look of impatience.

"You woke several times during the night, but you spoke as if you had no awareness of your surroundings. You sang a bawdy song and giggled."

"I did no such thing."

"You did. Then you fell asleep again."

"I assure you I would remember if I sang, for I cannot sing and would never willingly subject anyone to my song."

Payne laughed. "I can understand your feelings, for I heard your singing."

"Since I have already admitted my tonelessness, you needn't agree with me." Elf narrowed her gaze at him. Uncertainty filled her. "Did I really wake before now?"

Payne nodded. "You had us both worried."

Elf glanced at Nigel, then dropped her gaze. With gentle fingers, she felt the back of her head. A large bump rose from her scalp. As she probed the area gingerly, she felt the dried blood that covered a thin wound on the bump. Her fingertips brushed a large tangle, and she grimaced. She wanted to wash the blood from her hair. Once she sat in her uncle's dungeon, who knew when she would feel clean again?

Payne watched her. As she grew aware of his scrutiny, she withdrew her hand. She turned her gaze to him.

"What can we tell your uncle?" he asked.

"You haven't told him yet? Is that why I lie in a bed and not in his dungeon?"

"No, I wasn't speaking of the Black Knight. How do we explain your absence from the castle?"

Elf shrugged. "He won't miss me."

"Surely if you are gone for days, he will note your absence."

"Perhaps." She turned her gaze to the wall. "My uncle has never much concerned himself with me."

"I cannot believe that."

"Why? I am not important. When my father died, Uncle Matthew took me in. I was not a man he could train to be a knight, nor was I his daughter with whom he could make an advantageous match. Oh, I made myself useful—I was more skilled at running his house than my aunt or cousin—but he cared for his family. Me he tolerated."

"I find it hard to imagine you tolerated being ignored."

Elf laughed. "I wasn't ignored as much as deemed not worth worrying about. My uncle agreed to my entering the convent, but then delayed it when he realized how well he ate when I took charge."

She noticed Nigel's interest in her story and frowned. She asked, "Does he know about the Black Knight, too?"

"Little escapes Nigel's notice, especially when it disturbs his sleep."

"Humph," snorted Nigel. "You act as if I had no brain at all."

"When shall you turn me over to my uncle?"

"I haven't said that I shall." Payne raked his fingers through his hair. "In any event, I have a few days to decide yet. I can't take you home until you have recovered from the fall."

Although she tried to prevent it, a tear trickled from beneath her eyelids. Despite her brave words, she was frightened of her uncle's reaction.

With the tip of his finger, Payne wiped the drop from her skin. "I was but teasing. I had hoped you didn't think me so callous as to threaten you, no matter how ill-conceived your ideas might be."

Elf couldn't decide whether to feel relief or anger at his comment. "I don't know what to think. I cannot ask you to guard my secret, but neither do I wish to face my uncle's wrath." She tried to sit up, but grimaced as pain shot across her brow.

"How many times must I tell you to lie still?" Payne lifted her hand. "You need not fear Nigel's or my betrayal."

"Thank you," she whispered.

"Can you not see she needs to sleep?" Nigel snorted. "She's ill and should rest now. I'll think of something to say to Matthew."

Payne placed her hand on the bedding. "Sleep, Elf. Close your eyes and try not to worry about your uncle. I shall protect you."

She didn't know why she should, but she believed him. Elf closed her eyes, for she was truly tired. Within moments she felt the slightly dizzy whirl of thoughts that accompanied the onset of sleep. Her last coherent thought sent a smile across her lips. *It would be so easy not to fight him.*

In the next days, Elf allowed Payne to coddle her. He brought her food when she was hungry, drink to slake her thirst, and let her sleep when she felt tired. By the third day, the pounding had ceased in her head, she could walk with no fear of losing the contents of her stomach, and she hated the feather tick that was so soft beneath her. The mattress was her biggest source of irritation, for Payne didn't allow her to rise very often, and when she did, he hovered about her like a bird with its fledglings. Oh, he had been most solicitous to her, but she no longer wanted the attention.

No, that wasn't entirely true. She liked his attention, which frightened her more than facing her uncle.

She closed her eyes at the thought.

"Is your head still troubling you?" asked Payne.

Her eyes flew open again as heat crept into her cheeks. "No. I was just thinking I should be getting up soon."

"There's time enough for that when you are well."

"I am well." Elf sat up in bed, pulling the covers to her chin. "If you could get my clothes, I think I could return to the castle. I have to face my uncle sometime."

"Nigel is there now fetching you something to wear."

"I have something to wear." She pointed to her trousers and tunic.

"Oh, no. I cannot let you return in those things."

With a sigh, Elf lay back.

"You see, you aren't strong enough yet."

Elf frowned, then cast off the blankets and strode to him, ignoring her state of undress. A thin shift covered her from shoulder to knees. Tilting her chin, she shot her gaze at him. "I most assuredly am. I am quite tired of lying here, and I wish to return home."

"Nigel and I both agree you mustn't move about too soon. An injury to the head is serious and—"

She grabbed his arms and shook him. "I am well. Do you understand me? I am well."

Payne arched his eyebrows. "Obviously, we have a difference of opinion."

Letting out a puff of air in disgust, Elf dropped her hands. Shaking him hadn't done more than bring the head pounding back.

Payne put his hands on her shoulders. "Be patient."

"Hah. You're one to talk. Your arm is still stiff from our hedgehog adventure."

"My arm is fine." Payne stretched out his arm to the side and rolled his shoulder.

She couldn't help but notice the breadth of his reach. And wonder how it would feel if he wrapped those arms around her, if he were to pull her close to him and lower his lips to hers, if he held her as if he couldn't let her go. Without thinking, she lifted her face toward him and leaned against him.

Payne closed his arms around her. "Lady Elf, are you ill?"

Mortification flashed through her. Heat flooded her cheeks, and she knew a raging blush colored her skin. Had she just thrown herself into his arms?

She met his gaze with a boldness she didn't feel. The concern she saw in his gaze stole her breath. He was truly worried about her. No one had ever shown such concern for her in the past. She smiled at him, enjoying the strength of his arms. They provided the haven she imagined they would.

For a moment, Payne didn't know how to react. His worry died with her smile, but he made no move to let her go. He wanted to hold her, to press her more tightly against him. Her eyes flashed with an invitation he knew he should ignore, but he wasn't sure he had the strength to. Nor did he want to.

He lowered his head to her, never removing his gaze from the sparkle of her eyes. As his lips brushed hers, she closed her lids and welcomed his kiss with a tiny sigh. She tasted of honey and wine, sweet and heady. He let his hunger stir as he sampled her savor before giving in to the urge to indulge of the repast she offered.

Her eager response to his kiss heightened his need for her. He slid his hand up her side, brushing against the rounded curve of her breast. The smooth skin tempted him. He slipped his hand into her shift and cradled the warm flesh in his palm. Elf gasped, but didn't pull away.

With the side of his thumb, he brushed her nipple. The aureole puckered around it, thrusting it forward for more attention. He stroked it, then rolled the pebbled tip gently between thumb and forefinger.

Elf sucked in her breath, but before she could say anything, he stole the words from her mouth by deepening his kiss. His tongue glided against hers. His senses reveled in this new taste. A soft, contented sigh rose from Elf and settled over him like a fine fur pelt. This woman awakened feelings he believed long dead, dreams he thought dormant since he was a youth. He wanted to hold her forever.

"What are you doing?"

Nigel's strident voice cut through the dreamlike haze of his thoughts. Payne pushed Elf away from him. She blinked at him a few times, then her mouth opened to a horrified "O".

"I asked what you think you are doing," Nigel scowled at him. "Aren't you in enough trouble with the Baron without seducing his niece?" Nigel glanced at her then turned away. He coughed and thrust a bundle at her. "Would you please get dressed, Lady Elf?"

Elf looked down and reddened. She grabbed the bundle of clothes from Nigel and sought a haven from their sight.

"We'll wait outside until you're dressed." Payne turned Nigel to the door and led him from the tent.

Outside, Payne inhaled deeply. The air was cooler, but he wasn't sure that he felt any relief. To his dismay, he found himself wishing he were still in the tent with Elf. He shook his head. He had never been in danger of forgetting himself or the tasks he had set for himself.

Nigel stepped up and shook a finger in his face, disrupting his tenuous grip on tranquility. "I have never questioned your actions, boy, but—"

"I know, Nigel. You can't say anything to me that I haven't already said to myself."

"You're facing enough trouble with her uncle when you tell him you've failed to capture the Black Knight. How are you going to explain that you've seduced his niece?"

"I haven't seduced her, Nigel. I only kissed her." Payne raked his hand through his hair.

"Hah. If I hadn't walked in at that moment, you wouldn't have stopped with just a kiss."

Payne couldn't challenge Nigel's words. His body still waited for the release denied it.

"She's going to a convent," Nigel continued. "You've heard her say it, you've heard her uncle say it. The wrath of the Baron is enough. We don't need the wrath of God as well."

"She doesn't belong in a convent. She should have a husband and babies—"

"That is none of your concern."

"I know." He rubbed his forehead. "Our job here is almost done. We leave soon in any case."

"With our coffers heavier. Or have you forgotten what you've worked for?"

"No, I haven't forgotten. When Meredith pays me, we shall leave." *Before she entangles herself further in my life,* he added to himself.

Elf emerged in the next minute. "I am ready to face my uncle now."

Payne raised an eyebrow. "And just what do you plan on telling him?"

"I'll just tell him I was the Black Knight. He can't very well throw me into his dungeon . . . can he?" Her voice sounded less than confident.

"As if the Baron would believe his niece could outsmart his men," said Nigel with a sniff.

"Why shouldn't he? God gave me the power to reason as well as any man, and He gave me the stature as well."

Remembering the weight of her breast in his palm, Payne smiled. He may have given her the height of a man, but she most definitely wasn't a man. "No, I believe I can convince your uncle that he need no longer worry about the Black Knight." He peered at her and narrowed his gaze. "That is if I have your word you will no longer ride out as the Black Knight again."

"But I promised Sally—" She clapped her hand over her mouth.

"I know all about Sally, and your promise to her. I shall find her and speak with her. And bring her food." He leaned closer to her. "You may also want to consider the others who have helped you in your foolish endeavor. If your uncle finds those who stabled your horse, he won't be as lenient as I."

She swallowed hard, then nodded. "I give you my word. The Black Knight shall never plague my uncle again."

"Good. Let's get back to the castle then. The sooner I convince your uncle the Black Knight is no longer a problem, the sooner Nigel and I can depart."

For a fleeting moment, he thought he spied a stricken look on Elf's face, but she lifted her chin and steeled her expression. "And the sooner I can enter the convent."

Chapter Twelve

Elf grew more nervous as they neared the castle. Payne had assured her he could convince her uncle that the Black Knight was no longer a problem, but she wasn't as certain. Sometimes Payne's confidence annoyed her. He seemed too sure of his success. She was more doubtful of his capability. After all, she had experienced one of his mistakes all too well and nearly found herself married to Coxesbury.

Elf walked beside the cart. She wanted a chance to prove her recovery complete. Payne kept pace beside her. Nigel drove the cart, with Merlin and her horse tied to the rear. As they followed the road to the castle, she noticed a band of travelers in front of them. She wondered who was coming to visit her uncle. She knew of no expected guests. The travelers had several wagons with them. Whoever they were, they carried a lot of baggage.

Payne eyed the pennants that flew from the wagons. "Of all the cursed luck."

"What is it?" asked Elf.

"Do you not recognize the heraldry on the flags? The stag? It's Coxesbury."

"What is he doing here?"

"I imagine he's here to retrieve you." Payne shook his head.

Elf darted behind him.

Nigel chuckled. "He won't claim you on the road."

"Most likely he'll want to speak to your uncle and make his offer for you then," said Payne.

"Wonderful." Elf pursed her lips in disgust.

The band in front of them halted. As the trio came abreast of the travelers, Elf saw Baron Coxesbury standing beside Tedric. Tedric shrugged as if in apology, but Elf turned her gaze without acknowledging him. She frowned at the Baron.

"Good day, fair lady." Baron Coxesbury gave her a half smile that made her stomach turn. "I really should be cross with you, but that would be no way to start our life together."

Elf narrowed her gaze. "We are not starting a life together."

The Baron chuckled. "No, not yet. First I will speak to your uncle. He might be pleased we have an alliance after all."

"Why do you speak as if the matter is done with?" Elf eyed Coxesbury with suspicion.

"Do not trouble yourself, Lady Elfreda. We shall have time for your questions when we return to Pellingham."

"I'm not going anywhere with you."

"You are stubborn. No matter. I shall settle this with your uncle. Marriage is no concern for ladies."

" 'Tis our only concern. We aren't allowed any other concerns save the running of a household." Elf stomped her foot. A small cloud of dust rose from beneath her sole.

"As it should be. I'm pleased to hear you know your duties. I shall be delighted to teach you your wifely ones as well." Coxesbury leered at her as the men around him laughed.

Elf glared at him. "You will never touch me, you foul—"

Payne's hand shot out and covered her mouth. "Shall we see her uncle?"

Squirming under Payne's hold, Elf kicked his shin. He didn't loosen his grip, but she was gratified to hear a small grunt of pain.

"You must teach me your methods of controlling a woman, Payne. They seem quite effective, although I really should object to you touching my wife," said Coxesbury. "I haven't decided how to deal with you yet. Out of some misguided sense of honor, you went against my wishes. But I think I know a way you can make it up to me. You must back my claim. My drunken priest was too ill to travel with us, but when he arrives he will give witness to the marriage vows spoken between Lady Elfreda and myself."

"What vows?" asked Payne.

"Does it really matter? I will double your fee if you confirm my story."

Payne raised his eyebrows. Elf thrashed under Payne's hand until he wrapped his free arm around her and held her still. She shot daggers of anger from her eyes, wishing they had real power. "An interesting proposition."

"I'm glad you think so. I would so hate to have a misunderstanding between us." Coxesbury turned to Tedric. "Ride with me through the gates, Tedric. You say they know you here?"

"Aye, the Baron and I have shared ale and stories." Tedric grinned. "I think he might be pleased that Lady Elf has found a match."

"Lady Elf?" Coxesbury frowned. "That will never do. She's as tall as a giantess. I won't have my future wife be the butt of jokes. You will remember to address her as Lady Elfreda."

"As you wish, my liege." Tedric bowed his head.

Elf watched from within the confines of Payne's arms as the travelers moved toward the castle. When they were out of sight, Payne released her.

"How dare you?" Elf whirled to him. "I believed you. You said he wouldn't get me. How dare you make promises you will not keep? How dare you speak of honor when he is paying for your word?"

Payne's mien darkened, but his voice remained calm. "I have not lied to you."

"Then how do you explain his bribery?"

"I didn't say I would accept his offer."

Elf gaped at him. "But you sounded as if—"

Payne started toward the castle again. "I cannot help what you choose to hear, Lady Elf."

Elf grabbed her skirt and ran to him. "If you expect me to apologize—"

"No, I would never expect you to apologize." Payne continued to walk without looking at her.

Letting out a puff of air, Elf struggled to match her steps to his. "You held me back, kept me from talking. What was I supposed to think?"

"Thinking might have served you better," he said. "You weren't thinking when you replied with such cheek to the Baron. His temper knows little restraint. If you had continued with your insolence, the Baron most likely wouldn't have let us continue on our own. Now he believes that I have disciplined you, and that he controls me."

"Oh." Elf fell silent. His logic rankled her. It didn't help that he was right.

They rounded the last curve in the road before the castle.

Through the barbican, they saw Coxesbury's party in the bailey. The guards waved Elf and the two men through without stopping them. Elf hurried to the keep, trying to avoid Coxesbury. She knew her uncle would receive him. Her fear was that he might believe him.

As she expected, no one questioned her long absence. The only comment was made by the servant who helped her dress on occasion, and even she didn't realized Elf had been gone from the castle for more than one day. Elf had to admit her eccentric behavior had its useful purposes.

She changed her chemise and gown and washed her face before she sought out her uncle. What would she tell him? How could she prevent Coxesbury from making his claim on her? Good heavens, what if the toad already had?

She hurried to the great hall and breathed a sigh of relief. No one was there yet. Her uncle probably readied himself in his chamber. The surprise visitors must have caught him unaware.

What could she do? Shadows covered a bench in a recess along the wall. She took a spot on it and waited, searching her mind all the while for a solution to the Coxesbury problem.

All too soon the hall filled with people. Servants set up tables on trestles and draped cloths over the wood. The noise grew as Coxesbury's men enjoyed ale and mead. Coxesbury himself came after a short while. He had changed his attire. She didn't think it was any sort of improvement.

She pressed herself into the shadows of the wall. No one had paid her any heed if they had noticed her at all. Maybe she could spend the day watching the events from the edges of the room. If she were lucky, the shadows would engulf her and never reveal her again.

Coxesbury took a place at the head of the room on the dais. Elf nearly snorted with disgust. Even when imposing on his host's hospitality, Coxesbury acted overbearing.

Payne entered the hall soon after. Elf's gaze flew to him. Clad in black from head to heel, he dominated the room. Elf sighed. His strength was no pretense. He was a man a woman would be proud to have as her husband.

Payne searched the room before he stepped further inside the hall. His gaze fell on her at once. She shook her head, hoping he would understand she didn't want to be seen. He looked at her for a moment, then turned away and found himself a seat away from Coxesbury and his unruly men. A pretty young servant girl rushed to him and pressed a goblet into his hands. He quaffed from the vessel, then smiled at the girl and whispered something to her, which made the girl laugh.

Elf frowned. That girl should be serving the others and not waste so much of her time and attention on Payne.

Coxesbury noticed Payne. He nodded at the knight, then smiled. Elf seethed. Although Payne had reassured her, it still looked to her eyes as if they understood each other too well.

Uncle Matthew came in a few minutes later. He had donned his finest tunic, though Elf couldn't understand his need to impress Coxesbury. His men followed him and took their places around the room. Throwing out his chest, he elevated himself to his tallest stature.

"Welcome, Gilbert. Your visit is unexpected. I trust you aren't here to cause any unpleasantness."

Coxesbury rose from his seat and raised his goblet. "Matthew. To your health. I thank you for the welcome and assure you that you will not regret my visit. Come, drink with me to seal our friendship."

A servant rushed to hand Uncle Matthew a silver chalice. Matthew carried it to the table and took his place at the head. He raised his vessel to Coxesbury's. "Friendship."

Coxesbury lifted his goblet. "And to a continued link between our families." The two men drank.

The men in the hall joined in the toast. Elf noticed Payne did not. He watched Coxesbury and raised an eyebrow. How silly that a raised eyebrow should bring her such relief.

Conversations drifted around her. As food became ready, servants placed trenchers on the tables. Her stomach growled, but she didn't wish to relinquish her place in the shadows. As Coxesbury ate, the table in front of him became littered with specks of food. The dogs gathered around his place, often fighting over a morsel that landed on the floor instead of his mouth. When he drank, a thin trickle of ale dribbled down his chin. Elf vowed anew that she would never become his wife.

An hour later the eating and drinking had slowed. Uncle Matthew pushed his chair from the table and leaned back in it. "I am glad you bear me no ill will, Gilbert. 'Twas the king who dissolved Agnes's betrothal to you."

"Aye. There is no blame on you, my friend. I only regret that we were unable to unite our families with a marriage."

Elf's heart began to race. Coxesbury was about to ask her uncle for her hand.

"Yes, well, some things cannot be helped. I have but one daughter, Gilbert, and she is now wed."

"Perhaps, but you have a niece . . ." Coxesbury leaned closer to Matthew. "Have you considered a match for her?"

Uncle Matthew sat upright. His eyes widened. "Elf?"

"The Lady Elfreda has no husband and would bind our families together." Coxesbury smiled. His teeth seemed gray in the dim light.

A shudder ran through Elf. She couldn't marry this man.

Uncle Matthew stroked his chin. "I have promised her she may join a convent."

Elf started to breathe a little easier. Perhaps Coxesbury couldn't sway her uncle.

"Think, Matthew. What good does the girl do you in a convent when you can use her to your advantage?"

"Aye, but she has no suitors. In fact, she scared the last one off so fast he forgot his dog. Never did come back to claim the cur." Matthew chortled.

Heat stained her cheeks. She didn't regret chasing the fool off, but she didn't like being the source of her uncle's merriment.

"What if I were the suitor?" Coxesbury's gaze settled on Matthew's face.

"You? Why would you want Elf? You always thought she was a giantess, a monster . . . well, unsuitable anyway."

Coxesbury shrugged. "I need a wife, and who better than the niece of my friend? Besides, I can always bed her in the dark."

The men laughed around them. Even Uncle Matthew tried to hide his chuckle without much success. Elf nearly shot out of her seat. How dared they speak of her with such irreverence?

Payne stood behind the two men. Elf hadn't noticed him step forward, but his scowl frightened her. "Lady Elf doesn't deserve such callous words."

Uncle Matthew looked up at Payne. "Good heavens, you frightened me. I wasn't aware you had returned. Did you discover the Black Knight?"

Payne nodded. "I did."

"The Black Knight?" asked Coxesbury.

"A thieving scoundrel who has plagued me for several months," said Matthew. He turned to Payne. "Well."

"The Black Knight shall never ride again."

"Good to hear. Who is he?"

"Perhaps this should wait for another time when there are fewer distractions." Payne bowed.

"Yes, excellent idea." Matthew quaffed some ale. "So you truly wish to wed Elf, Coxesbury?"

"Elfreda is a far more dignified name," said Coxesbury between his teeth.

"You would have her? Let's tell her the good news." Matthew smiled at his guest, then turned to a servant. "Send for Elf."

"No need, uncle, I am here." Elf rose from her seat.

"Why are you hiding in the shadows, girl?" Uncle Matthew frowned at her. "You've heard then?"

"I have."

"What say you?"

Elf glanced at Payne. He stood behind the two men, his face grim. Hell's minions, why couldn't he have offered for her instead? If she had to marry, Payne was the preferable choice. She might have easily said yes to her uncle then.

She froze and held her breath. She *knew* how to thwart Coxesbury. Payne might never forgive her, but she wouldn't have to marry Coxesbury.

"I cannot marry the Baron, Uncle."

"I know I promised you to the abbey, but Coxesbury would make a fine husband. Don't you want children? Consider his offer, child."

"I cannot consider his offer. I cannot break my vows."

"You have taken no vows. I haven't even contacted the abbess yet."

"Not my vows to the convent. My vows to Payne."

"Payne?" Her uncle's brows shot skyward.

"Yes, uncle. We are handfasted."

Chapter Thirteen

Elf felt the heated gazes of the entire room upon her. Never had the hall been so silent. The only sounds were the crackle of the fire and the chewing of the dogs. She lifted her head higher and glanced at Payne. He hadn't protested yet, but neither did she see any hint of amusement in his eyes. She decided she didn't have the courage to face him.

Her uncle had not stirred. Elf turned to him and waited for his reaction. Finally, he gulped and said, "Handfasted?"

Elf nodded. "Yes, it is the custom in the north, and since I didn't think you would mind . . ." Elf held her breath. That part wasn't a lie. She didn't like to lie as a habit, but the alternative was unbearable.

Uncle Matthew turned to Payne. "Is this true?"

Her gaze flew to Payne's face. His golden eyes blazed with anger. Her heart sank. If he denied her story, if he wouldn't support her . . .

"Yes, it is a custom where I come from."

Her eyes widened, and joy filled her.

Uncle Matthew let out a shout. He thumped Payne across the shoulders. "What excellent news. We must celebrate the union of our two families." He raised his goblet. "More ale."

The buzz returned to the room as servants bustled to fill his lordship's request. Elf sneaked a glance at Payne. He hadn't turned his attention from her. His glare boded no hint of clemency for her. She cringed. His glare hardened.

Turning from him, Elf caught a glimpse of Coxesbury. From the white that rimmed his lips, she guessed his anger was great. His cheeks held mottled red splotches, and his lips were so pinched together that she doubted even an arrow could penetrate them.

But she had thwarted him. A giddy glee filled her. She wouldn't have to marry the Baron. She had won her freedom.

She froze. A glance back at Payne confirmed her error. She hadn't won her freedom; she had simply donned a different yoke.

Uncle Matthew thrust a goblet into Payne's hands and lifted his own vessel. "To my new nephew. May his strength ever grow, especially as he now has the demands of a woman to see to."

Raucous laughter filled the great hall. Payne lifted his goblet as well, but his face never lost its stern expression. Elf sighed. She supposed it was unfair of her to trap him this way, but he had promised to save her from the Baron.

No, that flimsy excuse didn't absolve her of the guilt that swamped her. She would have much penance to do the next time she saw the priest.

"I insist we have a real wedding. Exchanging vows is fine, but I will see my niece before the altar, pledging her vows." Uncle Matthew clapped Payne's back again. "Tomorrow, lad, we'll see you in the chapel and well wed to my niece."

Payne nodded, but Elf saw no sign of softening in his features. Instead, he downed the remnants of his ale and held out the goblet for more.

Elf wanted nothing more than to disappear from the hall. She didn't like the attention, nor did she wish to remain in the presence of Payne or the Baron, although for different reasons.

She tugged on her uncle's sleeve. "Uncle, with your leave I shall retire to my room for the night."

Her uncle guffawed. "Don't think I'll be sending your bridegroom to you until I've seen you wedded. Though I wager it's too late by now."

Heat seared her cheeks at the laughter that greeted her uncle's observation. She fought the urge to hide her face and lifted her chin a notch. "I am more than happy to respect your sensibilities, uncle."

Uncle Matthew roared again. "Get your rest, girl. Tomorrow we celebrate a wedding."

Elf hurried from the hall and bounded the circular stairs to her room. She shooed away the maidservant who tried to help her undress, just as she brushed away the offer of food. When at last she was alone, she threw herself on the bed and released her sobs.

She was getting married on the morrow. It didn't matter that the world already considered her wed. Tomorrow she would swear before God to obey her husband. Her life would become the property of someone else, worth only as much as he deemed. She now realized the consequences of her spontaneous solution to her problem.

A momentary pang of guilt assailed her as she thought of the web of deceit she had dragged Payne into, but her desperation outweighed her remorse. Better Payne as a husband, than Coxesbury. She could only pray that Payne would forgive her and not punish her, as would be his right.

Payne surveyed the hall. He felt more than saw Nigel's

gaze upon him. Right now he didn't want to face him. Payne turned his attention to revelers. The men drank and ate in noisy abandon. Few women attended the hall. He imagined the ladies of the castle would prefer to abstain from such company, and the female servants would prefer not to put themselves at risk. The women who did roam the hall seemed to welcome the attention of the many men.

He glanced at Coxesbury. The man's gaze hardened under his scrutiny.

Coxesbury rose to his feet. "I pray you, Lord Meredith. A word."

"Ah, Coxesbury. I had almost forgotten you were here. You will stay for the wedding?"

"I wish to express my concern over your haste to bless this union." Coxesbury shot a glance to Payne.

"Haste? Of course I need to deal with haste. You don't know how hard it is to handle the girl. She's liable to change her mind if I don't get her to the altar. Or worse, Payne might come to his senses." Meredith guffawed.

Payne stiffened. The urge to punch Meredith grew in him. Instead, he said, "The handfast is a solemn vow."

"I do but jest, my boy. I can't begin to tell you how happy I am over this union. The Golden Bear, my nephew. And you save me the trouble of getting the dowry together for the abbey. It's yours now."

"Dowry?" Payne frowned. "I ask for no dowry."

Coxesbury snorted. "Fool," he muttered.

"You don't have to ask. Her father left her lands. Candlewood Keep is a small castle, but the lands are rich."

Lands? He no longer heard the buzzing of the room as the Baron's words registered. Elf came with lands. How long had he been working toward owning a holding? Seven years, eight years? If he received Elf's land upon marriage, he could use the money he had saved to make improvements to his castle.

His castle. Even the thought was enough to send a shiver of expectation through him.

He shook his head to clear his mind of the temptation. Elf had forced him into this marriage. She had steered and trapped him into a union he hadn't planned or wanted. Her dowry was just compensation for her trickery.

On the other hand, he had given his oath to protect her from Coxesbury. His thoughts stole to the memory of holding her in his arms, the softness of her skin, the heady taste of her lips.

Marriage to Elf might be compensation enough.

With an angry shake of his head, Payne lifted his goblet again. He caught a glimpse of Nigel's face and lowered the vessel. Nigel frowned at him, then drained his own ale. He rose from the table and approached Payne. "I'm going to see that the horses are well fed." He turned to leave.

"Nigel?" Payne stared after his friend, but Nigel didn't stop. Payne furrowed his brow. Why was Nigel so annoyed? This situation was not of his own making.

"Drink up, nephew," said Meredith with a laugh. "Tomorrow you don the yoke of marriage."

Payne didn't taste the ale as it snaked down his throat. Tomorrow would bring a wedding, a wife and a castle. His mind whirled from the news, not from the effect of the drink. His mood swung between excitement and fury. His goblet remained empty for the rest of the evening.

As the revelry faded and the men sought places to bed down, Payne picked his way through the castle toward the chamber he occupied. He would sleep well tonight. Tomorrow he would be a landed knight.

A smile curled his lips, then just as quickly faded. He pressed himself against the wall and waited. The muffled whispers of men breezed somewhere in front of him. A rush of wariness seized him. He hadn't lived so long without trusting his senses.

Pulling a knife from his belt, he advanced with the stealth of a fox until he saw the vague shadows of two men. They huddled together as they whispered. One man was clearly shorter than the other, and by his demeanor the shorter one was in charge.

Using surprise as his weapon, Payne roared, then ducked under the grasp of the big man, whose arms flailed in the air in a vain attempt to fell his attacker. Payne grabbed the smaller man by the neck, and twisted his captive until he stood with Payne's knife at his throat.

"Damn you, Payne." Coxesbury's voice hissed through the darkness.

"Your surprise for me failed, Coxesbury," said Payne. He didn't loosen his grip on Coxesbury.

"No surprise," gritted out Coxesbury. "I only wanted to talk."

"Now, why would that require an armed knight? Tell your man to drop his sword and leave." Payne pressed the edge of his blade against Coxesbury's throat.

"Do as he says." Coxesbury's voice was growing hoarse.

The taller man dropped his weapon and retreated into the darkness. Without releasing his grip on the Baron, Payne kicked the sword to the edge of the chamber door.

"Now we shall have a little chat." With the knife at Coxesbury's neck, Payne led him to the chamber. "Open the door."

Coxesbury lifted the latch, then Payne kicked it open with his foot. He shoved Coxesbury into the room. As Coxesbury stumbled forward, Payne retrieved the sword and followed the man inside.

Coxesbury almost righted himself before he pitched forward onto the bed.

Payne latched the door behind him. Without taking his gaze from Coxesbury, he slid his knife into its sheath on his belt. He held the retrieved sword in his right hand. A single taper glowed on a table. Payne used it to light the sconces on the wall. "I take offense when someone who owes me money tries to kill me." Payne lifted the sword and pointed it at Coxesbury. "No, let me correct myself. I take offense when anyone tries to kill me at all."

"Fool," spat Coxesbury. "I could have your head for this."

"I don't think so. Edward wouldn't like to see one of his strongest knights beheaded."

"You aren't handfasted. You lied."

"I never lied. Matthew drew the wrong conclusion. In any case, it doesn't matter. I shall wed Elf tomorrow."

Coxesbury's nostrils flared. "I would have paid you well for Lady Elfreda."

"She isn't mine to sell." Elf's name on Coxesbury's lips angered him.

"It's not too late. You can still back up my claim for her. I'll call my priest here to swear we were wed. She would be a Baroness." Coxesbury's gaze darted to the door and back. "I'll triple what I owe you."

Payne crossed to the man, who flinched backward. "I'm giving you warning, Coxesbury. If I see you near Elf again, I shall kill you."

"Your wits are addled. She isn't worth making an enemy of me."

"If I hear of you speaking her name, I shall kill you."

Spittle gathered on Coxesbury's lips. "You don't know what you are saying."

"In fact, if I am ever close enough to smell you again, I shall kill you."

The color drained from Coxesbury's face.

"Get out."

These last two words, although spoken in a whisper, had the effect of a whip's lash on Coxesbury. He jerked backward, then ran to the door. Fumbling with the latch, he opened it. "You'll regret this."

Payne didn't bother to respond. He merely swung the sword toward Coxesbury. Coxesbury let out a cry that sounded much like a puppy's yelp, and dashed into the dark hall.

Payne gave a short laugh, then closed the door. He wasn't sure if he had chosen the wisest path, but he had enjoyed himself nonetheless. Coxesbury had to learn Elf was under his protection now.

And tomorrow she would be his wife.

Nigel pushed the door open. "Was that Coxesbury I saw fleeing down the hallway?"

"Yes. He thought he could frighten me. I showed him otherwise."

"Wish I could have seen it." Nigel lay on the pallet near the window. "Are you really going to wed her tomorrow?"

"Yes."

Nigel scowled. "And then?"

Payne raised an eyebrow. "Didn't you hear? She comes with land. Nigel, I'll have a castle."

"Humph. And you'll have a wife."

Payne didn't know what Nigel wanted of him. "I promised her protection."

"And you'll get yourself a castle in the bargain. Nicely done, I'd say." Scorn tainted Nigel's words.

"I said I'd wed her before I knew of the dowry."

"What are you going to do with her?"

"Do? She'll be my wife, my chatelaine. I imagine we'll have much to do at Candlewood Keep. Matthew told me the castle has been unoccupied for years."

"So we'll be traveling then?"

"Of course. I want to get to Candlewood as soon as possible."

Nigel grunted. "Have you told her?"

"No. But she'll understand. I must see to the needs of my castle." Payne removed his belt and tunic. "I think we should sleep. The sun rises quickly this time of year."

"And you exchange your vows tomorrow." Nigel turned his back to Payne.

"Nigel, what is the reason for your umbrage?"

Nigel faced him. "Boy, there is much you still have to learn."

"You speak in riddles. Can you not see that I shall finally have what I've worked so long for?"

"Aye, but I wonder if it's what you need."

Chapter Fourteen

Elf didn't recognize half the crowd that filled the pews of the chapel. They were here for the wedding, not for her. She adjusted her girdle on her hips, then sighed as she spied her shoes. Her gown hung short, showing more of the under skirt than she wanted, but she could do naught about it. The dress wasn't hers. She owned no gown as fine as this one. Her collection of gowns had meant to serve her only until she joined the convent. A wedding gown was something she had never wanted.

She peered down the aisle. Payne stood at the altar, in black as usual. Her uncle beamed at the crowd as though he was responsible for the spectacle about to commence. Coxesbury sat in the second row. The grim set of his lips told her he didn't enjoy the prospect of her wedding.

The corner of her mouth lifted into a half smile. She enjoyed thwarting *him* even if she couldn't enjoy her wedding.

In less time than she could imagine, she stood beside Payne at the front of the church and then knelt before the priest. She bowed her head and tried to listen to his words. The thudding of her heart made them impossible to hear.

Soon Payne's voice rose strong and loud vowing to cherish and protect her. She nearly laughed. Marriage should protect her, just as he had promised.

But when it was her turn, she found no humor in making her vows before God. Her voice didn't resonate through the chapel as Payne's had. In fact, the priest leaned forward to hear her.

All too soon the ceremony ended, and Elf found herself on Payne's arm. Dear heaven, she was his wife, his to do with as he pleased.

So why did she feel a sudden thrill rush through her?

Her feet carried her beside him, yet she had no sense of movement. In truth, she had no sense of anything. A numbness had seized her. She believed she smiled as they entered the great hall; she thought she heard a cheer ring out; she imagined she smelled a feast, but she wasn't sure. When someone thrust a goblet into her hands, she didn't taste the wine as she drank.

The guests appeared to be enjoying themselves. Elf watched in fascination as they drank and ate, ostensibly in her honor. They didn't suffer from numbness as she did.

The raucous crowd laughed and sang. Elf couldn't understand their gaiety. She tried. She pretended she sat with them, watching the new bride glowing under their attention, but then she'd remembered *she* was the bride and the thought froze her anew.

Within a few minutes, every noise grated in her ears and she wanted nothing more than to duck under the table and clap her hands over her head. Instead, she sat in her chair and stared at the bounty in front of her.

Payne glanced down at his wife. She was quiet—a state he wasn't used to seeing in Elf. God knew he wouldn't be standing in front of the room right now if she hadn't spoken in her brash manner yesterday. Was it just yesterday he had shackled himself with the chains she had forged?

And won himself a castle in exchange?

He didn't expect the shot of guilt that jolted him. He looked at Elf again. She sat so still and quiet, so unlike herself.

He wasn't enjoying himself, either.

Lord Meredith stood and lifted his goblet, mindless of the wine that sloshed over the side and dribbled onto his hand. "To the health of the wedded couple."

The room echoed the toast. Payne nodded his acknowledgment. He noticed Elf neither lifted her vessel nor drank.

"And to the passion that kept her from the convent and brought the Golden Bear to my family." As Meredith quaffed his wine, laughter rippled over the room.

Payne eyed his new uncle. Why was Elf's marriage considered such a miraculous feat? Could no one see her intelligence and beauty? Perhaps she was a little forward, but he could understand her behavior if she had been the butt of such ridicule for years.

He glanced at her again. Her gaze had not shifted from the empty spot she stared at, nor had she touched the food and drink in front of her. Only the slight pink in her cheeks gave evidence that she heard her uncle at all.

The urge to shield her from the room filled him. He wanted to spirit her away and prove to her she was worth two of any of these callous guests. He could take her to his room and—

Not his, *theirs.*

That thought sent another jolt through him, although not of guilt.

Before he could act on his urge, Meredith clapped him on

the back. "Payne, I can't tell you enough how this union pleases me."

Payne arched an eyebrow.

"The thought of Candlewood going to the church never thrilled me, may God forgive me. I mean no disrespect to the church, but it was my mother's property. When she died, my sister inherited it, and when she passed, Elf got it. I spent many a happy week there as a child.

"The keep isn't very big, but the lands are rich and fertile. Of course, I haven't seen the place in years. When Elf came to me, the men that serve Candlewood came with her. They've served me in the meantime, but they will travel back with you."

Men? The keep came with knights? Payne swallowed before he spoke, fearing his voice might betray his excitement. "How many men?"

"A dozen. And their families, of course."

Not only had he gained land, he was a lord. No title, to be sure, but he had men to lead, land to protect, peasants to rule. Add to them the men who had sworn to follow him if he should ever call on them, and he already had a formidable force to protect his land.

He looked out over the great hall. They couldn't leave today, that would be unseemly, but tomorrow . . . with first light. "I am eager to see Candlewood."

Meredith said, "We should be able to assemble everyone by the end of the week. As a wedding present, I shall send grain, meat, and ale with you. But no more talk of the morrow. Now we must enjoy the celebration. We have time to plan later."

Payne struck down the rush of disappointment he felt. In spite of his eagerness, he should have realized he couldn't leave immediately. Anger at himself grew. He had let emotions overcome his intelligence, but now others would depend on his wisdom and sense for their security. He wouldn't let his emotions control his thoughts again.

He searched the room for Nigel. Nigel knew the workings of a castle better than he. As his gaze sought the older man, Payne sent silent thanks to his father. When Payne had left Castlereigh, his father had ordered Nigel to accompany him. Payne wondered if his father meant to give him such a companion, then realized that his father's gesture was perhaps the only way the man could express his fondness for his son. His half-brother had protested his father's action, but Nigel had left with Payne. And now Nigel could help him with the administration of Candlewood.

He spotted Nigel sitting against the wall, scowling. He was staring toward the crowd. What had roused the man's ire? Payne continued his visual search of the hall. There. Coxesbury whispered to his men. He didn't need to hear the words to know he had made an enemy today.

He needed to speak with Nigel. As he turned from the table, his gaze fell on Elf. By the saints, he had forgotten this was his wedding. Chagrin raced through him. Elf still sat without moving, looking as forlorn as she had earlier. No, she definitely wasn't enjoying her wedding feast.

Nigel could wait. Payne held out his hand. "Come, Lady Elfreda."

Elf shot her gaze to him, as if he had startled her. "My lord?"

"Come." His hand still awaited hers.

She didn't move for a moment, then she placed her palm in his. The coldness of her skin surprised him. As she rose, the crowd cheered and called out bawdy jokes. She didn't deign to give them her attention.

He led her from the hall and didn't stop until the noise from the revelry was no more than a low buzz. "Is this better?"

Her large green eyes stared up at him. "Better?"

"It was clear to all that you weren't enjoying yourself."

Elf sighed. "No, I wasn't. But I didn't mean to pull you from the festivities."

"You didn't. I pulled you." He grinned. "Besides, I wasn't enjoying myself any more than you."

"But it's your wedding feast."

"And yours, and if neither of us wishes to partake in the celebration, we have every right to leave. It's *our* wedding after all. We can do as we choose."

She gaped at him for a moment, then laughed. "I haven't thanked you yet."

"For what?"

"For marrying me. I can't imagine you're thrilled to be bound to me. I have been thinking on our situation, and I believe I may have a solution."

"Indeed?" He raised his eyebrows.

"Yes. You have my leave to take me to Candlewood and then continue as you would had you not married me."

Payne kept his silence for a moment. Her words stirred the banked embers of his anger. "Do you not think a castle needs its lord?"

Elf shrugged. "I have run my uncle's house for so long, I imagine I can maintain my own home."

"Did you also see to this castle's protection?"

"No, but I'm sure I can learn that." She pulled in her lower lip between her teeth, worrying it.

"I have no doubt you could," he said in an even tone. She was mistaken if she believed he would let her deny him his castle. "But such action is unnecessary. I am the lord of

Candlewood and will see to its safety."

"But you—"

"You seem to forget we also exchanged vows today. There is more to our union than just the upkeep of the castle."

She blinked, then blushed and hung her head. "I thought perhaps you wouldn't want . . . I mean, you don't have to honor the vows. You weren't exactly free to choose—"

Payne reached out and tilted her chin so that she had to look at him. "No one could have forced me to take vows I didn't intend to keep. I vowed to protect you. Marriage may have been an extreme solution, but it is a solution."

Elf stared at him. She didn't speak and she didn't pull away. He bent his head to hers. "You are my wife. You should learn I discharge all my duties."

Before she could react, he brushed his lips against hers.

She invited him in with a gentle parting of her lips. His tongue slipped inside, tasting her, sliding across the textured smoothness of her tongue, savoring her.

He had expected to show her his willingness to honor his vows. He didn't expect the reaction of his body. His blood roared and his pulse raced at the headiness that accompanied her flavor. His loins tightened at the thought of having her in his bed.

She pressed herself against him. His arms tightened around her, as if trying to eliminate every space between them, as if trying to mold two bodies into one.

It wasn't close enough. With a low growl, he released her. "Not here. Come."

He led her up the circular stairs to her room. He had climbed these stairs before. Memories of the first night he saw her flooded him. "You're alone this time, I take it?"

She nodded.

"Good." He threw open the door.

A chambermaid knelt by the fire. The woman gasped. "Oh, my lord, I didn't expect you so soon." The bed was turned back and a gauzy shift lay upon the sheet. Flower petals strew the bed and a flagon of wine stood on the bedside table.

"Leave us," said Payne.

"But the fire—"

"I'll take care of it."

"Yes, my lord." The maid giggled and rose from the floor. "I can help Lady Elf with her gown if you—"

"Go," roared Payne.

"Aye, my lord." The maidservant laughed again as she closed the door behind her.

Payne eyed Elf. She stood in the center of the room and stared at the bed. He stole up behind her and put his hand on her shoulder. She jumped beneath his touch, then whirled to face him.

"You must think me a frightened goose," she said with a toss of her head. Her attempted casualness failed when her voice cracked. She winced.

Payne almost laughed. He had never seen her less sure of herself than at this moment. And he had never felt more desire to hold her and protect her from everything, even herself, than at this moment. "Come here, wife."

Instead she took a step back. "I don't think I can."

He scowled, but then noticed the tears in her eyes. With a step, he was by her side. Cupping her face in his hands, his gaze probed the depths of her eyes. "Tears? From the Black Knight? I thought you feared nothing."

"I'm not crying. I never cry." She sniffed and frowned. She shook her face free and dashed a drop from her cheek. "Moreover, I'm not frightened."

"I didn't believe you were." Payne crossed to the table and

poured two goblets of wine. He handed her one. "Tell me what troubles you."

Elf lifted the vessel and drank. When she lowered the goblet, wine sparkled on her lips. He struggled to concentrate on her words and resist the urge to lick the drops from her.

"I just . . . this all has happened so fast. I never thought to marry."

"You must have expected it when you claimed we were handfasted."

"Yes . . . I mean, no. I don't know. I said the first thing I could to prevent Coxesbury from asking my uncle for my hand. I wasn't thinking."

"And now?" He didn't know what he wanted to hear.

"And now I've ruined my life and yours." She was crying in earnest now. "I never wanted to marry."

Her words brought him no ease. He took the wine from her hands and placed it with his on the small table. "You wanted to join the convent."

"Yes."

"Why?"

His question startled her. Her tears stopped, and she took in a sharp breath of air. "Why?"

"Yes, why? Did you want to serve God? Did you wish to help the poor? Did you wish to tend to the sick?"

"I—I—" she stammered.

"Or did you just think to escape?" Payne paced in front of her. "Did you just want to leave behind the people who belittled you and prove to them you were better than they?"

Elf gasped. "I never—"

"I have heard the way they talk in front of you. And I have seen you pretend you don't hear." Payne stopped in front of her and grasped her shoulders. "Tell me your reason. If you truly want to go to a convent, I'll take you myself."

Elf stared at him. Her eyelashes still glistened with her tears, but her eyes were now dry. At last, her shoulders slumped and she let out heavy sigh. "I would have made a formidable nun."

Payne wanted to let out a whoop. "Yes, you would have, but I pity the abbess who would have had to teach you obedience."

Color rode her cheeks at his comment. "How can you say that? I am *not* headstrong."

"Remind me to tell you of the legend of the Black Knight sometime."

Elf fell silent. After a moment, she sent him a shy smile. "Perhaps I am a bit headstrong."

He laughed. "A bit. And now you will have your own home to run. You shall be the chatelaine, nay, you *are* the chatelaine of Candlewood."

Her eyes brightened. "My own home," she breathed.

"And I am the lord of Candlewood."

Elf didn't respond for a moment. Then she nodded. "Aye. You are my lord and husband."

Desire struck him like a battering ram.

Chapter Fifteen

Did he know how her heart pounded? Elf didn't have the courage to look at him. She couldn't bear to see pity in his eyes. He had married her, true, but she didn't fool herself into thinking he wanted the union. Whereas she—well, she wondered if he felt the same glorious lightheadedness she did when he kissed her.

Payne's hands brushed against her back. He was loosening the laces of her gown. His hands slipped lower and unclasped the girdle on her waist. The links clinked as he placed the belt on a stool. Her overgown fell off one shoulder. He reached to the other to sweep the material from it as well. The dress pooled around her feet.

Her undergown was a simple garment. Long sleeves fell to her wrist, and the hem brushed the floor. Payne stood behind her and pulled the loose end of the bow that secured the back of the gown together. Cool air whispered across her shoulders as Payne released the other bows that trailed down the back of her dress. She didn't breathe as his finger traced the curve of her spine through her shift. In the next moment, her undergown melted into the garment pool on the floor.

Clad in nothing save her stockings and shift, Elf faced Payne.

His golden eyes flashed in the candlelight. "Dear heaven, you're beautiful."

"No, I'm not."

"Let me show you." He stepped to her and took her in his arms.

A strange giddiness gripped her as his lips met hers. She knew the room didn't spin, but her blood raced, and she felt her heart beating between her legs. Her spirit sang as he lifted her into his arms, carried her to the bed, and lay down beside her.

He kissed her and touched her. He ran his hands up her legs and pulled each stocking off her with more of a caress than a tug. Her shift came next, until she lay bare to his gaze. She tried to cover herself with a sheet, but he stopped her.

"Don't hide yourself from me." He rolled from her, and a sly smile curved his lips. His gaze captured hers. With deliberate slowness, he removed his tunic and trousers until he, too, stood bare for her scrutiny. Her gaze drank in his broad shoulders, muscled chest, tapered waist, his narrow hips where his . . .

She couldn't breathe. She doubted she would ever breathe again.

Raising her gaze to the relative safety of his chest—she couldn't look into his eyes—she felt the mattress sink under his weight. She stared at the pale scars that marked the lightly haired skin. She placed her palm against his chest. His heart thumped beneath her hand, and his warmth spread through her from the point of contact.

They lay skin to skin, his heat mingling with hers. His mouth captured her lips and soon their breath swirled together, each breathing the other's essence. The throbbing between her legs quickened, filling her with a longing for something she didn't understand.

Payne's hand reached down and cupped her breast. With a grin, he bent his head. She gasped as his mouth closed over her nipple and teased it to a pebbled peak. Then he lavished the same attention to her other breast.

His tongue teased her until she could scarcely breathe.

His hand traveled across her belly, lower until he reached the apex of her thighs. He reached the source of throbbing, and teased the bud he found there until she thought she could no longer make sense of her world. He slipped a finger into her feminine valley as she bucked beneath him.

"So hot, so wet," he whispered in a thick voice.

He rolled her beneath him and pressed himself up on his arms. She felt his hardness against her thigh and without thinking spread her legs for him.

"Look at me, Elf. I want you to see me."

Elf gazed deep into his eyes. He guided himself into her, easing himself deeper, and paused. Why had he stopped? She wanted more of him, to feel him deep within her. Then with a sudden thrust, he broke through her maidenhead.

A flash of pain erased the pleasure-filled haze that had surrounded her.

"I regret the pain you must feel, but I don't regret that I am the one who caused it," Payne whispered in her ear. "You must trust me now to show you the pleasure."

He withdrew slowly, then entered her again. Elf relaxed when she realized no pain accompanied the movement.

Payne bent his head and took her nipple in his mouth. She gasped as desire jolted through her again. From the center of her core, a sensation grew that she could only describe as a tickle. But as Payne rocked above, the urge to meet his thrusts overpowered her. She tilted her hips, and the tickle grew until she abandoned all effort of naming what she felt. She only knew she enjoyed it and she wanted more.

The tickle crept into every inch of her body, tingling inside her, filling her with a yearning for some unknown end to this delicious torture. The tingling grew until she gasped for air, and yet felt no distress at her inability to breathe.

Elf didn't believe the tingling could grow any more without hurting her, but Payne moved faster above her, and she no longer cared if she was hurt.

And then the tingling ceased, and her body exploded into stars. She believed she screamed, but she couldn't hear herself.

As she drifted back to her senses, Payne gathered her in his arms. "Well, my little Elf, I wonder what other surprises you will bring."

She pressed her cheek against his chest and snuggled deeper into his embrace. "Surprises?"

"Yes. It was quite a nice surprise to find my handfasted wife isn't averse to passion."

She blushed. "Are women supposed to be?"

Payne laughed. "I wouldn't know, never having been a woman. I rather enjoy indulging in passion myself."

Elf thought for a moment. "Well, I believe I would enjoy making a habit of this behavior also. How long do we have to wait to do it again?"

"Patience, my lady. This was your first time to lie with a man. You're bound to feel a little sore come the morn. Were it otherwise, I wouldn't hesitate to show how soon."

"Oh." She let out a soft sigh of disappointment. A moment later she spoke again. "And if I promise not to complain on the morrow?"

Payne let out a guttural moan. "Woman, I am only a man,

and I hold a desirable woman in my arms. You cannot tempt me without consequence."

Elf smiled as his heart beat grew more rapid under her cheek. With mischievous intent, she traced a line down the rippled warmth of his belly, lower still, until she felt his manhood stir against her hand.

He sucked in his breath with a hiss. She looked up at him and saw him staring at her. Since he hadn't told her to stop, she wrapped her fingers around his hardening shaft. She gave him a wicked smile. "Soon?"

"Not long, my lady." Payne rolled on top of her and stole her next teasing remarks with a kiss. Moments later, Elf felt the tickle start anew.

When Elf woke the next morning, she shivered slightly. A light rain was falling, bringing its chill to the chamber. Glancing beside her, she saw an empty spot. Payne had already risen and left the chamber. She couldn't blame him for leaving. While she had slept, the morning had nearly fled.

She stretched her arms and gave a slight wince. She was indeed sore, but with a smile she acknowledged she would gladly suffer the twinges of muscles unaccustomed to use for the pleasure she had shared with Payne in the night.

Rising, she found her shift on the floor where Payne had discarded it. She slipped it over her head and let if float over her hips. Grabbing a simple gown and overgown, she dressed herself in little time, and left the chamber to search for her husband.

The hall was empty, save for the few servants still cleaning after the previous day's festivities. She followed the passage to the kitchen where the cook gave her an apple and a piece of bread to tide her over until the midday meal.

Munching on her snack, she grabbed a cloak and stepped

into the courtyard. The rain fell harder now, but it couldn't stop her from finding Payne. How would he greet her? Would he kiss her again? She felt the tickle anew at the thought.

She pulled the hood over her head and headed for the stables, wondering if perhaps she would find him there. She was disappointed, but fed the core of her apple to Merlin after scratching the horse on the nose.

The clang of metal from the exercise yard drew her attention. Elf crossed to an area saved for the use and training of the knights. She saw a group of men fighting each other with blunted swords. Their movements lacked the intensity she had witnessed at the tournament.

Her gaze moved over the men with disinterest until she spied the last pair. Her heart quickened as she recognized Payne. Withdrawing to a spot along the stone wall, Elf watched her husband as he turned his opponent's thrusts away with apparent ease, then pressed his own attack with grace and speed. Although tunic and hauberk covered him, Payne's lithe movements brought the image of the naked man to her mind. A surge of warmth effused through her.

"All right, men. That's enough for now. Good work. Be prepared to move in two days." Payne's voice resonated through the yard.

Move? Were they leaving so soon? Payne had said nothing to her about leaving yet.

The men ceased their mock battles, and the low buzz of convivial comradeship filled the air. She knew these men. They had been loyal to her father and now served her uncle. Their faces shone with excitement. As their pages helped the men with their weapons, Payne walked toward her.

Elf couldn't help but smile as he neared her. He stopped, nodded to her, then walked past her.

Her smile evaporated as fast as a drop of water dancing on a hot pan.

Dumbfounded, she stared after him as he strode to Nigel, who stood in a shaded archway. Payne wiped the sweat from his brow. "What did you think of them?"

"They show promise. Of course, we don't know how they would do in battle, but these are good men. You are fortunate to have them."

Payne nodded. "When we get to Candlewood, we'll set up a training schedule. We'll be a little vulnerable until we settle, but I don't imagine that should take us very long. It depends on the state of the keep and battlements."

"What of servants?" asked Nigel.

"Candlewood has a village." Payne wrinkled his brow. His gaze fell on Elf. "My Lady Elf, perhaps you can answer."

Elf crossed to them. Anger simmered just below the calm she portrayed. "My lord?"

"Whence has Candlewood obtained its servants in the past?"

"I do not know, my lord. I was far too young when I left to remember."

"Perhaps Lord Matthew will part with some of his help until we can find servants of our own. Let's not worry about comforts until we must." He and Nigel started walking, leaving her behind. "Nigel, can you think of anything else I need for the men?"

Anger seethed in her blood. She hadn't expected a declaration of love from him, but she had expected some show of tenderness after their wedding night. Elf circled in front of Payne, halting his stride. "You might want to consider where they sleep tonight."

Payne gave her a puzzled look. "Tonight? They bed where they always have."

"Good. Since your concern is for your men, you may join them there, and leave me my bed." She pivoted and stomped away with her head held high, leaving Payne with a look of bewilderment decorating his face.

Payne watched her disappear, then turned to Nigel. "Why is she angry?"

"You didn't hurt her last night, did you?"

"By my troth, I did not." He hesitated, then shook his head. "No more than I had to."

Nigel held up his hand. "Spare me your tale of conquest. How did she appear this morn?"

"Asleep."

"Pardon?"

"She was still sleeping when I left the bed. I thought to let her rest."

"There you have it."

"Nigel, I cannot understand your riddling speech."

"Women are much like a pampered dog. Give them attention and they behave for you. Ignore them and they sulk."

Payne snorted. "Surely Elf must realize I have more important things to do than to pander to her whims at this time. I have a castle to run."

Nigel shrugged. "I don't pretend to understand women. I was only making a guess as to the behavior of your bride."

Payne stared in the direction of her departure. "She will value my work when we are settled at Candlewood."

Chapter Sixteen

Elf gazed out over the line of men, women, carts, and wagons that snaked down the road. She sat atop her mare near the center of the procession, where she would be the best-protected in case of attack. She almost snorted at the thought. Who would be foolish enough to attack the Golden Bear's lady? But she understood her new position. These men served her as well as her husband and they wouldn't like to see her riding at the head of the line as she longed to do.

Elf sighed. The light would not last much longer this day, and Payne was eager to reach Candlewood. They had left her uncle's castle three days earlier. She could see the frustration on Payne's face as they stopped each evening, but they couldn't travel as fast with such a procession as they had when they had traveled to the tournament. She could also see he didn't want to push the men too much. He would join her in the tent each night after seeing to the men, but she had not yet forgiven him. He had slept on a mat on the other side of the tent.

She sighed again. If she were honest with herself, she would admit she wanted him back in her bed. The memory of their wedding night sent shivers down her spine when she thought of it.

A hill rose in the distance. Elf smiled. She knew that Candlewood was visible from the top of that hill. Indeed, the pace of the travelers quickened. She glanced at the sky. The sun was lower in the sky now. They would make it to the castle, but not before dark.

Payne rode beside her on Merlin as they topped the hill. Atop a slanted ridge stood Candlewood. The keep rose from the highest point, but the castle sprawled over the ridge's various elevations. The last rays of the sun glistened off the castle's walls, and the stone glowed as if in flames. A thick stand of trees grew at the base of the castle, and the gleaming stones just above the tops of the trees gave the image of hundreds of candles burning.

"Welcome to Candlewood," said Elf in a low voice. Her gaze fastened on her husband.

Payne didn't stir. Merlin shifted beneath him, but Payne's gaze never wavered from the sight. Awe and disbelief reigned on his features.

Then the sun sank lower and the glow disappeared. The stones became gray in the darkening light, and the castle lost its glimmer. In fact, the castle lost its appeal. The curtain wall, which protected the lowest end of the rise, held half a tower, its other half-strewn in rubble at its base. Weeds choked the moat that wrapped around the broken wall. Her gaze traveled the slope toward the keep. A gaping hole yawned in the roof over the stables. Small plants grew from cracks, and straw from the nests of birds poked out of every hole. The keep itself loomed dark and unfriendly.

Payne's face no longer held awe.

"I suppose we should have believed my uncle when he said he hadn't seen Candlewood in years." Elf couldn't keep the disappointment from her voice.

A murmur rose from the men. Candlewood had been their home as well. She glanced at Payne.

"I shall fix it," he said in a voice meant only for her. Then he stood in the saddle. "Men, the sight of our home in such disrepair has surprised me, but Candlewood is our home. We shall overcome this setback. Candlewood shall glow again, and not just in the sunset, this I swear."

A cheer rose from the men.

"Now let us go home." Payne rode to the front of the line and led the procession toward the castle.

The road hadn't been leveled in years. Rocks jutted out from the dirt, making passage difficult for the wagons. Where no rocks obstructed the path, holes caused as many problems. The wooden bridge over the moat creaked in protest. By the time Elf reached the castle, she was weary.

She rode through the portcullis and glanced around her. Chickens cackled from their roosts above the gate. Litter covered the yard, lumber lay askew, and ample evidence of the habits of wild beasts rested underfoot. The men had already lit several small fires to light the yard and castle.

Payne lifted her from her mount.

"This isn't the homecoming I expected," said Elf as she glanced around the yard that bustled with activity.

"It will look better in the morning." Payne led her around the trash and into the keep.

"It can hardly look worse." Elf let out a humorless laugh. The great hall was dirty, but intact.

"I had Nigel find us a room. The solar wasn't serviceable."

"Oh." Elf walked without hesitation toward the stairs. The way the castle looked today didn't match her memories of Candlewood, but at least she knew where everything was. She stopped before she ascended. "Which room?"

"I don't know. We have to wait for Nigel."

Elf sat on the bottom step and put her elbows on her knees. She cupped her chin in her hands. She watched as the men and women swept aside eight years of dust and neglect to place their narrow pallets on the floor of the great hall.

"It will look better in daylight," said Payne. The look of concern on his face irritated her.

"If you say that to me one more time, I believe I shall scream. I have every right to mourn my memories. I don't intend to pout forever, just for a minute or two. Besides, I'm tired."

Nigel's appearance on the stairs saved her from the comment she was sure sat on Payne's tongue.

"I found you a room," said Nigel.

Elf rose and turned to Nigel. Payne followed her up the stairs to the next level. The room was small, but it was clean—almost. She didn't really want to see what the dark corners held. A cheery fire burned in the hearth. Her trunks stood along one wall. A thick layer of dust covered the bed, but Elf noticed the pallets on the floor. She smiled. Nigel thought of everything. "Thank you, Nigel. I'm sure I shall sleep in comfort tonight."

Nigel nodded his head. "I didn't think you'd want to sleep in any of the beds until they had a good airing. Good night, my lady."

"Good night." Elf waited until Nigel left the room, then turned her back to Payne. "Would you? I think it would be too much to expect a maidservant to come help me undress tonight."

She knew the instant he stepped behind her. His warmth diffused over her, but when his fingers undid the laces of the overgown, a shiver skittered down her spine. She hadn't let him into her bed since their wedding night, but neither had she forgotten a moment of that night. When the gown was loose enough, she stepped away from him and let the gown slide to the floor. She didn't dare face him. Heat burned in her cheeks as she folded the gown and placed it in her chest. Without glancing at him, she slipped off the undergown and placed it in the chest as well. Clad only in her shift, she climbed between the blankets on the floor.

Payne watched her with a crooked smile on his lips. "It seems Nigel isn't aware of our sleeping arrangements. He laid but the one bed."

Elf shrugged her shoulder. "It doesn't matter to me. I'm too tired to worry about it now." She rolled over and closed her eyes.

Behind her she heard Payne blow out the flame of the lamp. The light from the fire flickered on the walls. She watched his shadow grow as he stepped further from the fire. As the shadow undressed, Elf's heartbeat quickened. She slowed her breathing, but as she exhaled, the unevenness gave proof to her agitation.

Payne chuckled. "Have no fear, my lady. I am also too tired to fight with you this even."

"Good." She wanted to say something witty and biting, but nothing came to her. Instead she wrestled with the disappointment she felt.

"Good night, Elf." Payne lifted the covers and climbed in beside her.

She didn't stir as he settled himself. Within moments he stilled, and his breathing was even and calm. In disbelief, she rolled over, only to find his eyes open and an amused smile on his lips.

"Welcome home, Elf." Payne leaned forward and kissed her.

The desire she tried to subdue raged to the surface. She returned his kiss with a hunger she wasn't aware she had. With a groan, he wrapped his arms around her and rolled on top of her. He pushed her chemise off her shoulders and took a nipple in his mouth. She arched her back. Her hand traced down his spine until she reached the hills of his buttocks. He shuddered as she cupped the rounded firmness. His erection brushed against the skin of her thighs. With a soft moan, she opened her legs to him and waited, holding her breath until he settled between them. And still she couldn't breathe.

When he slid into her, her breath rushed out like a summer breeze. She lifted her hips to meet his thrusts, again and again, until her senses soared, and she could believe she flew.

His hand reached between them and found her swollen bud. He stroked her then, sending jolts of fire through her until she shattered. As her senses returned to her, he drove into her, quaking with his release.

A few minutes later, she lay in his arms, drowsy and content. Her cheek lay against his chest. She could hear his heart beating under her. With a deep breath, she closed her eyes. Just before she fell asleep, a thought flitted through her mind.

She was home.

When she awoke the next morning, once again she found Payne gone from her bed. With a sigh, she dressed and hurried downstairs. At least this time she hadn't overslept.

Elf found him in the great hall, giving orders to a group of women.

"I have already set the men to repairs, but the solar needs to be cleared first. The beds must all be cleaned and aired as well."

Elf stepped forward. "Forgive me, my lord, but I think we should begin in the kitchen."

Payne stopped and looked at her.

"We have a household to feed. We must store the foods my uncle sent and ready the kitchen. I can sleep on the floor as long as I need to. Our men and their women have needs more important than mine."

Payne stared at her, then grinned. His approval sent a wave of satisfaction through her. "As you wish, my lady."

Elf didn't miss the knowing looks the women shared with one another. The heat of blush crept into her cheeks, but she held her head high. "Until we can get servants from the village, we have much work to do ourselves." She led the women to the kitchen and assigned tasks to each one, including herself.

They righted the tables, scrubbed the wood, then rubbed in flaxseed oil until the tabletops gleamed. Elf found a broom, and after rousting a family of mice that had nested in the bristles, she swept the dirt from the buttery and pantry. The women talked and laughed as they worked. Elf overcame their initial reluctance to include her by working as hard as any of them, showing them she was willing to dirty herself for the benefit of Candlewood. By the afternoon, the kitchen was nearly clean. Elf sat back on her heels from where she had been scrubbing the stone floor of the pantry, and pushed a strand of hair from her damp forehead.

"You there. Wench. Where is your master?"

Elf turned at the rude voice. A man stood above her. She looked behind him and saw a trail of muddy footprints across the newly cleaned floor. She threw her hands in the air. "Couldn't you have wiped your feet before you tracked in all the dirt?"

"Watch your tongue with your betters, wench. I wish to see your lord," the man snarled at her.

Elf rose from the floor. She watched the man's expression

change from arrogance to surprise as she stood fully half a foot taller than he.

"Great heavens, what sort of beast sired you?" The man stepped back and gaped at her.

A murmur of protest rose from the women, but Elf raised her hand and shook her head. "You wished to see the lord? Allow me to take you to him." Her tone was deferential. As she turned to hand the scrub brush to the nearest women, she winked at them all. Their expressions changed from anger to amusement.

"This way, sir," said Elf and led the way to the great hall. "Sometimes it's hard to find the master. There is much to do here, and he's trying to oversee it all." Elf scratched her head. "I know. He must be at the tower."

She led the man out the door and down the slope to the curtain wall. Payne wasn't at the tower, and the man started to grumble.

"No, the stables must be where he is." Elf didn't wait for the man to say anything. She plunged back up the hill, through a gate, and into the yard. Indeed, men worked on the stables, but Payne wasn't there.

"Hmmm," said Elf drawing her finger along the side of her face. "He must be at the chapel."

"He'd better be, you stupid woman," muttered the man.

Elf grinned to herself, then led him back into the keep, up the staircase, through the maze of hallways to the chapel. With mock surprise, Elf said, "I can't imagine where the master is."

The man held his side as he huffed and puffed. "Dim-witted virago. You've led me on no more than a merry goose chase. Find your master now, and don't think I won't tell him of your idiocy."

"Of course, the barbican. The master would want to see to

the defenses of his home first."

"I can find my own way."

"No, sir. I wouldn't dream of letting you go alone." Elf smiled at the man as if he hadn't spoken. Without waiting for him, Elf rushed back through the keep, through the yard and into the barbican. The man struggled to keep pace.

Payne stood with Nigel as they surveyed the work of clearing the rubble from the gate. Elf strode to his side. Payne looked up at once.

"A visitor has come to see you, my lord." Elf bowed her head.

The man tottered up in front of Payne. He didn't speak for a few moments as he struggled to catch his breath.

Payne raised an eyebrow and eyed Elf with suspicion. "Elf?"

She just shrugged. "He wouldn't tell me his business."

"That's because I have no business with stupid wenches such as you. My lord, you have no idea the trouble this woman has caused."

Payne's gaze narrowed. "Who are you?"

The man swallowed once, drew in a deep breath, and bowed. "I am Kip of Tinnesby, the steward of Candlewood, appointed by Lord Matthew Meredith himself. I would ask your business here, Sir Knight."

"If you are the steward, then you are just the man I need to see." Payne stepped forward forcing the man's gaze up. "Are you aware that Candlewood doesn't belong to Lord Meredith?"

"Of course it does. Lord Meredith hired me to—"

"I know what Lord Meredith hired you to do. But Candlewood is no longer Lord Meredith's concern."

Kip gulped. "But I assure you, Lord Meredith—"

"Meredith held the land for his niece."

"Yes, but Lord Meredith said she was to enter the abbey."

"She changed her mind. She married. Me. My lady wife is Lord Meredith's niece. But you've met her." Payne waved Elf forward. "Lady Elfreda of Renfrey, this is your steward, Kip."

The man grew pale. "But she . . . I found her scrubbing the floor."

"Aye. She and all the women are busy cleaning the mess you left with your stewardship." Payne took another step forward like a lion stalking its prey. "You'd best learn my name as well. I am Payne Dunbyer of Castlereigh."

"The Golden Bear?" whispered Kip in horror.

"The same, but we were speaking of *your* stewardship. What excuse do you have for the state of the east tower?"

Kip backed up. "An earthquake. Toppled the tower. And lightning. A storm. 'Twas fearsome."

Payne continued to stalk him. "Let's pretend I believe you. Why didn't you have it repaired?"

"Lord Meredith didn't give me money to repair—"

"Ah, so he gave you money for Candlewood's upkeep, did he? How much of it stayed in your pockets?"

"I . . . I . . ." stammered Kip. He stumbled over a loose stone and fell. His backside raised a cloud of dirt around him. Scrambling to his feet, he put his hands out in front of him as if to protect himself from Payne's approach.

"And just how much money did you spend in keeping the castle clean? If I asked the women in the village, how much would they say they earned in the cleaning of the castle? If I asked the villagers, how many of them would they say you've hired for the upkeep of the castle?"

Kip opened his mouth, but nothing came out.

"Your stewardship is at an end, and you can be sure I'll report your industry to Lord Meredith. In fact, I'll do my best to tell all my neighbors of your incompetence. You'll be lucky if you can make your living begging."

Payne's hand shot out and grabbed the man by the neck. He lowered his head to Kip's so that a mere inch separated their noses. "And if I ever hear of you abusing any woman, especially my wife, you'll consider this your lucky day, because today you only lost your job."

As Payne released his grip, Kip let out a cry and fell to the ground again. He scrambled on all fours for a few yards, then shot to his feet and dashed from the gate.

Elf's hands covered her mouth. Payne faced her, and a look of concern overtook his features. "Did I frighten you?"

She removed her hands to reveal a bright grin and shook her head. "It was all I could do to keep from laughing."

"I'm happy you approve."

"I only wish I could have done it myself."

"From the state of his breathing, I imagine you exacted your own revenge." Payne gave her an expectant look.

Elf shrugged. "We merely took the long way to find you."

He laughed, filling her with a delicious contentment. "You have a smudge across your nose and cheeks. You've been working hard."

Elf rubbed her nose and looked down. Her skirt had flecks of dirt and a large wet spot near her knees. She groaned. "I'm glad I can't see my face. I suppose I do look more like a servant than the lady of the manor today."

"Never." He reached out and brushed her cheek with her thumb. "No lady of the manor has ever declared her place with more honor than you today. Consider the dirt on your dress a badge of honor."

Chapter Seventeen

When Payne awoke, he rolled from the pallet. He placed his feet on the floor with a thud. His floor, his castle. Drawing a deep breath, he grinned. He was ready to continue the work at the barbican.

Elf stirred in the bed and woke with a sleepy smile. "Good morrow, husband."

"Good morrow, Elf." His castle, his wife. Things certainly did look better in the daylight.

She stretched like a cat in the sun and yawned. Her guileless movements brought the desire to delay his work for a while and return to bed, but chiding himself, he dressed. He watched as she rose and washed her face. As she dressed herself, the desire to *undress* her grew, but a knock interrupted those inclinations.

Glancing back to make sure Elf was covered, he said, "Come."

Nigel opened the door. "You have visitors."

"What?"

"The villagers. They've come to see you."

"Whatever for?"

Elf looked at him. "You're the lord of the castle. *Their* lord."

"But I have work to do," said Payne with some irritation.

"I expect you won't get much done today," said Elf.

Payne gave her a look of exasperation before he left with Nigel. In the great hall, a chair stood on the dais. He raised an eyebrow. Twenty or so men fell silent as he walked into the chamber. They snatched caps from their heads and lowered their gazes.

Nigel led him to the chair. Before he sat, he addressed the men. "Good morrow. I am Payne of Castlereigh, Lord of Candlewood."

Several of the men glanced at him in surprise and murmured amongst themselves. He heard snatches of the hushed conversations. Mostly he heard the name, "Golden Bear." Payne almost groaned. He wondered if he would ever rid himself of that annoying appellative.

News of the castle's new occupants had flown through the village on the swift feet of gossip. Kip's well-deserved and much applauded dismissal only added to the curiosity of the villeins. By the end of the morning, Payne had met with over fifty men. He watched with relief as the last man took his leave. Then he rubbed his eyes with the heel of his hands.

"You didn't expect all your duties as lord to be enjoyable, did you?" Nigel emerged from his seat in the shadows.

"No." Payne rose from his chair. "There is much I need to learn. On the other hand, many that came wanted their former positions. Candlewood will shine sooner than I thought."

"Aye. And tonight we shall eat better than we have in days. Thank heaven, the cook returned." Nigel smiled and clapped him on the back. "Your mother would be pleased."

"I expect she would be." Payne allowed himself a moment

of satisfaction before he spoke again. "But we still have much to do."

Nigel nodded. "I'll get back to the men."

"I'll be there as soon as I find Elf. I want to tell her that her days as a scullery are over."

He searched for her first in the kitchen, but found only the cook giving orders to the many new servants. Elf had been right. This was the first room that needed cleaning.

He wandered through the castle looking for her. When he reached the solar, he thought it empty until he caught a glimpse of a green skirt through the window. His first thought was that Elf had climbed onto the walls, but then he realized she stood in some sort of private courtyard that he hadn't noticed when he first saw this room. He returned to the hallway and made his way to the door.

The little square opened to the sky. The floor was of stone, and benches lined the walls. A slender fountain stood silent in the middle of a moss and algae covered pool. Cracked urns held dirt, and the dried stalks of some long forgotten vine clung to the stones with the feeble grip of a dead tendril.

"This was my mother's favorite spot." Brushing a tear from her cheek, Elf turned as he stepped out. She reached forward and pulled out a handful of slime from the basin of the fountain.

The urge to take her in his arms and comfort her overwhelmed him, but he didn't. He was unaccustomed to such feelings, and the thought it might be a sign of weakness frightened him.

Elf dropped the green strands back into the pool. "She helped design the fountain, you know. A cistern catches water on the roof and helps spray the water into the air. I suppose it is clogged now." She wiped her hands on the apron she wore, then pointed to the back of the little courtyard. A single arch led to an open wooden staircase that curled its way to the highest point of the keep. Payne noticed the intricate carving on the balustrade. At one time, this spot must have been magical.

"There is another room up there. You can see the entire castle and even into the village from there. It used to be my favorite place to hide from the ladies who tried to make me work on my stitches."

"Show me."

Elf shook her head. "I can't. The top of the stairs is blocked. The roof has fallen in. I don't even know if the room is intact."

She sucked in a deep breath, then smiled at him. "Ah well, we have more important things to take care of. I suppose I can get to the airing out of the beds today." She stepped back into the hallway.

Payne glanced around at the small courtyard before following her. He hadn't realized there were little treasures such as this spot at Candlewood.

As Elf pulled another mattress off yet another bed, she let out a puff of air. She pulled the straw-filled tick toward the window.

"My lady?"

With a little cry, Elf dropped the mattress.

A woman rushed to her and bowed her head. "Oh, forgive me, my lady. I didn't mean to frighten you."

Elf laughed and touched the woman's shoulder. "Don't fret yourself. You only startled me."

The woman lifted her gaze. Elf looked into the soft gray eyes of the woman. She was about a decade older than Elf, but her face showed the lines of a much harder life.

"Why did you wish to see me?"

The woman bowed her head again. "I was wondering if you needed a servant, my lady."

"We need several. What is your name?"

"Margaret."

"My mother had a nursemaid named Margaret. She took care of me when I was a babe. I still remember her," said Elf.

"She was my grandmother." Margaret reached for the mattress and started to pull it to the window.

Elf stared at the woman for an instant, then hurried to help her. With two sets of hands, they were able to drag the mattress to the window in little time.

"My grandmother told me many stories of life in the castle," Margaret said. "You were but a young girl when she became too old to care for you. My mother had already married by that time and didn't wish to leave her family, but Granny raised me to take her place at the castle. I worked here for a little while." Opening the end of the mattress, Margaret shook the old hay from the tick.

Elf watched the straw flutter to the courtyard below. "And when my uncle came to get me, he didn't take you with us because I was old enough not to need a nursemaid any longer."

"Yes, my lady." Margaret shook out the material with a snap to remove the last wisps of hay from the mattress, then laid the fabric on the sill to air.

Wonder filled Elf for a moment. "You were the one who would bring me sweetmeats from the banquets and tell me the stories of what you saw."

"Yes, my lady. I wasn't sure you'd remember me. I wasn't here for very long."

"I remember thinking I was too old for a nursemaid, but I do remember liking you because you didn't treat me as a child." Elf grinned at Margaret. "What did you do after my uncle closed Candlewood?"

"I returned home to help my father. He is a weaver in the village. Then I married. I have two daughters of my own. My husband died last year."

"I'm sorry." Elf felt her heart constrict for the woman. "Where are your daughters now?"

"My mother watches them."

Elf fell silent for a moment. "I have no children, but I do have need of an attendant."

Margaret looked dumbfounded. "But I do not have the skills to attend a lady."

"Good, because you will find I'm not like most ladies. Between us, we'll figure out your duties."

Margaret fell to her knees. Tears welled up in her eyes. "Thank you, my lady."

"And this is the first thing we shall have to work on. My name is Elf." She pulled the woman to her feet.

With a tremulous smile, Margaret nodded her head. "Thank you, Lady Elf. You were a beautiful child, and now I see you have grown into your beauty."

"What drivel. I am too tall and my hair is too red."

"Your hair is burnished gold in the sunlight and your height will give you sons others will envy."

Elf looked at Margaret, unmoved. "Or daughters who will have trouble finding gowns that fit them."

Margaret laughed. "I forgot to tell you that I am quite skilled with a needle. We shall make those gowns fit."

In the days and weeks that followed, the flurry of activity never slowed at Candlewood. Rooms were cleared, cleaned, and readied for use. The chapel held its first mass in years, and tables filled the great hall at meals. The number of servants doubled, and in the mysterious way prosperity breeds its own repute, craftsmen appeared at the castle to provide their services. Stonemasons began their work on rebuilding the tower, and carpenters cut new beams for the stables from the woods. Farm lads cleared the orchard and vineyards, and gardeners once again clipped the overgrown hedges and bushes to open the gravel paths for use.

Elf breathed in the scent of the fresh rushes that strew the great hall. She didn't think she would ever tire of the smell after the stench that had pervaded the castle when they had first arrived.

But even the sight of the clean hall couldn't improve her mood. She knew Payne busied himself with furbishing the castle. In fact, he spent every spare moment in the strengthening of Candlewood. He was just as likely to be seen lifting stones that blocked a creek as clearing brush that had overgrown a patch of garden. He oversaw the work on the tower and the training of his men. In the past weeks, he more often than not stumbled into bed, nearly asleep before he removed his clothes. But that didn't excuse ignoring her. The demands on his time were great, but she was lonely. Oh, Margaret provided some company, but the woman often talked about how fine the lord was, and how happy the castle would be if a babe were born.

A babe? Even Elf knew they needed to do more than just sleep together to beget a child.

To be fair, Payne had been attentive once or twice, but the castle kept him far too busy to further the familiarity she wanted with him.

She glanced up to see the new steward bearing down on her.

"My lady, I have discovered some of our stores are missing."

Elf almost laughed. She knew she hadn't taken them. The Black Knight hadn't ridden since early summer. "What is gone?"

"A slab of bacon and some flour. It's not much, but it's vexing all the same. The cook claims not to have used the stores, but I'm not sure I believe him. He has been known to cook in a wasteful manner."

"Has it affected our ability to feed our own?"

"Not at all, my lady. We have plenty and with the preparations for the upcoming winter, it's hardly noticeable. I just didn't want you to think I'm shirking my duties."

"I'll speak with the cook, but if it isn't a large amount, I shouldn't trouble yourself over it. Thank you for bringing it to my attention." Elf nodded at the man.

"Thank you, my lady." The man bowed and retreated.

As he left, a page appeared at her side. "My lady?"

"I seem to be quite popular this morning," muttered Elf.

"Pardon?"

" 'Twas nothing. What did you wish?"

The boy bowed. "The master wants to see you in the solar."

Elf's heart began to race. Payne was waiting for her. She started to climb the stairs, then stopped. She hadn't been inside the solar since the day Payne had found her there. They still slept in the room Nigel found for them the first night of their arrival. Facing the page, she asked. "Are you sure he said the solar?"

"Yes, my lady."

"Thank you." Confused, Elf climbed to the top of the keep. As she turned down the hallway to the solar, the sound of gurgling water reached her ears. She walked into the chamber and froze.

The room was immaculate. The walls boasted new paintings, and the wooden floor shone with polish. From the bed hung new drapes. A table stood against one wall and a bowl of fruit rested on its surface. Her chests lined another wall, with the largest at the foot of the bed.

Margaret beamed at her from the corner. "Isn't it lovely, Elf?"

Elf blinked to make sure the image didn't vanish. "But who . . . how?"

"The master wanted to surprise you." Margaret clasped her hands together in front of her. "I can't wait to tell him of the expression on your face."

"Where is he?"

"Nigel needed him in the exercise yard, but he told me not to wait for him."

The room was beautiful, but his absence dampened her joy. She smiled at Margaret to hide her dismay. "It's lovely."

"There's more." Margaret took her hand and led her through a new door into the little courtyard. The stone of the fountain gleamed white again and the flume sprayed into the air. The pool beneath it rippled as the drops hit its surface.

Elf couldn't speak. She walked around to the staircase. The dark oak shone. As she climbed each step, she ran her fingers along the smooth wood of the railing. No trace of dust remained in the carvings of the balusters. At the top, she pushed open the door.

The door swung open without a creak to reveal the small room she knew was there. Cleaned and repaired, the room once again provided a haven from the bustle of the castle. The two windows now had glass panes. She touched them in wonder. Her often-neglected needlework was here. Two chairs encircled a table upon which lay a chessboard.

She sighed.

"Don't you like it?" Margaret had followed her up.

"Of course I do. It's just . . ." Elf paused. "I don't suppose you play chess, do you?"

Margaret laughed. "Don't be silly. That's for you and the master."

Right. She questioned whether the chessboard would ever be used.

"I remember how you used to hide up here when the ladies tried to teach you how to stitch on a tapestry," said Margaret.

Elf nodded. "My mother told me stories up here. In the winter, this room was always so bright when the sun shone." She gazed out the window over to the exercise yard. Even through the wavy glass, she recognized her husband.

She could understand why some wives sought lovers if they suffered the same neglect that she did. The trouble was she wanted no other man than her husband.

Careful, Elf. Don't give him your heart.

And in the next instant she recognized the warning to herself came too late.

Chapter Eighteen

The new mattress cradled her as straw never could. Elf hadn't realized how much she missed sleeping on feathers. The morning sun had risen and Elf stretched in the comfort of the new bed. She glanced around for Payne, then frowned. He wasn't there, and from the neatness of the covers on his side, she realized that he hadn't even spent the night in the bed with her.

Yesterday evening news had come that reavers had attacked the outlying fields and carried off two head of cattle. Payne must have spent the night trying to chase down the thieves.

Elf dressed, trying not to feel disgruntled about Payne's absence. When she descended to the great hall, she found Payne sitting at the head table.

"Elf, good morrow. We have a guest."

The man beside him rose, and she recognized him at once. Tedric.

"Good morrow, Lady Elf. I see I am too late to snatch you away from this beast and make you my own."

Elf didn't smile at his jest. "You only wanted to snatch me

away to give me to Coxesbury."

Tedric laughed. "True enough, but I was hoping you didn't remember."

"What brings you to Candlewood?" Elf sat beside her husband.

"Coxesbury has heard rumors of trouble in this part of his holdings, so he has moved the household from Pellingham to Brookstone. We are neighbors for a time, so I thought I'd visit."

Coxesbury was near? A shudder ran through her. As if he read her mind, Payne whispered to her, "He can't hurt you now. You are my wife."

She drew in a deep breath and nodded.

"So Coxesbury's been having trouble as well." Payne's gaze shifted to Tedric.

"Nothing big. Some of the farmers claim thieves have been attacking, but Coxesbury just thinks they're trying to weasel out of having to pay their tribute to him."

"He would," muttered Elf under her breath.

"Reavers stole cattle from us last night," said Payne. " 'Twould seem they move around a bit."

"Perhaps if you worked together . . ." Tedric stopped as Payne lifted his eyebrows. "Then again, perhaps not."

"I think not." Payne drew his fingers along his chin. "If it's the same ones who steal from Coxesbury, then they must be well organized. A gang of knaves poses more threat than a pair of thieves."

"True, true. I'll try to let you know if Coxesbury learns anything. It's the least I can do for a friend," said Tedric. "In the meantime, let me tell you how impressive Candlewood looks."

"We still have much to do," said Payne.

"Yes, yes, but you can leave most of it to the servants."

Tedric waved his hand in dismissal. "They will have to know what to do when you are away fighting in the lists."

"I won't be jousting any time soon."

Tedric's eyes widened. "You're giving up tournaments? Why?"

"They no longer hold the same appeal as they once did." Payne glanced at Elf.

Tedric nodded. "I understand. You now have a hearth and family. You'll leave many a knight disappointed that he can't take his revenge against you. How will you entertain yourself?"

"There are other things besides a tournament."

"I know. A hunt. Why don't we organize a hunt in honor of your new standing?"

Payne gave him a thin smile. "I will, when the work here is done."

"But the hunting is good now. Surely you can spare a day or two." Tedric jabbed Payne with his elbow. "I can borrow some dogs from Coxesbury. He'll never know."

"I'll know." Payne shook his head. "You can wait until next year when I'll have my own dogs and perhaps falcons as well."

Elf sighed. She wondered how many more tasks Payne would create for himself until he was satisfied with Candlewood.

A servant entered the hall and bowed before Payne. "My lord, you asked me to fetch you when the moat was ready to be filled."

"Yes, thank you." Payne rose. "Come along, Tedric. Maybe you can learn something about responsibility and the joy of accomplishment. Who knows? Someday you may win your own lands."

"I won't waste my time working if I do. I'll have servants

for that." Tedric followed Payne from the table.

"Perhaps, but you'll never instill their loyalty that way."

"That's your problem, Payne. You think like a warrior, not a lord."

They continued their argument into the hallway until Elf could hear them no longer. She shook her head. She knew better than most the value Payne placed on Candlewood.

A kitchen maid rushed into the room. "My lady, please hurry. They're going to kill each other!"

Elf jumped to her feet. "Payne?"

"No, no, my lady. 'Tis the cook and the steward. In the kitchen."

Elf shook her head and followed the frantic maid into the kitchen. The cook held a cleaver in his hand and swiped it in the air in the direction of the steward. The steward stood well back, holding a large wooden tray as a shield.

"A pox on you," yelled the cook. "I'll not have you disparage my cooking, or you'll have nothing but boiled turnips to eat."

"And I'll not have you wasting the master's stores," returned the steward, his voice meeting the cook's in loudness. "What have you done with the ham?"

"Nothing you blathering idiot. I keep telling you that you counted wrong."

If not for their serious expressions, Elf would have laughed. She hid her smile behind a stern frown. "What is the meaning of this din?"

The cook dropped his arm, but not the cleaver. "This dull wit claims I've been wasting food. I ask you, how could I have wasted food without the entire kitchen knowing it?"

Elf nodded and turned to the steward. "He speaks with logic. One of the kitchen servants would have noticed if the cook had taken the ham."

"My lady, that may be true, but it doesn't explain how the ham is missing," said the steward.

"If you'd have learned your numbers better, you'd know why," muttered the cook.

Elf raised her hand. "I trust the steward's numbers."

The cook opened his mouth in protest, but Elf continued before he had a chance to speak. "And I believe you haven't taken the ham. In fact, I wished to thank you for the meals you've been preparing for us. They have been delicious."

The cook sniffed. "I haven't made a real feast yet. And with him so stingy with the key to the spices . . ."

The steward looked outraged.

Elf stepped between them. "It seems we have a thief in the castle. I shall inform Payne when he returns, but I'll need the figures from you. I thank you for bringing this to my attention."

The steward nodded. "I'm merely carrying out my duties, my lady. His lordship has entrusted me with the care of the household."

"And you are doing an admirable job. I shall be sure to tell him he chose well with both of you."

The cook and the steward looked at each other and frowned, but they bowed to her. Elf didn't think they liked each other any better, but at least she had turned aside the crisis. She left the kitchen and let out her breath.

"Is something amiss, Elf?"

She jumped. "Margaret, you startled me."

"Forgive me." Margaret smiled. "You look as if you are tired."

"Not tired as much as incredulous. It's hard to believe men are so inclined to fighting, even over trivial matters. I just had to settle a petty dispute between the cook and the steward."

"What was it about?"

"A lost ham. The way they carried on, you'd have thought

they were fighting over the jewels of the Orient."

"What did you discover?"

Elf paused. She didn't want to tell Margaret of her history as the Black Knight, yet how could she explain her feelings that if someone needed the food so badly he would steal, she would rather let him have it?

Of course she would also prefer the thief ask her instead of steal, but she understood why he didn't. "Well, I'll have to tell Payne we have a thief, but he hasn't stolen much. We'll see if it happens again."

"Do you think you will catch him?" Margaret paled.

"Eventually." Elf patted Margaret's hand. "Don't worry. I'm sure he won't cause us any great harm."

Margaret crossed herself. "I hope not."

Poor Margaret. The thought of a thief in the castle seemed to alarm her. Elf supposed she herself might be more disturbed except that she had once been that thief. "Come. You can show me how to stitch something. Perhaps laughing at my inadequacies can help us forget this unpleasantness."

Tedric remained at Candlewood for the next two days. He grumbled in good humor that he had done more work during his stay with Payne than in his entire service to Coxesbury. What was more, Coxesbury paid him better.

"Why do you put up with him?" asked Elf as Tedric rode from the bailey.

Payne shrugged. "He was one of the first knights I met when I left the monastery. I endure him, but I don't trust him."

Elf gazed after Tedric. "Then why endure him?"

"He amuses me. I can't tell you the number of times he has tried to best me at a tournament and failed."

"Has he ever won?"

"Once, when I was green. He is a strong knight. Most men would fear facing him in the lists."

"But not you." Elf sent him a sideways glance.

"No, not I. Then again, I had little to fear when I fought in the tournaments."

"And now?"

Payne thought for a moment. True he had Candlewood now, but his gaze landed on Elf. Yes, he had too much to fear. "Now I would risk losing too much."

Her gaze met his, and he felt himself disappear into those green depths. She had more power over him than he cared to acknowledge. He, who had never known fear in the tournaments, now feared the power of a woman. He shook himself free of her gaze. "I must see to the tower." He turned from her and started away.

"Of course."

He heard her soft answer, but didn't respond despite the note of sadness in it.

When the sun disappeared, the work ceased on the tower. Payne chaffed at the slowness of the rebuilding, but understood the need for it. When it was complete, the tower would stand taller and stronger than before.

He fell asleep that night dreaming of the coming year when Candlewood stood whole again.

"Payne!"

In the next instant, Payne rolled from the bed, awake and ready to face the danger that roused him from sleep. Nigel stood in front of him.

Dread clenched at his heart. "What's wrong?"

"Fire. In the tower."

Payne grabbed his breeches and shoved his legs into them.

Elf woke. "Payne?"

"Wake the women. Get them to safety. There's a fire in the tower."

Elf blanched, but he didn't have time to comfort her. If the fire wasn't extinguished, it could spread throughout the castle. "Go, Elf," he barked and left the room.

He ran through the hallways until he reached the bailey. The dark night sky glowed orange in the east, but the brightness wasn't a portent of the sunrise. Merciful heaven, how was he going to stop the blaze?

He raced toward the fire. Already his men had formed a chain and were passing buckets from the moat to douse the fire. He shuddered to think they had filled the moat only a few days ago. How would they have found enough water with a dry moat?

The flames licked at the white stone, giving the walls an unholy yellow and orange pall. He grabbed a bucket and tossed its contents over a small pile of straw near his feet that had ignited. The sizzle hissed into a thin cloud of steam. For a moment, the magnitude of the blaze overwhelmed him, then he took charge.

As more men appeared to help, he formed several more lines to combat the blaze, then he himself took the head position of one line.

The fire grew as it fueled itself on the scaffolding around the tower, but as the wood disappeared, the fire seemed to shrink. Payne ordered men to wet the walls around the tower so that the fire couldn't regain its strength. His arms ached from hauling the water and throwing bucketsful on the inferno, but he didn't falter. After two hours, the flames died into a heap of smoking embers at the base of the tower. Only then did he allow his men a respite, but he continued to toss water on the hot spots.

The sun started its climb in the sky, and as the first rays hit

Candlewood, the stones glowed, except at the tower. The charred wall rose black from the ground. Payne viewed the odious image. Smoke rose from gaping holes that remained in the tower. Hot ash covered the ground in front of him, and the few scattered patches of white on the wall seemed like mouths gasping for breath.

He didn't know how long he stared at the destruction, but when he felt a hand slip into his he looked down. Elf stood at his side.

"Get away from here."

"I came to help," she said.

"You can't help. It's over." His voice was harsher than he intended.

Elf gazed up at him. The hurt in her eyes only made him scowl more. She withdrew her hand. "It's my castle, too. You should be grateful we lost only the tower." She turned from him. "A few of your men are injured. Send them to me. Margaret and I shall tend to them."

As he watched her leave, a great weariness seized him. His hands were as black as the charred stone. Blisters had broken on his palm and blood now filled them. His shoulders ached from carrying so much water. He gritted his teeth against the urge to groan. Around him, many of his men sat on the ground, their faces blackened from the heat. The stonemason didn't trouble to hide the tears in his eyes, and the master carpenter cursed.

Payne straightened his shoulders, wincing as he stretched the muscles he had overused. "Good work, men. You saved the castle. Go clean up and get some rest."

Some of the men rolled to their feet and ambled off, but others remained on the ground, lying where they dropped.

Nigel walked up beside him. Payne almost didn't recognize the man. His face was as black as night, and he walked with a slight stoop to his shoulders. For the first time, Nigel looked old.

"If I look half as bad as you, I must look a fright," said Nigel. "There is nothing golden about you now."

"I'm not in the mood for jests, Nigel."

"No, but you should be. You saved most of the castle, and your men are still alive. Now is the time to celebrate."

"I don't have the strength to celebrate."

"Neither do they." Nigel nodded toward the men. "But they will."

Payne rubbed his forehead. "Very well, I shall reward them. God knows they deserve it."

"Always knew you had more intelligence than your brothers gave you credit for." Nigel looked up at the smoking ruins. "There is naught else we can do here."

"I'm not leaving yet."

"As you wish. I want a bath and a bed."

"Go. I'll be along soon."

Nigel nodded and staggered away.

Payne gazed at the tower. He knew he was tired, but something troubled him. Heat still rose from the embers, but he pressed forward. Gazing up, he gave thanks for the dark clouds that filled the sky. Rain would help cool the last coals. Pity the rain couldn't have come last night when they needed the help.

He stopped. That was what was troubling him. How had the fire started? There was no lightning last evening. His men wouldn't have lit a fire in this part of the castle. In fact, this was the only part of the outer wall that could have caught fire. With its scaffolding and gaps, the tower was the only vulnerable part of the castle. If he were planning an attack, he would strike at the tower.

As he peered through the rubble, his conviction grew. A

single charred log jutted out from ashes. The natural shape of the log showed no trace of human touch. No such wood was used for the construction, but it would have been the perfect size for laying a fire. A gust of wind stirred the charred remains. With creaks and snaps, the unstable scaffolding tottered and fell in on itself. Payne could no longer see the evidence, but he could picture it in his mind.

This was no accident. Someone had tried to burn Candlewood.

Chapter Nineteen

Elf stared at the ceiling. After having been awake most of the night, she had helped the men with burn injuries all day. She was exhausted.

So why was she having trouble sleeping?

She closed her eyes, tried to relax, then rolled onto her side yet again. She stared at Payne in the dark. His chest rose and fell in sleep. His dark hair curled onto his face, and despite the scar, his face looked almost boy-like. The urge to stroke his cheek overwhelmed her, but she didn't dare touch him.

How could she have let herself fall in love with this man?

That question was too easy to answer. He had proven his worth time and time again. All she had to do was think of the room she now slept in, and warmth surged through her anew.

She could kick herself.

Tossing the covers back, she left the bed, not caring if she disturbed him or not. She donned a simple gown over her shift and stepped outside to the courtyard. The moon's reflection shone in the water of the pool. She sat on the edge of the pool and let her fingers play in the water.

The trouble was she could never be as important to him as he had become to her. Elf sighed. He had proven that today. Well, even if she loved him, she didn't need to spend every minute fretting about it.

She rose from the edge of the pool. She wouldn't be able to sleep. Where could she go? Perhaps she could find something to soothe her nerves in the buttery.

She wandered through the keep with a silent tread. When she reached the kitchen, she froze. Someone was in the pantry.

The words of the steward flashed through her mind. Someone was pilfering from their stores again.

Elf hid behind a large barrel and waited for the thief to come out. She didn't wait long. The moon provided ample light to see thief's face.

"Margaret?"

Margaret yelped and dropped a shank of ham. She whirled to face Elf.

Elf crossed to Margaret. The older woman began to cry.

"Forgive me, my lady." Tears coursed freely down her cheeks.

"You are the thief? I don't understand." Elf shook her head. "Do we not give you enough to eat? Are your children hungry?"

"No, my lady. You and the master are kind and generous. It isn't for me at all." Margaret wrung her hands.

"Come." Elf put her arm around the woman's shoulders and led her to a table. She gave the woman a chair then pulled a second over for herself. "Are you in trouble? Tell me. Perhaps I can help you."

Margaret gulped. She lifted the edge of her skirt and dried her eyes. "I'll gather my things and leave at once."

Elf patted her hand. "Have I asked you to leave? Tell

me. Why you were stealing?"

"I wasn't stealing it for myself. I swear by all that is holy, I wouldn't steal for myself."

"You are a good woman, Margaret. I know that."

Margaret drew in a ragged breath. "My sister married a man from a neighboring village."

"I didn't know you had a sister."

"She doesn't see us much since she left, but about a fortnight ago she came home. She told us that Baron Coxesbury had taken up residence at Brookstone."

Coxesbury again? Elf sensed that she wouldn't like this story. "I know Coxesbury. Go on."

"He isn't the kindest of masters. When he arrived he took his supplies from the villagers. They had just started to put up their supplies, but now they needed to feed themselves with the food meant for winter. Coxesbury didn't listen to their protests and in fact taunted them with the feasts he threw each night, tossing the remains to the dogs or the pigs." Margaret's face became mottled with anger. "He wouldn't even give the food to the people he took it from."

With an angry swipe, Margaret wiped a tear from her cheek. "When the village's priest complained to the Baron that the people would starve, the Baron laughed and ordered more food for his table.

"Oh, my lady. My sister was hungry when she came to us. I took the food so she could feed her family. I didn't take much. When you told me the theft had been discovered, I stopped, but she came back today. She brought her son with her. The poor boy is as skinny as a reed. I had to get her more food." Margaret's crying started again.

"Is your sister still here?"

Margaret nodded. "But she must go home to her husband tomorrow."

Elf stood and retrieved the shank and handed it to Margaret. The woman gaped up at her. Then Elf walked into the pantry and filled a sack with turnips and leeks and bread. She pressed the sack into Margaret's hands. "Take this to your sister. Then come back here. I'll hear nothing of your leaving."

"Bless you, my lady."

"We'll find a way to help your sister and her village. Now go."

Margaret took the food and dashed out of the kitchen. Elf returned to the chair and tugged on her lower lip with her teeth. She stilled. A slow smile spread across her face.

"And I know just who can help us," she whispered into the night.

Payne studied the damage. The acrid smell of the damp cinders burned his nose. The fire had consumed all the wood in the tower, but the stone was intact. They would have to replace the floors and beams again.

Two months' work wasted. Payne turned to the two men who waited behind him. "And you saw nothing that night?"

"No, milord. We failed you," one said.

Payne shook his head. "No, I think it would have been easy for one man to come across the moat and light the fire without being seen."

"Still, it was our watch and we didn't see anything." The second man stood as straight as a pike and never lowered his gaze.

"No, it was my error. I was too arrogant. I should have placed more men on watch," said Payne as he gazed back at the ruin. "Thank you both. You may go."

The two men bowed and returned to the keep.

More than ever, the vexing thought that the fire had been

no accident nettled Payne. But he had no proof. And the fire had destroyed anything that might have helped here.

He glanced toward the woods on the other side of the moat. If someone had set the fire, they must have arrived from somewhere—if they weren't his own household. And the only path open to a stranger was the woods.

Payne hurried through the barbican and into the woods opposite the tower. He didn't know what he was looking for, but he examined the area, searching for any signs of activity.

The lower branches of some trees and shrubs hung at twisted angles, but these he dismissed as the possible work of animals. He delved deeper into the woods. Only the sound of blackcaps and nuthatches were louder than the crunching of his steps on the forest floor. Looking over his shoulder, he could no longer see the castle. His steps became more careful. If something was to be found, he should find it soon.

There. Ahead of him appeared a small glade, more a thinning of the trees than a true open space. The ground was trampled, and he found the definite curve of a horseshoe in the dirt. A small pile of horse dung lay among the grasses, and a branch held the marks of reins rubbing against the bark.

Payne knelt to examine the ground. From the number of prints, he would surmise two horses had been there. No cleared trails passed anywhere near this spot, so he couldn't dismiss the evidence as the remnants of travelers. If he looked closely, he could see the trace of the path the horses took through the trees. This wasn't an area where one would ride for pleasure, and he knew he hadn't organized any hunts.

Brushing the dirt from his hose, he straightened. He couldn't know when the signs had been made, but his gut told him they weren't there before the fire. He didn't know how his discovery would aid him in catching the brigands, but at least he knew he needed to increase his caution.

From the corner of his eye, he saw something glitter on the ground. He squatted to see what had caused the flash. A silver button lay among the leaves. He picked it up and placed it in his palm. The button had an oak leaf in its center and a laurel wreath around its edge. Above the leaf, a small ruby cabochon sparkled. This button belonged to no common person. If he could find the owner of this button, he would find his criminal. He dropped the button into the small pouch at his waist.

A prickling sensation on his neck froze him. He wasn't alone. Staying close to the ground, he waited for some other hint of the trespasser's presence.

He heard the snapping of a twig and the twang of a bowstring before he saw the figure in the woods. Rolling to the side, Payne wasn't fast enough to prevent the arrow from hitting him, but it lodged in his thigh, not in his heart.

Ignoring the pain in his leg, he crept forward until he found refuge behind a large stone. Payne called out from behind his natural shield. "Your aim was poor."

The man didn't answer his taunt.

"Your first mistake was giving me warning. You should keep silent when you're attacking your prey." Payne gripped the shaft of the arrow and gritted his teeth. With a quick snap, he broke the narrow wood near the hole in his breeches. Sweat beaded on his forehead as he lifted his head to search the woods for the archer.

"But your biggest error was that you didn't kill me. You should know better than to wound a bear, for you will only make him angry. And I am angry."

Payne pulled his dagger from his belt and waited. To his left, he heard the softest rustling of the bushes and smiled. He knew the archer hadn't left the wood, and he knew the man came to finish his job. All he had to do was wait. He held the blade between his thumb and forefinger and tested its balance.

Once more a slight rustle came from his left, closer now. Payne grinned. He jumped to his feet and saw the shadowy figure of a man not too far from him.

The bowman straightened in surprise. A mask covered his face.

"Damnation," said Payne.

The man lifted his bow again, but before he could draw, Payne threw the knife. It embedded itself into the man's left shoulder. Screaming, the man dropped his bow and bolted from the wood.

Payne took two steps, then stopped. He couldn't keep up with the man as long as he had the arrow in his thigh. "We'll meet again, my friend." His voice filled the wood. "And I'll expect you to return my knife."

The archer no longer tried to hide the sounds he made. Payne heard the whinny of a horse, then the crashing of the man's retreat through the brush. Payne waited a moment longer, then limped back to the keep. As soon as the man on watch saw Payne's injury, he sounded an alarm. Payne described what had happened and sent two men after the bowman, but he didn't expect his men to find anything now.

Nigel propped himself under Payne's arm. "You shouldn't walk."

"What am I to do, Nigel, fly?" Payne limped forward.

"Let the men carry you." Nigel grunted under Payne's weight.

"I can walk." He leaned on Nigel's shoulders.

"Stubborn boy."

Elf ran from the keep. When she saw the blood trickling from his leg she let out a little cry and hurried forward. "Dear heaven, what happened?"

"I was shot," answered Payne with more amusement in his voice than pain.

"I can see that." Elf placed herself under his other arm and helped Nigel lead Payne into the keep. At the door, she waved one of the men over and gave up her position to him. "Get him to the solar," she ordered. "I'll get binding for the wound."

Payne soon lay on the bed. Nigel had removed the breeches. Blood oozed from the wound, but Payne paid it no mind. He knew the blood would flow even more when they pulled the arrow from him.

Elf rushed into the room, carrying a basin. Margaret followed, her arms filled with towels and cloth.

Payne grabbed the sheet and covered himself. "Woman, if I knew you'd be inviting all the ladies, I would have dressed."

"Don't be silly. Margaret is here to help me." Elf dabbed at the blood with a towel.

"Wait until I remove the arrow." Nigel pushed her hands aside, then bent his head to examine the wound. " 'Tisn't in too deep. I'll pull it instead of pushing it through."

Elf blanched.

"Are you ready?"

Payne nodded.

Nigel grabbed the broken shaft. "On three. One, two . . ."

Nigel pulled. Payne let out a roar. He knew Nigel's trick of not waiting to three, but the stab of pain still surprised him. He gritted his teeth to keep from moaning.

Nigel moved away from the bed with the broken arrow in his hand.

"Keep it," growled Payne. "I'll want to see it later."

Elf bent over him and tried to staunch the fresh flow of blood. Tears coursed down her cheeks. He reached up his hand and brushed a drop away.

"Don't cry, Elf. The worst is over. I'll heal now."

She drew in a ragged breath and tried to stop her tears. "I'm not crying over you, you stupid man. I'm crying at the waste of my best towels." She dabbed at the blood with a cloth.

Payne laughed. "And if I don't believe you?"

"I can't help that." She washed his leg. "I'll have to stitch this." Margaret handed her an already threaded needle. Elf pulled her lower lip between her teeth and bent over his leg.

If he wasn't careful, he would start thinking about where her hands lay and the last time she had touched him in such an intimate way. Too late. The thought had already settled in his mind. Payne let out a low moan.

"I'm sorry. I don't want to hurt you." She continued to stitch.

"You have no idea, wife." Payne barely felt the needle. His thoughts dwelled on what he would do once she had finished stitching and they were alone.

He had to admit having Elf to minister and worry about him was nicer than having Nigel.

"Done," said Elf. She sat back. "Bring the poultice, Margaret."

Margaret stepped forward with a small pot.

"What's that?" asked Nigel.

"Herbs and medicine to keep the wound clean," answered Margaret.

"I have my own," said Nigel.

"This is better," said Margaret and handed the jar to Elf.

"And just how would you be knowing that?" Nigel frowned at the woman and crossed his arms over his chest.

"We've used this in my family for generations," said Margaret.

Elf ignored the argument and soothed the salve over the wound. She placed a clean pad over her stitches, then tied it to his thigh. "Does it hurt?"

Not as much as trying to control his urge to take her on top of him. "Not much."

She nodded. "You should rest."

Rest was the last thing he wanted now.

Elf turned to the still arguing pair. "Go on, Nigel, Margaret. I'll take care of his needs."

"Do you promise?" Payne said under his breath.

When Nigel and Margaret left the room, Elf turned to him and stroked his cheek. "Who would do this to you?"

"I expect it was the same person who set the fire."

"Set the fire? Do you think the fire was deliberate?"

Payne nodded. "I found evidence of horses in the woods, and a button."

"A button?"

"In the pouch."

Elf rose from the bed, but he grabbed her hand. She looked down at him. "Do you need something?"

He nodded. A slow grin curved his lips as he pulled her back down on the bed.

A knock interrupted him. He released her hand with a scowl. "Come."

The two men he had sent after the bowmen entered the room.

"Did you find anything?"

"The shaft and the bow, my lord, and his blood. We found his trail, but he had disappeared."

Payne nodded. "I didn't expect you'd find him, but thank you. I'll be down later."

The men bowed and left the room.

"What about this button?" said Elf.

"Later." He pulled her to him and kissed her.

Elf's soft lips yielded under his, but then she pulled back. "Payne, your leg."

"What I plan to do has nothing to do with my leg."

Chapter Twenty

The moon was a sliver as the Black Knight rode away from the castle. Elf reveled in the freedom the men's clothes gave her. True, the woolen mask was constricting, but her limbs could move with an ease she never felt in her gowns.

She had left Payne sleeping in their bed. His leg was healing nicely, but Margaret had given him warm mead to help him sleep. The mead seemed to work, for he had merely rolled over as she left the bed.

She urged her mare into a canter. She had many miles to cover tonight, but had no fear that she wouldn't return before he woke. Brookstone wasn't that far. Still there was no need to tarry.

The sack of venison bumped against her leg. Elf smiled. She had missed these midnight outings. Margaret had protested her plan. She had wanted to take the food to her sister's village herself, but Elf convinced her the Black Knight was a better way. Margaret feared horses and the journey to Brookstone would take her a day by foot. On horse, Elf could achieve the same thing in a few hours. Besides, she wanted to ride out again. Of course she hadn't told Margaret that.

In little over an hour, she reached the fields outside Brookstone. She turned the mare and rode into the trees at the edge of the fields. She searched the darkness for the glow of a lamp. Slowing the pace of the horse, she skirted around the village.

Finally she spotted a small flame to her left.

"Is someone there?" The tremulous voice of a woman floated through the darkness.

Of course, Margaret's sister must have heard the horse coming. She wouldn't be as deaf as old Sally had been. Elf rode directly to the woman.

Margaret's sister dropped to her knees. "Don't hurt me, Sir Knight." She placed the lamp on the ground and crossed herself.

Elf shook her head. She hadn't wanted to frighten the woman, but expected she might. She waved her hand to indicate the woman should rise.

The woman's legs shook as she stood. "My sister told me to wait for someone in these woods. Would you be that person?"

Elf nodded.

"Why did you come?"

As Elf pulled a knife from her tunic, the woman gasped. Elf held up her hand and shook her head. The worst part of this ruse was the need to remain silent.

With a quick slash of the knife, she cut through a rope tied to her saddle. A bundle fell to the ground. Elf pointed to the sack.

"Do you want me to pick it up?"

Again Elf nodded.

The woman lifted the sack and offered it back to Elf.

Her mask fluttered as she exhaled in exasperation. Old Sally had understood her, but Elf remembered how difficult the first meetings had been. Holding her gloved hand upright, Elf shook her head. Then she turned her palm up in a gesture of offering.

"This is for me?"

Elf moved her hand in a circle.

"For everybody?"

Once again, Elf nodded.

The woman opened the sack, and her jaw dropped. "A side of bacon. Oh thank you, Sir Knight."

Reaching into her tunic, Elf removed a small pouch. She tossed it at the feet of the woman. The pouch jingled as it fell.

"Is this also for the village?"

Elf nodded.

The woman picked up the pouch and peered inside. "This is enough gold to pay the taxes for the entire village," she said in a reverent whisper. She tucked the pouch into her waist and smiled. "My sister wouldn't tell me why I had to come here tonight, but I'm glad I listened to her."

Grinning under her mask, Elf bowed from the saddle. Then without waiting for more conversation, she turned the mare and retreated through the woods toward home.

She reached Candlewood without any disturbance. Margaret waited for her by the hidden door. Elf wondered what her father would think if he knew she used it not as a means of escape in an emergency, but as a way to sneak in and out of the castle.

"Did you see her?" asked Margaret.

"Yes. I think I scared her, but the gifts made her smile." Elf dismounted. Goodness, to speak again was agreeable.

"You truly are a saint to do this for them."

She shrugged. "I enjoy sneaking out too much to be a saint."

Margaret laughed. "You'd best get out of those men's

clothes before someone does see you. I'll take the horse back to my father's stable."

"Thank you." Having an accomplice made being the Black Knight much easier.

Elf ducked her head and crawled through the little door. The narrow passageway was dark, but she had played in these tunnels so often as a child, she didn't need a light to find her way. The occasional rough patch caused her to stumble, but she moved forward and upward with confidence.

She slipped into the solar. A quick glance at Payne assured her he still slept. She removed the hose and tunic and placed them under other clothes at the bottom of the chest. The boots she hid in the opposite corner of the chest under an old blanket. Pulling her shift on, she climbed into the bed. Morning would come soon, and she needed some rest if she was to make it through the day without arousing suspicion.

Morning did come soon. Too soon. Elf squinted at the brightness as Payne left the bed. "Good morning, wife."

"If you say so." Elf flipped onto her side and tried to pull the covers over her head. In the past week she had stayed awake for a fire, catching a thief, caring for Payne, and riding out as the Black Knight. She didn't want to get out of bed this morning.

"Come, my lady. The day awaits."

"Let it," she grumbled, but she pushed the covers back and rolled from the bed.

Payne eyed her with a frown and placed his palm on her forehead. "Are you ill? Your eyes have dark circles beneath them and there is no color in your cheeks. You do not look well."

She glared at him.

A pounding on the door distracted them. "Yes?" said Payne.

Nigel burst into the room. He clutched his side as he panted his news. "Raiders. To the south."

Payne dashed to his chest and pulled on his breeches. "Rouse the men and ready Caesar."

Nigel nodded and ran out.

Payne stuck his arms through his leather tunic. "Stay here, Elf."

She no longer felt a hint of the drowsiness that she suffered from upon waking. "I won't go anywhere."

"Good." Payne darted from the room.

Alarm gripped her. Not today. She couldn't handle a calamity today. She was too tired.

Elf ran to the little courtyard and up the wooden staircase. She might have promised to stay in the keep, but she didn't promise not to watch. In the chamber at the top, she opened the window and peered southward. In the distance, she saw several men riding through the fields. Villagers scattered as the men drove their horses through them.

Hurry, Payne, hurry, she thought, as the distant cries of terror reached her.

Payne's hauberk clinked as he jumped atop Caesar. He didn't want to take the time to don his full armor, but the mail shirt would provide some protection.

"Let's ride." He urged Caesar forward and stormed out the portcullis. The thunder of the horse's hooves as they rode through the village stirred the fire in his blood. Battle he understood. Battle he excelled at.

Payne and his men reached the outlying fields in a matter of minutes. Six raiders tore through the fields toward the town. As he bore down upon them, Payne loosed his battle roar. The raiders looked up. At a signal from their leader, they ceased tormenting the peasants in the field, and scattered in the rows. Payne turned Caesar to follow the leader, but the man rode a horse built more for speed than battle. The raider retreated, flattening a path through the wheat as he fled.

With another roar, Payne trailed the raider to the edge of the field and beyond, but he could see the man was more intent on flight, not fight. He slowed Caesar and turned in the saddle to see how his men fared. They had had no more success than he. The other five raiders disappeared over the land.

"They have the luck of the Devil's whoresons," muttered Payne. He rode back to his men.

The damage to the field wasn't as great as he feared. Some of the crop had been trampled but most could still be harvested. Payne dismounted from Caesar and reassured as many of the villagers as he could. He could see the relief in their expressions, the joy at having escaped harm, the pride they felt at their lord. Yet he felt nothing but scorn for himself. He had failed to capture even a single miscreant. How could he prevent such an attack in the future if the knaves roamed free?

He had no inkling who the men might be. As he returned to the bailey, he tried to picture the clothing or any distinguishing marks or badges. All the men had worn simple tunics and hose. Not one wore anything more protective than leather. These men had never intended to fight, merely to frighten and deface. Still, something nettled him. What wasn't he seeing?

He handed Caesar's reins to Nigel. "I think he's disappointed we didn't have more of a battle." He ran his hand along Caesar's flanks, then froze. His gaze locked onto his saddle. On the edge of the wood, Nigel had painted a small golden bear. This was what had been bothering him. The raider likewise had a symbol painted on his saddle—an oak leaf with a wreath around it.

Payne hurried to the solar where he had left the button. Pulling it from the pouch, he examined the object in his palm. The symbols were identical. His first thought had been perhaps Coxesbury was behind the raids, but Coxesbury's coat of arms contained no oak leaves. If he could discover to whom the oak belonged, he would find his criminal.

Elf came into the solar from the courtyard. She spied him at once and hurried to him. If he hadn't opened his arms to catch her, she would have crashed into him. Tears rolled from her eyes and red stained her cheeks. "Elf?"

"You weren't hurt." She gulped for air between words. "I mean, I knew you weren't hurt. I watched from the tower, but I'm so relieved." Fresh sobs broke from her.

Payne closed his arms about her for a few minutes. Then he held her at arm's length. "You didn't cry this much when I was injured. Why are you crying now?"

Elf dashed the tears off her cheeks. "I don't know. I think I'm just tired."

"No one has cried over me since my mother died."

"I'm not crying over you." Elf sniffed. "I'm crying because I was frightened."

"As you say." He pulled her back to him and kissed her. When he finished, Elf no longer had tears in her eyes. In fact, she had very little to say. She sniffed once or twice and blinked in confusion.

Payne laughed as he sat on the bed. He looked at the button again.

"What is that?" Elf sat next to him and bent closer.

"I found this the day I was shot." Payne gave it to her. "Have you ever seen a coat of arms with an oak leaf?"

She shook her head and peered at the silver circle. "This

button wouldn't belong to any common man. I had thought perhaps Coxesbury was behind the raid."

"I had the same thought, but Coxesbury's coat of arms shows a stag rampant. This same design was on the saddle of one of the raiders."

"Do you think he was the same man who shot you?"

"No. My knife found a new home in that man's shoulder, so I don't think he'd be out riding today."

"Which means that somehow the two men are connected."

"Most likely." He fell silent.

Elf returned the button to him. "What will you do next?"

"Increase the guard again. And ride out myself."

A look of frustration crossed her face. "I suppose you must."

He raised an eyebrow. "I can't very well ease off and give the raiders an invitation to attack us."

"That's not what I meant."

"I didn't think so." He patted her hand. "You do look tired. Why don't you rest a while? I'll send Margaret to see if you need anything."

She stretched and yawned. "I don't need to rest."

"Stubborn woman." Payne pushed her back onto the mattress.

She let out a little cry, then laughed. "I suppose a little nap might revive me."

"That's better. Maybe someday you'll learn that your lord knows best."

"And maybe someday *you'll* learn that an overbearing lord doesn't win many hearts." She smiled at him, her eyes twinkling with her teasing.

There's only one heart I wish to win, my lady.

The thought grated on him. He turned from her before she

could see the fear in his eyes. He didn't want her heart. He didn't want to love her.

"I'll send Margaret." His voice sounded sharp.

"Payne, I was but jesting," said Elf, but he left the solar without responding.

Chapter Twenty-One

As Elf descended the stairs that afternoon, she saw a messenger hand a note to Payne. When he broke the seal to read it himself, she was surprised, until she remembered he had been raised for the monastery. Of course he knew how to read. He was practically a monk. Well, no he wasn't a monk, she corrected herself, thinking of Payne beside her in bed.

He frowned—he had frowned a lot today—then summoned the marshal. "We shall have guests tonight. Find them room."

"Yes, my lord." The marshal bowed.

"Guests?" she asked as she crossed the hall.

"Yes. We have visitors arriving in an hour." Payne crumpled the note in his hand.

"You don't seem pleased. Someone you dislike?"

"Worse. My brother."

Elf's eyes widened. "Your brother? The earl?"

"No, my other brother."

Elf searched her memory for the tales Nigel had told her of his family. Payne had two older brothers, and he was fond of neither. She let out a puff of air. This visit should prove interesting.

A half-hour later, she discovered how interesting when a powerful, stocky man walked into the hall. Stopping in the center of the hall, he glanced at the many faces. He placed his fists on his hips. "Where is he? Where's Payne?"

"I'm here, Royce." Payne stood in the archway. Elf had come in on his arm, but at the sight of the visitor, she dropped her hold and stepped back.

"Brother," bellowed Royce. He threw his arms wide and made a path through the men to Payne. Royce embraced his brother, clapping his wide palms on Payne's back.

Payne didn't return the embrace.

The man released Payne and bowed to Elf. "My lady. Royce Dunbyer of Castlereigh, at your service."

She nodded at him.

"This is my wife, Lady Elfreda of Renfrey."

"Ah, my sister." Royce took her hand and kissed it, then faced Payne again. "It's been a long time."

"Indeed."

Elf stared at the two men. Royce looked enough like Payne that no one could deny the relationship, even if they had different mothers. But Royce was heavier than his brother, and his black hair sparkled with silver. And although Royce was tall, the top of his head barely reached Payne's nose.

Payne led Elf to the head table. He waited until she sat, then took his place beside her. "Why have you come, Royce?"

Royce shook his head. "What sort of greeting is that for a brother you haven't seen in a decade?"

"One to which I still await an answer." Payne filled his goblet with wine.

Elf glanced at her husband, then faced her brother-in-law. "Won't you sit, Sir Royce?" She indicated a chair beside her.

"Thank you, my lady." Royce took a seat beside her. "Our brother heard you gained some land. He wanted me to see if we could speak of an alliance."

Payne nodded. "You never were one to hide what you wanted. I liked that about you."

"Well, that's one thing at least." Royce laughed.

Elf leaned forward. "And now, good knights, we shall enjoy our dinner without further attempts to best each other."

Payne smiled for the first time since he had seen his brother. "The lady has spoken. I am honor bound to fulfill her wishes."

"As am I." Royce lifted his goblet. "To the Lady Elfreda."

The men in the hall lifted their drinks.

Elf patted Royce's hand. "Please. My name is Elf."

"Elf then." Royce's eyes twinkled.

Elf would wager that the mischief that sparkled in his eyes was as much a sign of intelligence as amusement.

Nigel entered the hall and crossed to the table. "I heard we had visitors. I didn't know that meant riffraff."

"Nigel, you old goat. I thought you'd be dead." Royce grinned. "Have you taught my brother any manners to go with his brawn?"

"His manners are better than yours, you ungrateful pup," said Nigel.

"I take it you trained Sir Royce as well?" asked Elf. She shook her head. Only men would think insults an appropriate way to show fondness for one another.

"Yes, not that he would ever listen." Nigel sat beside Royce. "How are you?"

"I can't complain. William keeps me busy."

Elf saw Payne frown at that name. "Who is William?" she asked.

"The Earl of Thornheath, our eldest brother," answered Royce.

She nodded.

"Are you married yet?" asked Nigel.

"Never saw the need. William has his heir, and I have too much joy to spread among the ladies." Royce's comment brought guffaws from those listening.

"Any children, then?" Nigel asked.

Royce nodded. "A boy. A fine burly lad whom William is squiring."

Elf glanced at her husband. Could Payne—

He leaned to her and whispered in her ear, "I have no children I am aware of."

Her gaze shot to him in surprise. How had he known where her thoughts wandered?

The meal arrived, and conversation muted to the enjoyment of the food. Only Payne remained dour throughout the meal. Royce charmed her, plied her with sweet words, which only brought a deeper scowl to Payne's face.

When the meal ended, Payne filled his goblet with wine once again and sat back. "Now tell me what the earl wants."

Royce turned to his brother. "What is there to tell? William knows you are a powerful man. Who wouldn't want to claim the Golden Bear as their ally?"

"Flattery won't sway me."

"I didn't think it would." Royce gave him a sly grin. "But it is true. Your reputation is widespread. William only wants you to remember that he is your brother."

"Half. And believe me, that is a fact I cannot forget. Nor can I forget how he treated my mother."

"What if I told you he regrets the actions of his younger days?"

Payne leaned forward and stared into Royce's eyes. After a

few seconds of silence, he smiled. "I'd say you were lying."

With a laugh, Royce picked up his goblet. "You always were too clever." He took a swig from the vessel. "William has been boasting of his kinship to you, and finally realized you may not feel the same toward him. He sent me here to see if you would align yourself with him."

Elf looked at Payne. If Royce's words were an indication of how his brothers had treated him, she understood why Payne was less than fond of them.

"I have no answer for you yet." Payne drank from the wine. "But you are welcome to stay as long as you wish."

"My men and I thank you." Royce bowed his head to Payne, then he glanced around the hall. "You've done well for yourself, little brother. A castle, rich lands, a strong and beautiful wife."

Payne's gaze landed on her. He nodded. "Aye, I have done well."

In the week that followed, Payne trained with his men against Royce's in mock battles. The training confirmed to him that his men were as good as any in England. Nigel's work with them had proven its worth. Even Royce had to admit his men had benefited from the exercise.

Royce hadn't mentioned his errand again. Instead he seemed to enjoy the company of his famous younger brother. Despite the pleasant hours they spent, Payne still didn't trust him completely. He couldn't forget that Royce was William's vassal, and Payne wasn't ready to forgive his eldest brother yet.

One morning, two weeks after Royce's arrival, Payne rode out with Royce. Bringing the castle to preparedness hadn't left him as much time to ride his lands as he might have liked, but work on the tower progressed smoothly, and the castle now functioned without much intervention from him. He had more time for leisurely pursuits. Payne was contemplating organizing a hunt when he heard a sentry give a call.

He and Royce exchanged glances, then rode to the man.

The sentry pointed to the north. "Horsemen, sir. Three of them."

Payne called for five of his men to follow. Then he urged Merlin into a canter in the direction the sentry had indicated. He led them to the boundaries of his land. As reported, three men rode from the woods toward them. Payne stopped and waited for the horsemen to come to him.

Royce reined in beside him. "Do you know them?"

As the three figures approached, Payne recognized one of the riders. He nodded. "The man in the middle is Baron Coxesbury."

Royce let out a low whistle. "Didn't you serve him for a while?"

"Yes," said Payne between gritted teeth. "He never paid me."

Royce gave him a look of surprise, but couldn't say more for the men pulled up to them.

"Payne, good morrow to you, neighbor." Coxesbury's snakelike smile belied the polite words.

"What are you doing on my lands, Coxesbury?" said Payne.

"Forgive me, but we are seeking an outlaw. He has been seen in Brookstone twice these past two weeks," Coxesbury said.

So Brookstone continued to have its share of misfortune as well. Not that Payne would admit any troubles Candlewood had to Coxesbury. He wasn't ready to disclose information with this neighbor yet. "What has the man done?"

"He seems to think of himself as some sort of savior to my villagers. He brings food and money to them."

A coldness seized Payne, spreading from his gut through his limbs. He hid his unease behind a jovial tone. "He sounds like a wicked man, feeding the people."

"What a fiend," added Royce.

Coxesbury snarled. "I won't have their loyalty tested. If the fool thinks he can win over my village, he is mistaken."

"You still haven't explained why you are on my lands."

"He came to Brookstone last night. We followed his tracks this far. They continue toward Candlewood."

"Very well, I shall continue the search from here. Thank you for bringing this matter to my attention."

"I want to find this black knight myself," said Coxesbury.

"Black Knight? Is that his name then?" Payne struggled to keep his expression bland.

"That's what they are calling him. Apparently he dresses all in black and doesn't speak." Coxesbury eyed Payne's black garments. "You wouldn't know anything about him, would you?"

"Other than applaud his taste in clothing, I know nothing of any man who calls himself the Black Knight." Payne never shifted his gaze from Coxesbury's eyes.

With a grunt, Coxesbury tossed his head. "Move from our way. You've delayed us long enough."

"You will not pass." Payne leaned forward. "This is my land, and I no longer serve you. I have already said I will continue to search for this Black Knight. You may return home."

"Fool. Can't you see how the fiend undermines our authority? The villagers are too simple to see through his ruse. They think him some sort of hero."

Payne narrowed his gaze. "I don't like to repeat myself." At a hand signal from him, his men circled the three riders.

Coxesbury's gaze darted around the wall of men surrounding him. He gritted his teeth. "I am leaving." He turned his horse.

At another wave of his hand, Payne's men opened the circle and let the three riders pass.

As Coxesbury disappeared back into the woods, Royce asked, "Do you think it wise to goad him that way? He is one of the most powerful men in England."

"Coxesbury is a coward. I have said much worse to him than this." Payne smiled at his brother. "He wanted to marry Elf."

Royce lifted his brows. "Did you steal her from him?"

"Actually I abducted her *for* him."

"What?"

Payne laughed. "It's a long story."

"One I'd love to hear."

"Perhaps later." Payne clicked his tongue and Merlin moved forward.

Royce kept pace beside him. "Are you worried about this Black Knight?"

More than you know, brother. "I can take care of the Black Knight."

"My men are ready to help you."

"Thank you for the offer." Payne said no more. He turned toward the castle, his mood growing blacker by the minute.

Chapter Twenty-Two

Payne returned to the keep without waiting for Royce. He glowered at the steward. "Where is my lady?"

"I believe she is in the solar," said the man with a gulp.

Payne turned without thanking the man and climbed the stairs. The solar was empty. He nearly shouted with fury. Then the sound of the fountain penetrated his angry haze. Of course, she must be up there. Climbing the wooden stairs to the little room, Payne counted each step in an effort to control his rage, but he reached the top without the slightest success.

He heard her voice through the door. "Blasted needle."

Pushing the door open, he found her sitting in a chair and sucking on her forefinger.

"I must speak with you."

"Thank goodness. Now I have an excuse to put this thing down." She put her small tapestry to the side. The needlework looked more like a spider's web than any picture. "Margaret thinks she can teach me to use a needle, but I just don't have the skill. I was to enter the abbey, remember? I learned Greek and Latin rather than thread and thimble."

"I don't want to talk about tapestries—"

"Good." She folded her hands and looked at him.

Payne glared at her. "I saw Coxesbury today."

She grimaced. "What did he want?"

Payne pulled the other chair forward and placed his foot on it. "He was looking for a thief."

"Here?"

Elf opened her mouth to continue her protest, but Payne leaned forward and covered her mouth with his fingertips, muffling the sound. "It seems Brookstone has had a surreptitious visitor, someone the villagers are calling the Black Knight."

Elf's eyes grew wide. He felt her lips move under his fingers, but he didn't remove his hand. He leaned in closer. "The Black Knight has brought the villagers food and money on two occasions. They say he dresses in black and doesn't speak. What do you know about this?"

He removed his hand from her lips. She smiled at him. "What do you want me to know?"

"Don't play games, Elf. Coxesbury is furious."

"Well, he shouldn't have stolen the food from the mouths of his villagers." Her transformation from defiant to furious was instant, and she paced the room. Her voice shook with rage. "Those poor people are starving, and he has taken much of their winter stores."

"So you admit to riding out as the Black Knight?"

"Yes. And I'll do it again."

"You will not."

"You won't stop me." She crossed her arms over her chest.

"I can, but I won't have to. Or does your word mean so little to you?"

"My word?"

"You swore that the Black Knight would never ride again."

"No, I didn't."

Her answer robbed him of words. He stared at her and drew in a deep breath. "Do you deny your promise to me?"

"No, but I never promised the Black Knight wouldn't ride again. I promised the Black Knight would never plague my uncle again." She sat and gave him a smug look.

"That's not what I meant by asking for your word."

"Ah, but that is what I promised. So you see, I haven't broken my word."

"You think you're clever, don't you?" Payne leaned forward so that scarcely an inch separated them. "What of your duties to this castle?"

Elf frowned. "I haven't neglected any of my duties."

"You've taken food from the mouths of our people and given it to others. How is that different from Coxesbury?"

Elf shot to her feet. "How dare you compare me to Coxesbury? No one here is in danger of starving. We have plenty of stores for the winter."

But he was too angry to grant her this point. "Do you think it right to endanger yourself? Coxesbury won't pursue the Black Knight with the feeble effort your uncle did. He will hunt you down, and he won't care that you are a woman."

"I'll be careful."

"That's not enough. I caught you easily enough when I wanted to."

She gritted her teeth together. "I admit I became reckless at my uncle's, but you have warned me that Coxesbury will watch for me. Thank you. Now I know to be careful." Her gaze never left his.

"You will not ride as the Black Knight."

"Would you let those people starve?"

"I will take care of them."

"How?"

"I don't know how yet."

"Fine. If I hear you've helped them, the Black Knight shall remain at home." She met his gaze with unflinching haughtiness.

Payne clenched his fists. He had never felt such utter helplessness before. Or fury. How could she defy him? How could she stare at him without flinching? How could she be so stubborn?

Finally, in a low voice he said, "I will stop you. I forbid you to ride into Brookstone."

"You may try," she answered.

He stormed from the room. Of all the adversaries he had faced, why was his wife the one he couldn't vanquish?

He scowled at everyone he met as he made his way through the castle. Where was Nigel? He needed to find Nigel.

Nigel sat in the corner of the hall. He was drinking from a goblet and scowling himself.

"I have a job for you, Nigel."

Nigel winced. "Had I known, I would have kept a clear head."

Payne sat beside him. "What ails you?"

"It's that Margaret woman. She chased me into the stables, then proceeded to give me the scolding of my life for keeping you busy. She said I should be doing more of the work instead of passing it on you. That you haven't had a chance to organize a hunt or keep her lady company."

Payne raised an eyebrow. "What is with the women in this castle today?"

"Having your own problems, are you?"

"You have no idea. The Black Knight is riding again."

"What?" Nigel choked on his wine and coughed until his

face glowed red. When he could draw an even breath, he said, "Are you sure?"

"Heard it from her own mouth." Payne grimaced. "I tried to tell her how dangerous it was, how Coxesbury wouldn't stop until he captured her, but she wouldn't listen."

"She's rode into Coxesbury's lands?" Nigel clutched his head between his hands. "How did you stop her?"

"I haven't."

"What?" Nigel pushed his wine further from him as if the mere thought of a drink would send him into coughing spasms again.

"What could I do? Clap her in irons and keep her in the dungeon?"

"You could forbid her to ride. You are her lord."

Payne shot Nigel an impatient glance. "Do you really think Elf would obey me?"

Nigel hesitated, then snorted. "No. Maybe you *should* throw her into the dungeon." Nigel drew the goblet close again and took a deep draught. "So what shall you do?"

"I want you to watch her."

"Oh, no. I can't do it." Nigel shook his head with vehemence and waved his hands in the air.

"Can't or won't?" Payne eyed his friend.

A long, drawn out moan whistled between Nigel's lips. "All right. I'll watch her. How do you get me into such trouble?"

"I like you." Payne gave his friend a smile that he knew would bring a frown to Nigel's face. He waited for it. The expected scowl appeared in the next instant.

"Get away from me, boy, before I consider going home with Royce when he leaves."

Elf waited for some news in the next few days. She wasn't

due to return to Brookstone for two weeks, but she wanted to see if Payne would help the villagers. However, he was still angry with her. He rarely spoke with her, and she thought it best to let him stew by himself. Anything she might say to him would no doubt make him angrier.

As the week wore on, she ran into Nigel in the strangest places. She found him in the kitchen, in the garden, in the buttery. He always had an excuse for his presence, though she found some of them unlikely.

As the end of the two weeks neared, she wandered the castle. She still had not heard of Payne's plans for the villagers. Disappointment grew at the thought that Payne hadn't kept his word to her.

Hoping to discover something new, she found the steward. "Tell me, John, have you found any more food missing lately?"

"No, my lady."

"Oh." She frowned.

"And it's a good thing, too, what with the master wanting the extra food."

"What extra food?"

"The lord has asked me for two hams, butter, and ale. He intends to give them as gifts, I believe. He mentioned some deserving serfs."

Glee raced through her. Payne hadn't forgotten after all. "Thank you, John."

With a smile on her face, she turned to leave the hall and nearly collided with Nigel. She jumped back, startled by the encounter. "Honestly, Nigel. If I didn't know better, I'd swear you were following me."

The man reddened. "I . . . I . . ."

She narrowed her gaze at him. "You are following me, aren't you? Payne asked you to watch over me."

Nigel's blush deepened. "My lady, I—"

"Never mind, Nigel. I don't blame you." She sat on a stone bench along the wall. "I blame him for not trusting me."

Sitting beside her, Nigel gave her a half smile. "Well, you have to admit your behavior in the past has given him little to trust."

Elf sighed. "I suppose."

"And now that you're the Black Knight again—"

Elf's gaze whipped to him. "He told you?"

"Yes, my lady, but I would have known anyway. The villagers are talking about you, and I was there when Payne caught you last time." Nigel patted her hand. "Don't be too hard on him. He's concerned for your safety."

"He needn't be. I was never caught before, well, except by him, of course, and I won't be caught now."

"He won't let you ride out again."

"And I shan't. I gave him my word. *If* he helps the villagers."

Nigel looked at her in disbelief.

"I won't." Elf stood. "But you don't have to believe me."

Nigel scurried to his feet. "I do believe you. But I shall keep watch over you, nevertheless."

Elf stared at him for a moment, then laughed. "I suppose I can't fault you. Very well, then. But you don't have to skulk around any longer. You may as well watch me in the open now that I know."

Elf sat at the head table during dinner, and searched the hall for Margaret. When she spotted the older woman, Margaret shook her head. Elf sighed. She had hoped that Margaret would bring word from her sister. This eve was the night Elf had arranged to meet Margaret's sister, but she had thought Payne would deliver the food before now. Perhaps he meant to go tonight. She would have asked him earlier, but he had yet to forget or forgive her actions. He even welcomed his brother's company over hers. Every time she had tried to speak with him, he merely asked if she had given up her foolishness.

She glanced at him. Payne was eating without any difficulty she noticed. The thought of making the rounds of the Black Knight didn't seem to trouble him. Elf couldn't contain her curiosity any longer. She leaned toward him. "My lord?"

Payne turned to her.

"My lord, you are aware that tonight—"

"Yes, and I shall take care of the matter after the meal." He lifted a chunk of meat with his knife. "Which I intend to enjoy unless you wish to interrupt me longer."

"No." Elf sat back. He was so stubborn. And galling. And—

"My lord." A page ran into the hall. "Some of the villagers are here. Trouble, sir. In the north fields. Flooding."

Without a moment's hesitation, Payne shoved back his chair and rose from the table. He dashed from the hall, followed by his men and Nigel.

Elf stared after him. Her heart raced and her limbs felt weak. Another mischance. Who plotted against Candlewood?

Not knowing what to do, Elf retired to the solar. She climbed into the tower, but she couldn't see much except an expanse of water where once a field lay.

Payne didn't return. The hours passed, but she heard nothing of him or his men. She peered out the window, but the north fields were too far to see anything more than the sun reflecting off the water. In the next hours, the sun set and she could see nothing at all.

Returning to the solar, Elf flopped down on the bed. A wave of helplessness washed over her. She was the Lady of Candlewood, but she could do nothing to help her people. She glanced around the room. Her gaze fell upon the chest that held her black attire. As she sat up, a slow smile spread across her lips.

She may not be able to help Payne in the field, but she could take care of another matter for him.

Chapter Twenty-Three

Elf noted the full moon and frowned. Light made her journey more dangerous. The shadows appeared darker, but there were fewer of them. With a shrug, she mounted the mare Margaret had waiting for her.

"Godspeed, my lady," said Margaret, handing her the reins.

"I shall return before morning. No doubt Payne will return before me, but you may tell him I am just delivering the food for him, since he could not."

Elf turned the mare toward the south and Brookstone. The moon lit her path enough that she could keep a quick pace and not worry over the hazards she couldn't see. The cool autumn air made her glad of the thick black cloak. It was less a hindrance now than a necessity.

When she reached the edge of the fields of Brookstone, she stopped. The woods were quiet tonight, more quiet than she had ever heard them. An owl hooted in the distance, but its muted tones told her the bird was far away. She clicked her tongue, and her horse moved forward with a slow gait.

Picking her way through the brush and trees that skirted

Brookstone, Elf tried to stay in the shadows, but the cursed moon shone like a beacon. Many shadows large enough to hide horse and rider pooled on the ground, but between them bright spots glowed as if lit by sconces. She looked for the small flame that signaled the presence of Margaret's sister.

A loud crack startled her. She jerked in the saddle and stopped her horse. She tried to peer through the trees to see the cause of the noise. The many shadows played games with her vision, and she could discern nothing unusual amongst the trees.

Probably just a deer, or a branch that fell from a tree.

But Payne's warning against Coxesbury echoed in her mind. Elf pulled her lower lip between her teeth. The woods were too still tonight.

Nonsense, you've just let Payne scare you.

Still, better to err on the side of caution.

She had made up her mind to leave, when she saw the light of the lamp. *Silly goose,* she chided herself, and turned her horse toward Margaret's sister.

Elf entered the small circle of light and waited.

"You've come then," said the woman. Her gaze darted from side to side before dropping to the ground.

Elf would have sworn she heard disappointment in the woman's voice. Drawing her knife, Elf slashed through the line holding the sacks to the saddle. The food landed with a thud.

"Thank you, good knight." Margaret's sister didn't lift her gaze from the dirt.

Elf scowled beneath her mask. She didn't expect much more in return for the food than a heartfelt "thank you," but Margaret's sister seemed to begrudge her even those words. The food sat where it landed. Margaret's sister made no move toward it.

Something wasn't right. Why wouldn't the woman look at her? A prickling sensation crawled up her spine. Elf tightened the reins, but before she could urge her horse into motion, an oily voice came from the woods.

"Yes, thank you so very much for providing food for my peasants. You've made my coffers heavier now that I don't have to provide for them." Coxesbury stepped into the light, his sword extended toward Elf.

Elf choked back a scream. No, Coxesbury couldn't be here. She glanced toward the woods, but his next words froze her.

"I shouldn't try to ride away. My men have you surrounded." He waved his arms. "Step forward, so the brave knight can see you."

From all sides riders came out of the woods until they formed a ring around her. Arrows and swords aimed at her from every angle. Cold sweat dripped down her back as she gazed into the triumphant faces of Coxesbury and his men.

"Throw down the knife." Coxesbury again pointed his sword toward her.

For a moment Elf wondered if she had the courage to throw the knife at him, but archers stepped forward and followed her motions. She threw the blade into the leaves.

Coxesbury turned to the woman. "Go home. You'll get your reward tomorrow."

With a small whimper, Margaret's sister grabbed her skirts and fled the scene.

"You didn't really think these serfs you help would stand up for you?" Coxesbury laughed. "Promise them bread, and you can buy their loyalty with ease."

Elf grew angry despite her fear. How dare he toy with the lives of his people?

"Dismount." Coxesbury grabbed the reins of her horse

and handed them to one of his men.

Elf didn't move.

"I said, dismount. I don't care to repeat myself again." Coxesbury jabbed the air in front of her with his sword.

Clenching her teeth to keep from crying, Elf slid off her horse and stood in front of Coxesbury. Despite the trembling in her limbs, she held her head high.

"I think we should reveal who our thief is." Coxesbury looked up at the mask and grabbed the cloth. With a hard yank that almost sent her to her knees, he threw the mask to the ground. His mouth dropped open.

Elf glared at him, hoping the hatred in her eyes shone. With her voice steady, she said, "Good evening, Lord Coxesbury. A pleasant night for riding, wouldn't you say?"

Coxesbury threw his head back and laughed. "Lady Elfreda. I should have guessed only you could be as stupid as this. Welcome to Brookstone. It's a shame you won't be treated as quite the guest, but then again, you can hardly expect chivalry when you've tested my hospitality with such antics."

"Your people are hungry."

In a voice turned stony with anger, Coxesbury said, "My people are exactly that—*my* people. What happens to them is of no concern to you." Coxesbury waved his hand again. "Bring her to the castle. We'll find her fitting accommodations there."

By the time Payne staggered back to the castle, the moon was high in the night sky. He wanted nothing more than to drop into his bed and sleep. Anger and frustration had taken their toll on him today.

He had found the cause of the flood. A dam of stones and logs had blocked the swiftly flowing brook that ran through

Candlewood's lands. But by the placement of the logs and stones, Payne knew that his enemy had struck again. Nature did not build as neatly as man. He cursed himself for his lack of foresight and vigilance. Although he had set guards around the village to prevent any more incidents, he had failed to protect the lands to the north. He and his men had cleared the dam, and the field had drained. The brook once again ran its course without hindrance, and the muddy quagmire that was once a field of carrots, turnips and leeks would dry. And he wouldn't let himself be caught unaware again.

With half closed eyelids, he walked through the great hall toward the stairs. In the next instant, he stopped. Margaret stood in front of him.

"My lord?"

He rubbed his eyes as he struggled to keep his impatience in check. "It is late Margaret."

"Yes, my lord. But I must speak to you of Elf."

His eyes opened at those words. "Is she ill?"

"No, sir."

"Then perhaps this news can wait until morning. She is sleeping as I would like to be."

"No, my lord. She isn't here." Margaret wrung her hands.

"What?" Payne blinked in confusion at the woman.

"She told me to tell you that she is delivering the food for you, since you could not."

All trace of sleep fled him. "Please tell me she wore a gown and took someone to accompany her."

"No, sir. She wore black trousers and a black tunic. And she rode alone, sir."

"By the cross, that woman will kill me." Payne fled back through the hall. "Nigel. Damnation, Nigel, where are you?"

"Here, Payne." Nigel blinked in an effort to banish the sleep from his eyes.

"Stand watch in the castle. I must ride."

"Now?"

"Yes, now."

Nigel looked at Margaret, who was wringing her hands. "What have you done this time, woman?"

Payne didn't have time to listen to Nigel and Margaret argue. He dashed past the older man and ran from the hall.

Within ten minutes, Payne rode through the gates of Candlewood and thundered toward Brookstone. He gave thanks to the brightness of the moon as he urged Caesar to a faster pace. He should find Elf with ease.

Caesar's speed brought him to the edge of the village in short time. He reined in the animal and slowed the steed's pace to a walk. Payne knew where he would find her. He just didn't know how he would keep from strangling her.

A sudden bark of laughter roused his wariness. With a slight squeeze of his knees, he stopped the well-trained warhorse. He slid from Caesar's back and stole forward by foot. A large circle of men and riders stood in the woods. He recognized Coxesbury's voice at the center.

"Well done, men. Though perhaps twenty men to capture one woman was a bit overdone."

The men laughed again.

Payne's blood turned to ice. He waited to confirm what his heart told him to be true. In the next moment, he saw two men lead Elf by ropes.

Blinded with anger, Payne drew his sword. His first instinct was to leap into the middle of group and kill every man who dared laugh at his wife. But the voice of reason stayed his hand. Though he harbored no doubt of his skills, if he attacked now, Coxesbury could order Elf killed before he reached her.

The thought of inactivity rankled Payne, but he re-sheathed his sword and watched in helpless fury as Coxesbury and his men led Elf away.

He rode back to Candlewood as fast as Caesar would carry him. He woke the stable boy and gave Caesar's reins to him. Then he strode into the keep.

Nigel, sleeping in a chair, waited for him. The older man's head jerked up at the sound of Payne's footsteps. He blinked a few times then rose. "Did you find her?"

"Yes." Payne pounded his fist on the table. "Coxesbury has her."

"Hell." Nigel ran his hand over his face. "What do you want to do?"

"I want to kill him." Payne heard his own voice as if from a distance. The cold tone didn't surprise him. He had never felt such a blood lust before.

"Shall I ready the men?"

"Let them sleep. I must make my plans first."

"You trust Coxesbury to treat her well?"

"I trust he isn't stupid enough to harm my wife. Unless he enjoys the thought of slow dismemberment." Payne's gaze narrowed. "Of course, I may just dismember him in any case."

Elf stared at the stone walls of her prison. Although Coxesbury had not thrown her into his dungeon, this room in the tower was little better. Although the wind whistled through the cracks in the stone and window, the musty smell of disuse clung to every corner. She wrinkled her nose and shivered. The tiny chamber held no comfort. The thin, straw-filled tick did little to pad the hard planks of the bed. A ewer of water stood in the corner. Coxesbury had ordered all tables and chairs removed from the room lest she use them to strike at her guards. He believed the bed too large for her to wield.

Unfortunately, he was correct.

She sank down on the mattress and squeezed her eyes shut. The sting of unshed tears burned in her throat, but she wouldn't give Coxesbury the satisfaction of seeing her cry—even if he wasn't here to see it. She was tired and hungry. And scared.

She drew in a deep breath. Payne had been right. She had been a foolish woman to think she could dupe Coxesbury. She could not have expected betrayal from Margaret's sister, yet she bore the woman no ill will. Elf had seen the fear in the woman's eyes, the reluctance in her stance. No doubt Coxesbury had threatened the woman with something.

The door flew open without a warning. "Settled, I see." Coxesbury strutted into the room, shutting the door behind him.

"What do you want?" she said, hoping her voice remained even.

"Just seeing to the needs of my guest." Coxesbury chortled at his own jest. He crossed the room to where she sat on the bed. "I always sensed you courted trouble. Just like an ill-trained dog."

"If you came here solely to affront, you needn't have bothered. Your words bother me less than your stench."

For a fleeting moment, Coxesbury's eyes narrowed. Then he laughed. "But you have a fire I have seldom witnessed in other women."

He lifted his hand and stroked her cheek. She whipped her head away from his touch. Coxesbury leaned closer to her and stroked her cheek again. A smugness curled his lips into a sneer. "I would strive to be kinder to me now, in your place. Don't you understand that I own you now?"

She couldn't control the tremor in her voice this time. "Payne will kill you if you touch me."

"Maybe. Or perhaps he will thank me." He bent forward until his cheek brushed hers, and his breath wafted under her nose. It was the odor of old cheese and beets in brine. "Mayhap he thinks you more trouble than you are worth. If so, you might need a powerful man such as myself to protect you."

Elf gagged. Struggling to regain control of herself, she took a few shallow breaths, which only served to make her more ill from the rancid smell of Coxesbury's breath.

"Consider what I have said, and I can make things much more pleasant for you." Coxesbury licked the rim of her ear.

A shudder of repugnance shook her. She pushed him away, sending him sprawling across the floor. Rising, she straightened herself to her full height and looked down at him. "I'd sooner bed a toad than ask for your protection. Of course, that *is* what you are offering, is it not?"

Coxesbury scrambled to his feet. He glared up at her. "You will regret your words, Lady Elfreda. We'll see how long it takes that fool husband of yours to come for you. Rest assured I shall be ready for him if he does." Coxesbury flung the door open and slammed it as he left.

Elf dropped to the bed again. She hugged her knees to her chest. Why hadn't she let Payne deliver the food? With a soft grunt, she admitted it was because she enjoyed the adventure of dressing and riding as the Black Knight. She had told herself that she was just helping Payne this evening by continuing her pretense. In truth, she had wanted to be the Black Knight just one more time.

The tears she had fought against won. She had been a fool. With all her heart, she wished she had listened to Payne and stayed at Candlewood. Now she didn't know if she would see her home again. More than that, she wanted to see Payne again. She wanted to feel his arms about her, to listen to his voice, to touch him.

This is a fine time to realize Payne was right.

Elf sniffed and dashed the tears from her cheeks, only to feel fresh ones fall anew.

For the truth was she believed Coxesbury might be speaking in fact and Payne wouldn't come for her.

Chapter Twenty-Four

Payne paced the floor in the solar. He wouldn't sleep tonight, nay, he couldn't sleep tonight. When he had lain across the bed, Elf's scent invaded his nostrils, bringing him no peace. He had sprung from the bed, afraid of the thoughts and images that had assailed his mind. He strode to the window and stared out. A few torches on the walls gave out their glow, but the moon bathed Candlewood in a silver light. The castle stood proud and strong and beautiful. He had accomplished much in these past months.

Gazing over the parapets, he saw the village beyond and the woods beyond that. All this was his.

So why did the sight fill him with impatience?

He turned back to the solar, and the sound of the fountain's splashing struck his ear. Elf's fountain. He crossed the room and saw only Elf's belongings—her chests of clothes, her tangled skeins of thread, her knife on the table. The castle might belong to him, but it seemed to remember only her.

Closing his eyes, he let his fear for her seize him, until tears came to his eyes. He blinked in surprise. He hadn't wept since he was a child, but the tears fell freely now. His arms ached to hold her again, to laugh with her, to whisper his love to her.

He loved her.

For a moment the thought stunned him, but he realized it was true. His irritating, stubborn, wonderful wife had captured a part of him no one else had ever touched. And now she was gone.

Pain washed over him, leaving him gasping for breath, until rage replaced it. He was familiar with rage. Rage he could use to his advantage. Coxesbury would pay for his actions.

As he stood contemplating his plans for the morrow, a knock came at the door.

"Come in."

The door opened and Royce walked in. Payne narrowed his gaze. "What do you want?"

"Nigel told me of your lady wife."

Payne felt a rush of irritation. "Nigel woke you?"

Royce shook his head. "No. I heard noises earlier. I found Nigel in the great hall readying your armor." Royce paused, then drew in a deep breath. "You can't attack Coxesbury."

"What?" He stared at his brother in disbelief.

Royce closed his eyes and looked pained. "You must rescue Lady Elf, but you cannot attack Brookstone."

"I don't need your advice or your permission." Payne pushed past his brother and started for the door.

"No, you don't, but you do need the permission of the king."

That stopped Payne. He whirled to face Royce.

Royce took two steps closer to him. "Hear me on this. Coxesbury is a powerful man, and he is one of the king's vassals. For all that you are a great knight, you have no liege." Royce placed his hand on Payne's shoulder. "Edward will not take an attack on Brookstone kindly."

"I fought beside Edward in France."

"I know, and I believe the king would gladly claim you as his vassal, but for all that he is not yet your sworn liege, as Coxesbury is."

"Coxesbury isn't loyal to anyone save Coxesbury."

"That may well be, but you still can't mount an attack against him without the king's permission."

Payne sank into a chair and dropped his head into his hands. After a moment, he lifted his gaze to seek his brother's. "What would you have me do?"

"Coxesbury is sure to want a ransom for Lady Elf. Go to him tomorrow and ask him." Royce gave him a sly grin. "*And* send a messenger to the king."

Payne rode into Brookstone Castle in full armor. Only three men accompanied him—Nigel, Royce, and one man-at-arms. His banner fluttered from the end of a pike. The steward, who ran from the keep, stared at them. His Adam's apple bounced in his neck.

"Tell your lord that he has visitors." Payne's voice rang through the bailey.

The steward nodded and retreated into the keep. Payne dismounted and handed Caesar's reins to a waiting stable boy. He strode into the keep, waiting only long enough for the three men who accompanied him to flank his sides.

Coxesbury sat with his hands folded in front of him, waiting like a cat before a mouse hole. He allowed no expression on his face, then his face cracked with a superior smile. "I haven't even sent my messenger to you, but I can't say your visit is unexpected."

"Where is she, Coxesbury?" Payne's hand itched to grab his sword and wipe that smile from the Baron's face.

"What if I told you she's in my dungeon?"

"I wouldn't believe you were that stupid."

Coxesbury laughed. "You're right of course. I wouldn't want to incur the wrath of the Golden Bear."

"Too late for that," muttered Nigel.

Coxesbury waved his hand, and a servant appeared carrying several goblets. "Can I offer you some ale before we talk?"

"I think not." Payne hadn't moved yet.

"At least sit down. I don't want to get a crick in my neck from staring up at you." Coxesbury rolled his head around as if it were sore.

"I won't sit at your table, Coxesbury." Payne gritted his teeth. He was used to action, not playing word games with a snake.

"How am I supposed to bargain with you if you refuse my hospitality?" Coxesbury shook his head.

"I want to see my wife."

Coxesbury shot to his feet. "You are in no position to make demands. Your wife is a thief."

"Just what did she steal?"

Coxesbury sputtered for moment. "She . . . she is a spy. She has endangered my holdings." Coxesbury's visage calmed as he spoke. The smug look returned to his face.

"I never realized a single woman was such a threat to you. Perhaps you're not as strong as you believe."

Coxesbury's face grew mottled as he stared at Payne. Payne enjoyed his small victory, but it was less than satisfying. "What ransom do you want for her?"

"What makes you think I'd settle for a ransom? She's a spy. I'm holding her for treason." Coxesbury sat again and leaned back in his chair. "I'll make sure she has a fair trial."

Payne wasn't sure he could control the rage that exploded

within him. If she stood trial, Coxesbury would find her guilty. And then he would execute her. "May I see my wife?" he ground out between clenched teeth.

"No," said Coxesbury. The grin on his face conveyed his enjoyment of the situation. "Now get out. I'll send word when the trial is over. *If* she is found innocent. There will be no need for you to come if she's found guilty."

Payne glared at Coxesbury, then nodded to his retinue. Without acknowledging the Baron again, Payne left the keep. He said nothing until they rode well past the gate. He stopped in a copse just out of sight of the portcullis. "Do you think we gave her enough time?"

Nigel nodded, then glanced back toward the castle. "Aye. Margaret's a clever one."

Elf lay curled up in a ball with her face toward the wall and her back to the room. She was cold, and the stench of the uneaten food on the tray added to her misery. She heard voices outside her room, but paid them no heed. Probably just a servant with another tray of food she wouldn't eat.

The door opened behind her, then closed. Elf didn't move.

"Oh, my lady, are you ill?"

Elf whipped her head around to face Margaret. Her mouth dropped open, then she sprang from the bed and threw her arms around the older woman. "Margaret? Is that really you?"

"Of course, my lady. But please release me before I drop this food."

Elf stepped back with a smile. Margaret clicked her tongue over the spoiling food on the ground and shoved it with her toes toward the door. She turned back to Elf and handed her the tray of two fresh meat pies, vegetables, and an apple.

"The master said you'd be hungry."

Elf sat on the edge of the bed and eyed the apple. "How would he know?"

"He said you'd be too stubborn to eat any food that Coxesbury sent up to you. This food is from Candlewood."

Elf grabbed the apple and took a bite, wiping the juice from her lower lip. She never thought an apple could taste this sweet.

"Are you well, my lady?"

Tears welled up in her eyes. "Oh, Margaret, I've been such a fool."

"Nay, my lady, just a gentle loving soul who tried to do good for others." Margaret sat beside her and placed her arm around her.

"Is Payne coming to get me?"

Margaret shook her head. "He cannot just yet."

The tears rolled over her lids and trickled down her cheeks in hot rivulets. "He hates me."

Margaret looked at her in surprise. "What makes you say such things? He is here as we speak."

"Payne is here?"

"Yes. He is trying to find out what ransom that monster wants for you." Margaret took a kerchief from her pocket and wiped the tears from Elf's cheeks. "He is doing all he can to free you."

A horrible new thought seized Elf. "He isn't going to attack Brookstone, is he? I couldn't bear it if he was hurt because of me."

Margaret chuckled. "He wanted to. In fact, he is dressed in all his armor. Quite frightening he looks, too. I believe he could tear apart these castle walls with his hands alone to free you."

"But how—"

"Trust him, Lady Elf. He told me to tell you that you mustn't lose hope. He promises no harm will come to you."

Elf frowned. Margaret's words brought little illumination of Payne's plans.

"Have patience, my lady. And eat. You must keep your strength up." Margaret rose and lifted the tray with the spoiled food. She held it as far away from her as possible, but still wrinkled her nose. "I best go now. If I tarry much longer, the guards may suspect something."

"How did you get in here?" asked Elf.

"Men don't notice servants, especially us older women." Margaret winked at her. "Keep your spirits up. His lordship will come for you soon."

Elf had so many more questions for Margaret, but she knew the woman was correct. Margaret had to leave. Giving her a quick kiss on the cheek, Elf whispered, "Tell Payne I am fine and that I am sorry."

Margaret nodded, then opened the door.

"What took you so long, wench?" said one of her guards. He peered into the room.

"She had made a thorough mess with her last tray." Margaret shoved the rotten food under the guard's nose. He backed away. "I had to clean it, didn't I? But I told her. I said if you do this again I won't clean it, and you can just live with the stench."

The second guard closed the door and Elf could hear nothing more than a few more murmured responses through the wood. She smiled. Payne hadn't forgotten about her after all.

That thought alone would warm her this night.

An hour had passed since they had left the castle, and Margaret had not yet returned. Payne glanced at Nigel, who paced back and forth, glancing with increasing regularity at the road. Royce whittled on a stick. Caesar shifted beside him. "Easy, boy."

"Don't you think she should have come out by now if she wasn't discovered?" asked Royce.

Nigel spun in his tracks and faced Royce. "I'll thank you to keep such thoughts to yourself. Margaret's just fine. She had a harder job than any of us, that's all."

Royce dropped the wood and placed his hands on his hips. A scowl formed on his face. "Now see here, old man—"

Payne moved to stand between the two men, but in the next moment Margaret appeared on the dirt road. She almost missed them in the trees, but Nigel took a step toward her, then coughed and looked away. "Here, Margaret."

"By my troth, man, you frightened me." Margaret frowned, but Payne detected a softening in her gaze as she saw Nigel.

"Ungrateful woman," said Nigel.

Margaret opened her mouth to respond, but Payne crossed to her. "Did you see her?" he asked.

"Aye, my lord. She is well. A little frightened, but well." Margaret dabbed at the corner of her eyes. "Leaving her was one of the most difficult things I've ever done, sir."

"I know." Payne ran his hand through his hair. "Are they treating her well?"

"Her room is small and the bed hard. Two guards stand in front of the door, but they are feeding her." Margaret clicked her tongue. "She wasn't eating though, just as you said."

"Elf is a stubborn woman." Payne shook his head. Margaret's words eased his mind about Coxesbury's treatment of his wife, but they brought him little comfort. He wondered how soon his messenger would reach the king. "Where is he holding her?"

"In the south tower."

A scourge take Coxesbury. By placing her in a tower, Coxesbury had made rescuing Elf more difficult. To scale a tower required more stealth and luck than breaching a dungeon. He could take fewer men and would have to penetrate farther into the keep itself. At least he had had practice abducting Elf twice before. The thought brought an ache to his chest. By the heavens, he missed her.

"What the devil took you so long?" asked Nigel with a growl. Payne's thoughts ceased at Nigel's outburst.

Margaret sniffed and lifted her nose in the air. "You didn't have to stop and help with the dishes, did you? No one questioned my presence as a servant because I acted like one. Before I left, I thought it best if I worked a little in the scullery. Now I can come back to see my lady again with little difficulty."

"Humph." Nigel snorted.

"Very clever, Margaret. I thank you for your efforts," said Payne.

"We'd best be off before someone discovers us," said Royce. He walked to the side of his horse and mounted.

Nigel mounted his horse, then swung Margaret behind him. She sniffed again, then placed her arms around him as if the thought of touching him was painful.

Payne nodded and took Caesar's reins, then he paused. He looked at Margaret. "Did my lady say anything else?"

"Aye. She said she was sorry." Margaret dabbed at her eyes again. "Oh sir, you must get her away."

"I will, Margaret. You may take an oath on it." Payne mounted Caesar. "Let's ride."

He let the others take the lead, then turned for a final look back toward Brookstone. He had to muster every ounce of strength he possessed to turn his back on the castle and leave Elf behind.

Chapter Twenty-Five

A trial. Elf knew Coxesbury would find some way to torment her, but a trial would make his torment legal. What chance did she have when the entire village would testify the Black Knight did indeed bring them food and money? Then when Margaret's sister testified that Elf was the Black Knight, Coxesbury would find her guilty. She could think of no way to defend herself. The truth would only serve to quicken the finding of the court, and if she refused to testify . . . she shuddered. Refusing to testify was against the law. And she didn't want to dwell on what pressing did to the body.

The door opened and a woman walked in. "You're to come with me."

Elf rose from the bed and followed the woman from the room. She noticed that her two guards fell in behind her. The woman led her down the stairs to a room closer to the hall. When the servant opened the door, Elf almost gasped. A filled tub stood in the room and fresh gowns lay on the table. She turned to the woman. "This is for me?"

"The master requests you join him in the hall for dinner. He said you may clean up before you join him."

Elf gave the servant an uncertain look.

The woman gave her no reassurance. "I am merely following my lord's orders. As you can see, there is no way to leave this room save the door. The window overlooks the courtyard and is too high to jump from. Your guards will be standing just outside to assure you don't escape. But to safeguard your solitude you can see that the door latches on the inside." The woman gave a curt bow, then left the room.

Elf watched her two guards take their position outside the room, then she shut the door and latched it. Reveling in her comparative freedom, she took off the clothes of the Black Knight. She had enjoyed the garb in the past, but now she wasn't sure she ever wanted to see it again. Dipping her foot into the water, she sighed. The bath was still warm.

Without further hesitation, she climbed into the tub and leaned back. She closed her eyes and let the water soothe her. The scent of lavender wafted under her nose. Someone had taken great care to see that her bath was enjoyable.

Her eyes flew open. Coxesbury. Her pleasure in the bath over, she nevertheless scrubbed herself clean and washed her hair. When she stepped out, she wrapped a towel around herself and examined the clothes. These, too, were a gift from Coxesbury.

She eyed her black trousers and tunic. They were wrinkled and showed definite signs of three days of constant wearing. As she reached for them, her gaze moved back to the fresh shift, the green undergown, and the rich copper-colored overgown. What had Payne told Margaret? That she was stubborn. Well, not tonight. Let Coxesbury pay for her gowns. Perhaps if he thought her subdued, she might find a means to escape him.

She dressed herself in the gowns and looked down. Short, as usual. But they were clean, and perhaps if she appeared in woman's garb at her trial, it might go better for her. With short, strong strokes, she brushed her hair, braided the lengths into two plaits, then covered her head with a wimple. She was ready to face Coxesbury.

She unlatched the door and stepped out of the bathing chamber. Her two guards flanked her. "And a good evening to you, too, boys," she muttered as they led her toward the great hall.

Tables filled the chamber, and a feast covered each one. Musicians played from the gallery, and entertainers danced and juggled between the guests. Elf frowned. Why would Coxesbury invite her to a feast?

As if he knew she thought of him, Coxesbury looked up. "There you are, my dear. Come. I've been saving you a spot here beside me."

Elf moved toward the head table and noticed that her guards stayed in the doorway. As she crossed to the dais, she grew aware of the many stares upon her. These were Coxesbury's men. They all knew how she had come here and what awaited her.

Coxesbury rose as she neared him. He took her hand and kissed it. "You look enchanting tonight, Lady Elfreda."

Elf snatched her hand back.

"Come, sit beside me as my honored guest."

What was Coxesbury contriving? She took her seat and gazed at the shared trencher.

"May I serve you some pheasant?" Coxesbury leaned forward and placed the fowl leg on the plate. "Some currant jelly?"

She watched in silence as he filled their plate with all sorts of savory foods.

"I'm afraid I can't give you a knife, but I'd be happy to feed you from mine."

"I'll use my fingers, thank you." Elf picked up a chunk of meat between her fingers and bit into it.

"Ah, that spirit I so admire in you shows itself." Coxesbury laughed, then speared a piece of meat for himself. "Does it meet your approval?"

"The meat could use more spices." Elf popped another piece in her mouth.

"Aye," said Coxesbury with a long drawn out sigh. "My household lacks a woman's touch. If I had a wife who understood such things . . . but a man in my position cannot marry on a whim."

"Mmmmm," said Elf, feeling some sort of response was required, but not knowing what to say. What did Coxesbury want? The longer she sat beside him, the more sure she was that he had some purpose in mind for her. She sipped her wine to give her some fortification.

The meal continued without further conversation. She watched as a trained bear entertained the hall, just before a magnificent swan made of spun sugar was brought before Coxesbury. The pageantry didn't impress her. Why would Coxesbury invite her, his prisoner, to such a rich feast?

The meal came to an end. "Did you enjoy yourself, my dear?"

Elf didn't know how to respond. "Do you have such festivities often?"

Coxesbury waved his hand in protest. "This was a simple meal. No festivity at all. Such a meal is how a proper lord and lady should eat every day. Quite impressive, wouldn't you say?"

Elf raised her goblet to her lips instead of answering.

Coxesbury leaned closer. "It's not too late for you to renounce your marriage to Payne."

"What?" Elf coughed as the wine went down the wrong direction.

"We could have your marriage annulled, and then we'd wed. All this would be yours. I would have Candlewood and the alliance I desired with your uncle, and you would be a Baroness, not just the wife of some untitled knight." He reached out to stroke her cheek.

"Are you mad?" Elf stood. "I will never marry you. You are a repulsive, loathsome, little toad of a man. Your title means less to me than dirt. Even without a title, Payne is more a lord than you will ever be, no matter how many holdings you might have."

Coxesbury shot to his feet. His mouth twisted into a snarl and scarlet mottled his face. His chest heaved with heavy panting. "You will regret embarrassing me in front of my men. You should have considered your position here. The penalty for treason is death. Your words will serve you little when your head no longer sits on your neck. Best save them for your trial." He turned to her guards. "Take her away."

Her guards stepped forward, but she didn't wait for them to reach her. She crossed the room to them and nearly laughed when they had to match their pace with hers. So much for letting Coxesbury think she was subdued.

Payne rode Merlin through the village. Royce rode beside him. To all outward appearances, they were here to check the tithe barn and the stores for the upcoming winter, but his thoughts were with Elf. Five days had passed since her capture, and he had still received no word from the king. Her trial would start in two days. He had paid well for that information. If the king's answer didn't arrive within that time, he would do whatever was necessary to free his wife.

"Payne?" Royce leaned across the gap between the horses

and tapped his brother on the shoulder. "You aren't listening."

"What?" Payne turned his attention to Royce. "I'm sorry, I wasn't listening."

Royce laughed. "I know. I was saying Candlewood has many riches."

"It shall produce better next year. We had much to overcome when we arrived this summer."

"You are fortunate to have such a holding."

Payne shook his head. " 'Tis Elf's land."

"And thus yours." Royce slanted him a glance. "Are you not satisfied with Candlewood?"

Candlewood meant nothing to him if he couldn't pass it on to his children. Elf's children. He reined in Merlin. "Forgive me, Royce. 'Twas foolish to think I could give attention to the tithe barn. My concern is for Elf." He turned Merlin and was about to ride back to the keep when two of his men rode from the edge of the wood. From a rope fastened to one saddle, they led a man between them, his hands tied together in front of him.

"Sir Payne," called one.

Payne waited until the men reached him.

"We caught this assassin in the woods."

"Assassin?"

"Aye, my lord. He carried a bow and sword. He covered the lower half of his face like an outlaw, sir."

"Take him to the dungeon. We'll question him there."

Within half an hour, Payne watched as his men questioned the man in the dungeon of Candlewood. Three torches lit the dank chamber. Payne leaned against the wall and examined the man who sat with a snarl on his face and a defiant tilt to his head.

"Who sent you?" said the jailer.

"I won't betray my lord."

"Honorable." Payne pushed himself from the wall and crossed to the man tied to a chair. He leaned over him. "Were you sent to kill me?"

"Why should I answer any of your questions?" The man gave him a look of impatience.

"You're right. I wouldn't answer in your place either." Payne straightened. "But I have other, more pressing concerns than dealing with you. Perhaps a few days alone will loosen your tongue. Lock him in a cell."

The two men-at-arms lifted the prisoner by his elbows. Payne gave the man grudging admiration for his loyalty, but he couldn't worry about an assassin now. Elf needed him and—

A glint from the man's tunic caught his attention. "Wait."

The two guards stopped, holding the man between them. Payne grabbed a button on the man's tunic. He yanked it free of the cloth.

"That is mine."

Payne ignored the protest. He took the button to one of the torches. In the uneven light of the flames, Payne saw what he had expected to see—an oak leaf surround by a wreath. "Have you lost any of these buttons in the past?"

"No. My lord just gave me that for my services."

"I see. I'll keep this for now." Payne placed the button in his pouch. "Take him away. If he wishes to talk, I'll listen."

Nigel followed Payne from the dungeon. "What is the significance of that button?"

"I found one the day after the fire. In the woods. It's the same sign as I saw on the saddle of one of the raiders in the field that day. If we could find whose symbol the oak is, we'd find who is behind the raids. And the attempts on my life."

"Most likely he's hiding behind some unused symbol."

"Most likely." Payne drew his hand down his face.

"You're tired, boy."

"I know," snapped Payne. "I haven't had a chance for much rest these days."

"And when you do, you're thinking of her." Nigel nodded. "When do we attack?"

Payne glanced at his friend in surprise.

Nigel shrugged. "I knew you wouldn't let a minor thing like the king's permission keep you from rescuing your wife."

"Her trial starts in two days. If I haven't heard by then . . ."

"I'll ready the men."

"I can't ask you or them to risk the king's wrath."

"You don't have to ask. We all want our lady back as much as you." Nigel gave him a smile that held little mirth. "We're ready to stand by you."

"Thank you."

Nigel left him at the great hall. Payne continued to the solar. The chamber was his least favorite since Elf's absence—in fact he had spent the last five days sleeping with his men in the hall—but he wanted to retrieve the other button to compare the two.

When he reached the room, he froze. Instead of the usual flood of dismay, scattered images flooded his mind—Elf dressed as the Black Knight, the raiders, the assassin, the mask the man had worn—jumbled images one on top of the other until they fell into an ordered pattern.

Payne smiled. He knew just what to do to help Elf.

Chapter Twenty-Six

Elf refused to wriggle on the hard bench. Nor would she slouch. Cold leached from the hard stone behind her, but she scarcely noticed it. Across from her above the hearth, the black-eyed stag of Coxesbury's crest stared down at her. It held a shield with five lozenges. She stared without seeing the fleur-de-lis, the oak leaf, the lion, the sparrows, and the cross. Coxesbury had many lands to call his own.

To her left, the villagers of Brookstone filled the hall, sitting on benches like hers, shoulder to shoulder. Elf glanced to either side of her. She sat alone.

Glancing back to the crowd, she took in the myriad faces, each one different from the next. Some wore the ruddy complexion of daily work outside, others the bent shoulders of hard labor. A large monk sat among the group, but the hood of his cassock hid his face. Margaret's sister was here, but the woman never met her gaze. A child played with a whirring top on the floor beside his mother. Elf let a rueful smile touch her lips. The poor boy probably had to accompany his mother today.

Coxesbury sat opposite the villagers on the dais in a wide chair. He wore a splendid yellow and red tunic trimmed in gold braid. Payne never needed to dress in such profuse colors. He was impressive enough in black.

Coxesbury smirked at the crowd, then turned his gaze to her. She could almost touch the cold triumph in his expression. She lifted her chin a notch and hoped her dismay wasn't apparent.

The truth was, she needed a miracle today to keep her from execution.

Turning to his herald, Coxesbury nodded his head. The herald stepped forward. "Oyez, oyez, oyez. The trial of Lady Elfreda of Renfrey is to begin. A jury from the hundred has been gathered for a fair trial."

Fair trial, indeed. Elf could hardly keep from snorting. The villagers feared Coxesbury too much to rule against his wishes. She was guilty before her trial. She eyed the jury opposite her. They looked anywhere but at her.

Coxesbury stood. "Let us hear from the sheriff first."

A portly man ambled forward. He bowed to Coxesbury. "My lord."

"Sheriff William, you have collected the tallage for the year, have you not?"

"I have."

"Was there anything unusual this year?"

"Aye, my lord. The villagers paid their taxes in gold."

"Each of them?"

"No, my lord. They were all paid by one woman."

"Who was that?"

"Goodwife Baxter. She paid for the whole village."

"Indeed?" Coxesbury raised an eyebrow. "Thank you, Sheriff. You are dismissed."

The man ambled back to his seat. As he passed Elf, he grinned at her, showing the gaps where his teeth once rooted. He drew his finger across his neck and grinned wider.

Elf repressed a shudder. She didn't need this unwashed churl to laugh at her.

"Goodwife Baxter will step forward now," said Coxesbury.

Margaret's sister stood and walked forward. Her gaze never rose from the floor.

"Are you the Goodwife Baxter?"

"I am." Her voice was barely audible.

"Do you remember the day the sheriff came to collect the taxes?"

"Yes, my lord."

"Usually the men of the village line up for their turn to pay the sheriff." Coxesbury waited for her response.

"Aye, my lord."

"This tax day was unusual, was it not?"

"Aye."

"How? What happened on this tax day?"

"No one was there save myself."

Coxesbury arched his eyebrows in a show of surprise. "You stood alone? No one came to pay this year's tallage?"

"No, my lord . . . I mean, aye, my lord. I mean I came to pay the taxes," Margaret's sister stammered.

"Did you pay the taxes for the village?"

She nodded.

"Speak up. We cannot hear your head rattle."

"Yes, my lord. Forgive me, my lord." Goodwife Baxter's gaze fell even lower.

"Did you pay the tallage for the village?"

"I did, sir."

"The *entire* village?"

"Aye."

"And you paid in gold?"

Again Margaret's sister nodded.

"Don't nod. Answer me when I speak."

"Yes, my lord." Goodwife Baxter's words quavered.

"Where did you get the gold?"

"From the Black Knight, my lord."

"Ah, the Black Knight. Explain to us how you met this Black Knight."

"My sister told me to be in the woods and wait for someone to come to me. I did as she asked."

"When was this?"

"I cannot recall exactly. Perhaps two months ago."

"Continue."

"I waited in the woods until a knight came out of the darkness."

"What did the knight look like?"

"He was dressed from head to toe in black. A mask covered his face."

"And his hair?"

"I don't know, my lord. He wore a hood."

"You must have seen something?"

Goodwife Baxter shook her head. "No, my lord."

Coxesbury let out a low growl. "What did the knight say to you?"

"Nothing. He didn't speak." Margaret looked up for the first time.

"The Black Knight didn't speak?"

"No, my lord. He made gestures."

Coxesbury snorted with impatience. "Are you saying you never heard the Black Knight's voice?"

"No, my lord."

"Very well. What did the Black Knight give you?"

"Food. And money."

"What did the Black Knight tell you to do with the food and money?"

"Nothing, sir. He didn't speak."

Elf could almost hear Coxesbury's teeth grinding together.

"Then how did you know what to do with the gifts?"

Goodwife Baxter shrugged. "I used my own judgment."

"And you chose to pay the taxes. Very well. How many times did you meet with the Black Knight before the capture of Lady Elfreda?"

"Twice."

"So the Black Knight came onto my lands two times before we caught her."

"Aye, my lord."

"Tell us about the night a week ago."

"I went to the woods as expected and as you wished. The Black Knight came and brought his gifts, then you came forward and encircled us."

Coxesbury leaned forward. Elf saw the eagerness in his eyes. "What then?"

"You pulled the mask from the knight's face."

"And whom did you see?"

Elf thought she saw a tear splash to the floor as Margaret's sister dropped her gaze again. "The Lady Elfreda."

The low murmur of multiple conversations filled the hall. Several heads turned to her, others pointed.

"Quiet. I will have quiet," shouted Coxesbury, but the grin on his face belied his annoyed shouts.

The noise died down once again until she could hear only the whirring of the top.

"What is that sound?" asked Coxesbury glancing about the room.

A woman jumped up from the bench. "Forgive me, my lord. I had no place to take my son." She snatched the top from the child, who promptly began to wail for his missed toy.

"Great heaven, give the foul creature his toy back."

The mother handed her son the top. The lad quieted and popped his thumb in his mouth and hugged the wooden object to his chest.

Elf would have smiled at the boy's antics, were she not so worried for the child. She glanced at Coxesbury to see how he would react to the child. The look on his face wasn't what she expected at all.

Coxesbury crossed to the boy. The child clasped the top tighter to his chest. "Do you know who I am, boy?"

The young lad nodded.

"Then you know if I ask you a question you must answer me as your lord and master." Coxesbury pointed to the top. "Did your mother give you this top?"

The boy shook his head.

"Your father?"

"No," whispered the boy.

"I thought not." Coxesbury faced the crowd, puffing out his chest. "So that you may know the wisdom of your lord, listen to how I knew. I have seen the simple toys you make for your children. This top has intricate carvings and a whistle. It is painted in many colors. Such a top belongs in the house of a noble, not a villein."

Coxesbury turned his attention to the boy again. "Who gave you this top, boy?"

"The Black Knight. My momma telled me."

Elf eyed the boy in confusion.

Coxesbury laughed. He faced Margaret's sister, who still sat at the front of the room. "Thank you, Goodwife Baxter. You may sit."

Margaret's sister returned to her place. Coxesbury turned again to the little boy. "So you've heard of the Black Knight."

The boy nodded.

"What do you think of the Black Knight?"

The boy took his thumb from his mouth long enough to answer. "I like him."

Coxesbury addressed the crowd. "Do you see how Lady Elfreda's actions infect even the very youngest of Brookstone? She has invaded your lives for months now."

He turned back to the boy. "When did you get that top?"

The boy scrunched up his face, then grinned. "Today morning."

"Nonsense. You've had it several weeks now."

"Forgive me, my lord, but my son is correct. He received it this morning," said the boy's mother.

"Then you saved it for him until today."

"No, my lord. The Black Knight gave it to me last night."

"What?"

Elf couldn't believe what she heard.

Coxesbury's face grew red. "You are mistaken. The Black Knight couldn't have delivered anything last night because she was in her chamber."

"Forgive me again, my lord, but the Black Knight did come last night." The boy's mother looked apologetic. "He brought the top for Tommy. And a ham."

A man stood clutching his hat in his hands. "Aye, my lord. He came to my house, too. He brought me some venison and two groats." The man held up two silver coins.

"That is impossible. Lady Elf was locked in the tower this last night." Coxesbury glanced around the room.

"He brought us bread," said another voice.

"I received some pennies," said yet another.

Coxesbury sputtered, opening and closing his mouth like a fish. Then he pointed at the man with the groats. "You there. Stand forward."

The man lumbered to the front of the room. He twisted his

cap between two meaty fists.

"Who are you?"

"Festus, my lord. The blacksmith."

"Do you know of the Black Knight?"

"Aye, my lord. He brings us food and money and the like."

"How many times?"

Festus thought for a moment, then ticked off his fingers until he had counted them all. "Five, yer lordship."

"Five?" Coxesbury looked as though he were about to succumb to apoplexy.

Five? Elf didn't understand. She had only come twice before her capture on her third visit.

"Did you see the Black Knight?"

"Not the first three times. But I saw him plain as day these past two nights." The blacksmith nodded.

"What did he look like?"

"Don't rightly know. He was dressed in black from head to foot. And he wore a mask."

"Well, what size was he?" Coxesbury shouted this last question.

"Big. About as big as me, I think. But he seemed bigger. He was on a horse, ye ken."

"What did he do?"

"Rode right into the middle of the village. Never said a word, but knocked on our doors. When we came out, he passed out his gifts." Festus shrugged his shoulders. "Came these last two nights, and never said a word."

"Do you all agree with the blacksmith?"

A chorus of ayes rang out in the hall.

Coxesbury fell into his chair on the dais. He dropped his head into his hands. "Impossible," he muttered.

It *was* impossible. Elf looked around the hall. She had been in that uncomfortable chamber these past seven nights with two guards in front of her door. Who had been passing for her?

Coxesbury stood again and pointed at her. "Lady Elfreda, step forward."

Elf rose from her seat. On trembling legs she walked across the floor until she stood in front of the dais. She faced Coxesbury and drew a deep breath.

In a low whisper that only she could hear, Coxesbury said, "You will not escape my justice." He sneered at her. Then preening as only a peacock could, he straightened and faced the court. "Lady Elfreda, you will tell us of your part in this farce."

A voice from the benches filled the hall. "I don't think that will be necessary."

Elf snapped her head around.

The monk rose from his seat and threw off his cassock. Payne. His face was grim, and his eyes flashed at Coxesbury. He strode to the center of the hall, ignoring the gasps of the villagers. He slipped the robe from his shoulders and let it fall to the floor. He stood in his customary black, facing Coxesbury. Elf could feel his anger. Even Coxesbury flinched on the dais.

"I've come to take my wife home."

Chapter Twenty-Seven

Coxesbury flared his nostrils. "You have no right to interrupt these proceedings."

Payne didn't spare Coxesbury a single glance. He saw only Elf and never slowed his steps toward her. His sword brushed against his side, but he wore no armor. He felt no fear of Coxesbury, only concern for his wife. "From what I've heard this morning, these proceedings are over."

"Despite what you wish," said Coxesbury with a hiss, "your wife is guilty, and I haven't sentenced her yet."

Payne did stop at those words. He turned slowly and pierced Coxesbury with his gaze. He took a step toward the maggot with each word. "Let's look at the evidence. You claim a man who calls himself the Black Knight is a traitor. You don't know what this person looks like, or what he sounds like. So you laid a trap."

Coxesbury glared at him. "And I caught the Black Knight."

"You caught my wife, whom you've kept imprisoned this past week. Yet the Black Knight has appeared two more times while my wife was locked in your castle. It seems to me that either you've caught the wrong Black Knight, or the security of your castle leaves much to be desired." He paused. "Unless, of course, you want us to believe that Lady Elfreda escaped twice and returned for more of your hospitality of her own free will."

A few twitters rippled through the hall.

Coxesbury's face flooded with color. "Then how do you explain her capture?"

"You failed to consider that Goodwife Baxter's sister is my wife's tiring woman. The Lady Elfreda made you the victim of a harmless prank." Payne leaned over Coxesbury until that man fell back into his chair. "Do you really want everyone to believe that a *woman* can outwit a Baron of your repute?"

Coxesbury gaped at him.

"I thought not." Payne crossed to Elf. "Come, wife. Let's go home."

Elf stood and placed her hand on his arm. He led her from the hall without giving Coxesbury another glance. Two of Coxesbury's men stood in the archway. They raised their swords to stop them, but Payne just glared at them until they let the pair through.

He didn't speak as they walked out the doorway and through the bailey. Then again, neither did she. He wondered what she might be thinking. Her face was pale, and no hint of a smile teased her lips.

She hadn't looked at him since they left the hall.

"Your horse, brother." The stable boy handed him Merlin's reins, then looked at him in confusion. "Weren't you a monk?"

"I was. I changed my mind." Payne lifted Elf onto the pillow of the saddle, then climbed up himself.

As they rode from the castle, something nettled his mind—something he should have remembered, something in the great hall. The more he tried to seize on the image, the more it slipped away. With a shake of his head, he dismissed the thought. He would think about it later. Now he would enjoy his victory and revel in the feel of Elf's arms wrapped around his waist.

A surge of satisfaction rolled through him. He had succeeded; he had taken his wife from in front of Coxesbury and had done nothing to risk the anger of the king. He let out a whoop.

Elf jumped on the padding behind him. He turned to look at her. Tears coursed down her cheeks.

Payne stopped the horse and jumped down. He lifted Elf off the saddle and hugged her to him. "Hush, Elf. It's over."

"I'm so sorry," she said. The words were muffled against his chest. "I've been such a fool."

"Never that, my lady." Payne stroked her hair. "You are safe now. I shan't fail you again."

"You fail *me?*" Elf hiccupped and stared at him. "You didn't fail me. I wouldn't listen to you."

"And I didn't fulfill my promise to you. I should have delivered that food for you."

"But I should have waited—"

"There is time enough for your reproaches at Candlewood." Nigel appeared on the road in front of them. He frowned at their tender scene. "Come along. We are still too close to Coxesbury to discuss the issue now."

Margaret followed just behind Nigel. When she spied Elf, she said, "Oh, my lady," and burst into tears.

Elf looked up at Payne. "Margaret?" she said with surprise in her voice.

"We didn't dare leave her behind," whispered Payne.

"You're safe. I knew the master would save you," said Margaret as she ran to Elf.

Payne and Elf stepped apart. He watched with some humor as the smaller woman hugged Elf with much ferocity.

"Nigel, I told you to wait at the clearing," he said.

"I know, but you were taking so long. I couldn't keep that woman under control much longer." He pointed at Margaret.

Margaret released Elf and placed her fists on her hips. She frowned at Nigel. "Watch your mouth, you clod. You were the one pacing. Couldn't stand still for a moment, peering up and down the road, mumbling under your breath."

"Woman, I'll thank you to keep your thoughts to yourself." Nigel turned his back to her. "Do you see what I've had to put up with?"

Payne laughed, then held up a hand. "Let's get Elf home." He took hold of Merlin's reins, then stretched his hand toward Elf. Still sniffing, she stepped to him and slipped her hand into his. He lifted her palm to his lips and kissed it. "I missed you."

Nigel cleared his throat and muttered something Payne couldn't understand. Margaret beamed at the two of them. Then the small group walked to the clearing, where three horses waited for them. One of Payne's men guarded the animals.

Still grumbling, Nigel lifted Margaret onto a horse.

Elf gave her a puzzled look. "I thought you couldn't ride."

"I can't, my lady. But I had to get here somehow. Nigel held the reins for me. All I have to do is stay on top of the beast." Margaret gave her a worry-filled smile.

Payne hid his amusement behind a cough, then turned to Elf to lift her onto Merlin.

As he put his hands about her waist, she tilted her head and frowned. She pushed away from him. "Listen."

He stilled. The distant thunder of horses' hooves rumbled

toward them. "Coxesbury," he shouted.

Elf glanced at him. Fear glittered in her eyes.

"I won't let him take you, my love. I swear." Payne faced the road and unsheathed his sword.

Elf's eyes widened. *My love?* She mouthed the words without a sound.

Nigel threw Margaret's reins to her, then pulled out his own sword. "Ride, woman. Ride for help."

"I can't ride," said Margaret.

"You must." Nigel stepped back from animal.

"But I cannot leave my lady—"

"Go!" screamed Elf. "Bring help."

Margaret opened her mouth as though to protest, but then snapped it shut. Her brow wrinkled in concentration. She clicked her tongue and gave a shake to the reins. As the horse jumped forward, she let out a short shriek, but stayed on the saddle. As she rode from the clearing, her grunts and gasps floated back to them until the oncoming thunder drowned out the sounds.

The third man drew his sword and joined Nigel, ready to fight for his lord. Payne turned to Elf. "Go. There's still time if you ride Merlin."

"No." Elf stepped beside him. "I won't leave you. I . . . I love you."

"By St. Swithin's bones, not now." But he swept her into a one-armed embrace and kissed her.

The thunder ceased, and dust swirled around them. Payne held Elfin a tight grip as a cackle split the air.

"I do so hate to interrupt such a charming scene." Coxesbury glared at the small group from atop his mount. "You didn't think I really would let you walk away from me, did you?"

Payne counted Coxesbury's men. Six, not including the

Baron, and he doubted Coxesbury would risk himself. Six men against three. And Elf. He had to keep her safe.

He eyed the men again and paused. "Tedric."

Tedric bowed to him from his horse. "I shall miss our battles in the future."

"So this is to be the last?" said Payne with little sorrow at the thought.

"Indeed." Tedric leaned forward on his saddle. His posture bespoke confidence.

As if considering a new thought, Payne stroked his chin. "You know, Tedric, you needn't die for Coxesbury."

Tedric barked out a harsh laugh. "I won't be the one dying here today."

Payne shrugged. "So you might believe."

Coxesbury gave a signal, and five of the men dismounted. He and Tedric remained on their horses.

"If you see a chance, run to the trees for cover," Payne whispered to Elf, but his gaze never left the advancing soldiers.

"But I—"

"I cannot fight *and* worry about you, my love. I need to know you're safe."

Before Elf could answer, Coxesbury gave them a wicked smile. In a low, even voice he said, "Kill them."

Jumping into a ready stance, Payne thrust Elf behind him, and yelled, "Stay behind me until you can run to safety."

The words had hardly left his mouth when the first sound of metal upon metal filled the air. Elf let out a cry, but didn't move from her position behind him. *Good girl,* he thought.

With a quick slash and thrust, Payne took care of the first man. He heard the grunts of Nigel and his soldier beside him, but he didn't spare the time to look at them. Payne stopped the jab of the man in front of him with his blade, then used the hilt to drop a second man with a blow to the head. *That's two.*

He heard the guttural cry of his man at arms. From the corner of his eye he saw the man fall into a pool of blood. Nigel ran his sword through his opponent, then spun to ward off the attack of the man who had killed one of their own. Payne turned back in time to see his opponent charge him. He bent his knees. As the man reached him, Payne hoisted him onto his back, tossed him to the side, then used his dirk to slice the man's throat. A gurgle whimpered from the enemy's lips before he died.

Nigel was still fighting the last man. Payne faced Elf. "Go, now."

She hesitated only an instant before she fled to the trees. Payne waited until she was away from the skirmish before he gave his strength to Nigel. Together, they finished off the last man.

Nigel knelt beside their fallen companion. He reached for the man's neck, then shook his head. As he rose, Nigel clutched his own arm.

"Are you hurt?" asked Payne in a low voice.

"Aye, but not enough to stop me from fighting." He transferred his sword to his left hand.

"Go find Elf. Keep her safe."

Nigel peered into his eyes for a moment, then nodded. "Watch your back."

"I intend to."

With a speed that belied his injury, Nigel dashed into the trees.

Payne faced Coxesbury. "Any other cleaning you would have me do?"

Coxesbury's face reddened. "I didn't expect those men to succeed. But you will die today."

"That's not in my plans. I do however intend to repay you

for the death of my man." Payne readied himself. "Or will you retreat like the coward you are?"

"Oh, I won't fight you. Not when Tedric here is so willing to do it for me." Coxesbury waved his hand toward the knight. "Really. You don't expect me to soil my clothes for you."

Tedric dismounted.

Payne eyed Tedric, but directed his words toward Coxesbury. "So you intend just to watch the sport? I hope the ending won't disappoint you too much."

"I won't be disappointed. You are already tired. Tedric is more than your equal."

Tedric unsheathed his sword.

"Tedric has never been my equal." Payne and Tedric circled each other. Payne didn't take his gaze from Tedric. "It's a pity you have no shame in wasting a life in this way."

Coxesbury laughed. "There's no waste. When you die, I shall have Elfreda and her lands. Our sons will grind your name into dust with their deeds."

"Elf will never have you." Payne watched Tedric's eyes. His eyes had always given him away.

"I shall enjoy bedding the wench. I shall teach her obedience, and I shall make her pay for the humiliation I suffered today."

Payne gritted his teeth. *Don't listen,* he told himself. *Watch Tedric.*

"But first she must be punished for her actions. Tonight she shall reward my men with her body. By the time she comes to me, your lowly touch will have been fucked out of her."

Payne roared. He lifted his sword toward Coxesbury just as Tedric lunged forward.

Chapter Twenty-Eight

Even as he swung at Coxesbury, Payne knew he had made a mistake. Tedric's blade sliced through the air. He corrected himself in mid-thrust by rolling to the side. The honed blade slid through the leather of his tunic. Steel met skin, and Payne cried out as the sword opened his side. But not enough to kill. Payne rolled to his feet and faced Tedric.

"First blood to you, my old adversary. You did well to take advantage of my anger. A pity your strike wasn't deep enough." Payne lifted his blade to ward off another blow. The clang echoed through the clearing.

"I have been looking forward to this day for many years." Tedric swung his sword again.

Payne turned the strike aside and stepped over the body of one of the fallen men. "I have no doubt."

Tedric circled him. "You don't seem to mourn our friendship."

"You were never my friend. You amused me, but I never thought of you as my friend. I am not that stupid." Payne let out a chuckle. His side was burning, and his breath came harder now, but he wouldn't let Tedric or Coxesbury see that.

Tedric's mouth curled into a sneer. "Your words wound me."

"I never considered you that stupid, either."

"Enough chatter," shouted Coxesbury. "Finish him."

Tedric lunged forward, but Payne evaded his attack by turning to the side, then striking Tedric on the back as he passed by. Tedric sprawled into the dirt, but before Payne could launch his own attack, Tedric jumped to his feet. Payne retreated a step. He sucked air in gulps now, but he wouldn't let Tedric's show of freshness dismay him. He knew who the superior fighter was.

Raising his sword, Tedric brought it down with a swish. Payne blocked its descent with his own blade and threw Tedric's arm into an arc.

As the futile battle waged on, Tedric's face grew mottled with anger. He leapt forward, swinging left, then right. Payne met every thrust and turned it into wasted effort.

"You seem to favor your left shoulder," said Payne.

"A minor injury, I assure you." Tedric's voice was uneven now.

Payne took heart at the audible sign of weariness. "I should hate to hear you using it as an excuse later, when you're explaining your loss to your friends over an ale."

"You won't. You'll be dead." Tedric stepped back for a moment. "I should have finished you in the woods that day. The knife was poor compensation for my disappointment."

Before Payne could react to these words, Tedric struck again. The clearing sounded more like the inside of a busy smithy than a battle between warriors. Tedric moved with speed and agility, but Payne met every attack with a calmness and strength that flowed from him like a mighty river. Tedric's impatience showed itself in a snarl that intensified with each thrust. He grew wild in his attacks, jabbing at a furious pace, stumbling over a body, but righting himself at the last moment.

From the corner of his eye, Payne saw Coxesbury dismount. He didn't fear Coxesbury, but fighting another man while still battling Tedric would be difficult. Turning himself, he placed Tedric between Coxesbury and himself. Now the Baron couldn't move without being seen.

Tedric's eyes narrowed. Payne almost smiled. A change was coming, Tedric's eyes told him. Tedric whirled. Payne saw the glint of something in Tedric's left hand before he saw the knife flying through the air at him. But he had known it was coming. He had fought Tedric often enough to know the man threw to the right with his left hand. Payne stepped neatly to his right and listened to the knife whistle past.

"You've wasted a weapon. And I want my knife back." Payne raised his sword and launched his own attack. He no longer waited for Tedric. The time had come to end this.

Trying not to cry, Elf ran into the woods. She stopped just far enough not to be seen, but close enough to hear the battle. She spotted some bushes that would conceal her well, but then didn't crawl between their branches. How could she hide while Payne was in danger?

As she turned back, she heard a roar of pain and anger, and her breath froze in her throat. Her heart told her it was Payne, and fear sent a weakness through her.

She took a few steps toward the clearing, then stopped. She couldn't help him if she returned, and he as much as said he couldn't fight if he had to worry about her safety. Her legs buckled beneath her and she slid to the ground. Drawing in a ragged breath, she hugged her knees to her chest and let the tears fall.

She heard nothing of the battle for a few moments—or had

it been hours—then the sound of the conflict returned anew. Elf lifted her head. It wasn't over. She stood, uncertain whether she wanted to return to the clearing, not knowing what she would find. Was Payne alive? He was a powerful warrior, but—

The sound of footsteps reached her. Grabbing her skirt, she fled behind a tree. Nigel burst through the woods.

"Nigel," she said.

Nigel stopped and turned toward her.

"Is Payne . . ." The words choked her throat.

"Payne is still alive, but it's not over yet, my lady." Nigel grimaced. He dropped his sword and clutched his right arm.

"You're hurt."

" 'Tis nothing." Nigel released his arm and reached for his sword. "I have to get you to safety."

"No, I won't leave Payne."

"You can't help him. He faces Tedric as we speak."

As though the words had the power of prophecy, the sound of swords clashing reached their ears.

"Merciful heaven," whispered Elf. She faced Nigel. "But he's defeated Tedric in the past."

"Aye, but not after fighting three men to their deaths." Nigel lifted his sword in his left arm, letting his right arm hang uselessly at his side.

The sound of the fighting intensified. The ring of metal upon metal grew frenzied.

"I won't leave him, Nigel." Elf lifted the overgown until she exposed the soft material of the undergown. She tore at the hem until it ripped. She felt no remorse at destroying the lovely cloth. Coxesbury had given it to her. When she had torn several long strips from her skirt, she said, "Come here and remove your tunic."

Nigel stepped forward and removed his woolen tunic. His

shirt of linen clung to his body from sweat. None of it bothered Elf, except for the bloodstained sleeve.

She ripped the sleeve from the shirt and gasped. A long gash lay open on his forearm. Blood trickled from it. "We'll have to sew this when we get home. Until then, I'll tie the wound together." She wrapped a cloth strip tightly around his arm and tied it, then she repeated her actions until all the strips were gone. Reaching for more of her skirt, she tore away a large square, which she folded into a triangle. She tied the cloth around Nigel's neck to form a cradle for his arm.

A breeze touched her legs. Very little of the underskirt remained. *Good. The less there will be to burn when I get home.*

The clangs of the battle grew ever more frequent. Nigel cocked his head at the sounds.

"Give me your sword," said Elf.

"What?" Nigel scowled at her.

"Your sword. I will go help Payne."

"Are you daft?"

Elf gave him a determined smile.

"Forgive me, Elf, but I can fight better with my left hand than you ever could with your right." Nigel shook his head.

"You are injured." She extended her hand, waiting for Nigel to place the sword's hilt in her palm.

"Payne would kill me." Nigel took a step back.

Elf let out a grunt of impatience. "Well, I'm not waiting here."

She started back toward the clearing. She turned around to see Nigel gaping at her. "Are you coming?" she asked.

Nigel ran to her side. "Payne will flay the skin from my back when he sees I've let you return," he muttered.

"My skin will probably come after yours." Elf pushed

through the bushes toward the man she loved.

With every step, Payne pushed Tedric back. He had let Tedric control the fight until now, let Tedric lead with his attacks, while Payne defended himself. No more. Now he controlled the fight. Payne gave Tedric no respite from the onslaught of his blade. Tedric could do no more than keep his feet under him and protect himself. He was fighting for the wrong reasons—money and pride. Payne was fighting for his life and his love.

Sweat dripped down his face and into his eyes, but he paid no heed to the stinging of his eyes and blurring of his vision. He was tired, but he had right on his side.

Tedric thrust at Payne in an attempt to regain the advantage, but Payne knocked the sword aside with his gloved hand. Tedric was scrambling now. He swung in a wide arc that Payne avoided with ease.

"Get him, you fool," shouted Coxesbury.

"Shut up," answered Tedric with a vicious snarl. His breathing was ragged and his eyes blinked in an effort to keep the sweat out. He swiped his arm across his brow.

"Tired?" asked Payne in a low voice.

"No." Tedric jumped back a few feet and drew a deep breath. Then releasing a cry of rage, he ran forward, his sword uplifted.

Payne swung his blade in a tight arc. Steel met flesh, and Tedric screamed as he watched his severed hand fall to the ground, still clutching his sword. Payne pushed him to the ground and strode to the far end of the clearing. He turned back to Coxesbury, then sank to his knees, drawing in as much air as he could.

Tedric writhed on the ground, keening his pain. His left hand gripped his wrist as blood flowed through his fingers. He climbed to his knees.

"You won't win your land now," whispered Payne without a hint of sympathy.

Coxesbury grabbed his sword, then ran up behind Tedric. "Idiot. You are of no use to me now." He plunged his sword into Tedric's back.

"No!" shouted Payne, but he was too far to stop Coxesbury.

Tedric's eyes widened in surprise. He lifted his gaze to Payne. For a moment Tedric didn't waver, then his lips curled into a smile. Payne could read the entreaty in Tedric's eyes, and he nodded. In the next instant, Tedric's eyes lost their light and he fell forward into the dust. They had lived as adversaries, but Tedric had died asking for redemption.

Payne still struggled to catch his breath, but he wasn't finished here yet. He rose to his feet with deliberate slowness. Coxesbury climbed onto his horse. Payne didn't care. He walked to Tedric's body and looked down at it.

"Don't tell me you'll mourn his death," Coxesbury cackled. "You're a bigger fool than I thought."

"I mourn any unnecessary death." Payne's voice was quiet, yet it filled the air. "But you can be sure I won't mourn yours."

He knelt beside Tedric and rolled the slain knight to his back. A glint of silver caught his attention. He pulled a button from Tedric's tunic. An oak leaf surrounded by a wreath graced the silver. He closed his fingers around the button, and remembered what he should have seen at Elf's trial. The crest on the hearth. The oak leaf on one of the lozenges. The guards at the door had all worn such buttons.

He flung the button at Coxesbury, who flinched at the tiny object. "Clever of you to give your men a different herald than your own."

Coxesbury snorted. "Stupid of you not to know that the oak is the symbol of Brookstone."

Payne lifted his sword. "You couldn't be content. Why? Why did you try to destroy my lands?"

"I wasn't about to let you have Candlewood." Coxesbury circled the glen like a caged animal. "Marriage to Agnes would have brought me more power than you can even dream of."

"The king disallowed your marriage."

"A pox on the king. The king wouldn't dare touch me. Meredith would have made me his heir, then I would have killed him. So you saved a life, after all." Coxesbury laughed. "For a little while anyway. After I wed Elfreda, I shall have to kill Agnes and convince Meredith to make Elfreda his heir. Oh, I shall be of such consolation to my dear uncle."

"But I won't marry you." Elf stepped from the woods with Nigel. For a moment, Coxbury met her gaze. Then she saw the bodies that littered the ground and gave a little cry. Covering her face, she turned her head.

Payne glanced at her. "Go back, Elf. Nigel, get her out of here."

"Yes, go Lady Elfreda. I wouldn't want to see you distressed when your husband's body joins the others," said Coxesbury. He lifted his sword and kicked his horse into a run.

Elf screamed as Payne held his sword in two hands to repel the blow that came from above.

Chapter Twenty-Nine

Elf watched in helpless horror as Coxesbury bore down on Payne. She held her hands over her ears as the two blades met. Covering her ears didn't mute the sharp metallic crash. Payne staggered under the blow. Elf bit her tongue in an effort to keep from calling his name.

The weariness on his face alarmed her. Sweat plastered his hair to his neck and face. He clutched his side as Coxesbury turned his horse. When Payne braced himself for the next blow, Elf saw the spreading red stain on his hip.

"He's bleeding. Oh, Nigel, he's hurt." Elf struggled to keep her voice quiet.

"Aye, my lady. I saw." Nigel's voice was grave.

Coxesbury thundered forward. This blow sent Payne to his knees. Payne rose more slowly this time.

"What can we do to help?"

"I don't know, my lady. Until Coxesbury is unseated, he has the advantage."

"There must be something we can do." Elf glanced around. She picked up a rock and hurled it at Coxesbury. It hit the horse's flank. The horse danced about a bit, but

Coxesbury remained in the saddle. He turned to make another pass at Payne.

Payne glanced around. Jabbing his sword into the earth, he grabbed a thick, fallen branch and took his stance again.

"What is he doing?" Elf watched in disbelief as Coxesbury rode toward Payne.

The sword fell again, but this time Payne used the log to block the blow. Coxesbury's blade bit deeply into the wood. Payne pivoted, never releasing his hold on the branch. Coxesbury's blade never slid from its wooden vise. Payne's action yanked Coxesbury from the back of the horse. He released his blade too late to keep his seat. The horse bolted down the road.

"That's the way, lad," shouted Nigel.

But Payne dropped the wood and fell to his knees. He reached for his sword and pulled himself up.

Coxesbury scrambled to his feet. The wood still held his sword. He grabbed another weapon from one of the fallen soldiers. He faced Payne. The sheer hatred on his face frightened Elf.

Payne lifted his sword as Coxesbury attacked. Payne met every thrust with steel, but he stumbled more than once.

No, I won't let him die. Anger washed over her, purging the fear that had once claimed her. She swallowed hard, then grabbed a sword from a dead man's hands. "No!" she shouted and ran out into the clearing.

"My lady!" Nigel reached out to grab her, but missed.

At her cry, Coxesbury looked up. At that moment, Payne hit him with the end of his hilt. Coxesbury staggered forward, dropping the sword, but he remained standing. He whirled back to face Payne, but found himself blocked by Elf. She held the sword at his chest.

Coxesbury laughed. "Get out of the way, Elfreda."

She didn't move. "My name is Elf, and I do not give you leave to use it."

"Elf, step away," Payne said.

The sword was heavy in her hand. She wrapped her other hand around the hilt.

"You're no warrior," said Coxesbury with a sneer.

"Mayhap not, but I can run this through you without a knight's training." Elf took a step toward him.

"I think not." Coxesbury grabbed the sword by the blade and twisted it. She pulled back as hard as she could. The blade cut through the leather of Coxesbury's gloves, but as she pulled, she fell over Tedric's body and landed on the ground. For a moment she had trouble breathing and she feared she had hurt herself, for she heard a buzzing coming from the road.

Coxesbury cradled his hand. "You will regret this." He pulled a knife from his belt and advanced toward her.

"You'll not be harming the lady today."

Elf looked up. From the road, dozens of villeins, armed with pitchforks, knives, axes, and many things Elf had never considered as weapons before, surrounded the glen. Margaret's sister led the group.

"You won't harm the lady," repeated Margaret's sister.

Coxesbury looked over the crowd with a sneer. "Go home while you still have homes to go to."

"No," said a man who held a cleaver as if he knew how to use it. From his bloody apron, Elf assumed he was the butcher.

A second man stepped forward, wielding long iron tongs. "This lady has done us much good, unlike yerself, my lord." He said the last two words as if they left a sour taste in his mouth.

Elf clambered to her feet and moved to Payne. He placed his arm about her.

"I will have you all killed for this," shouted Coxesbury. He flashed them a look of triumph.

None of the villagers moved. The three largest men walked toward Coxesbury. "Don't see no soldiers here to kill us with," said one of them.

Coxesbury's look of triumph faded. His gaze darted from one face in the crowd to another. Not one held any expression of sympathy or friendliness or fear. He backed up until he touched Tedric's body.

Coxesbury whirled around. He spied Elf standing beside Payne, and his eyes narrowed. "This is all your fault."

Before anyone could stop him, Coxesbury threw his knife. She screamed. For an instant, she saw the glint of the blade, but in the next, Payne was pulling her to the side. A searing pain flamed in her arm.

"He has killed the lady," shouted a voice.

"Kill him!" came a yell from the crowd.

The crowd surged forward. Like a cornered fox, Coxesbury dashed from one side to the other, seeking a path of escape. Nigel blocked his retreat to the rear. The crowd closed in on him.

Elf buried her head against Payne's chest.

"Stop. This is not the way." Payne's voice rose above the din. "The lady is not dead."

Payne started for Coxesbury. The crowd parted to let him through. Coxesbury cowered at the center of the mob. He looked up at Payne. "Thank you for saving me from these primitive creatures. You understand that we cannot let the villeins act in such a manner."

Payne's gaze was cold. "Save your thanks. You should be praying I don't kill you myself." To the crowd, he said, "Tie him up. I'll deal with him at Candlewood. And you needn't bother being gentle."

The villeins cheered again and carried out the task with fervor.

"Stop. You cannot leave me to these—"

But Payne ignored Coxesbury's pleas. He hurried back to Elf's side. She cradled her injured arm in the other. Coxesbury's knife lay on the ground at her feet.

"How bad is it?" he asked.

Elf gave him a faltering smile. "Not so bad that I fear death, but 'tis something I don't care to repeat. 'Tis *your* job to be a hedgehog."

Payne let out a soft chuckle. "If you can jest about it, I shan't worry overmuch."

"What of you?"

"It hurts as if a hive of angry bees has settled in my side, but it's nothing less than I deserve. I was careless. I shouldn't have let Coxesbury goad me—"

"What did he say?"

"It doesn't matter now." He kissed the top of her head.

Nigel joined them, his face grave. "I hear horses."

Elf listened. She heard them, too. A large number by the sound of the hooves. *Please, no more,* she prayed.

The horses weren't coming from Brookstone.

Payne pushed Elf behind him. The crowd fell silent as a group of knights dressed ready for battle appeared beside them. The horses snorted when the knights reined them in.

"Payne," called the knight at the head of the group.

Elf let out her breath. She recognized that voice.

"Here, Royce," said Payne.

Royce jumped from his horse. "Brother, I feared the worst." He ran to them and hugged them both.

"Ouch," said Elf.

Royce stepped back and looked at her. "Dear lady, you are injured. Forgive me."

"Not as badly as Payne," said Elf.

Royce looked over at his brother. "It seems I've come too late to help."

"You came to help?" Payne eyed his brother in disbelief.

"As soon as Margaret told us what had happened."

"Why would you risk the king's displeasure?"

"You are my brother." Royce shrugged.

Payne stared at Royce. Elf knew he didn't know what to make of this display of brotherly affection and loyalty. She smiled. "Thank you, Royce."

Royce didn't avert his gaze from his brother for a long moment. Then Payne stretched his arm forward. Royce looked down at it and gripped his brother's forearm in a clasp of kinship and fealty.

Elf wiped a tear from her eye.

Payne waved to the crowd. "Thank you all for your help. Your deed here today shall be remembered by myself and my family. No harm shall come to any of you because of it. I give you my solemn vow."

The crowd shouted their approval.

"And you thought the Black Knight was a foolish idea," whispered Elf. She grinned at him, her pain nearly forgotten.

"I haven't changed my mind," said Payne. "And we'll discuss how well you take orders later."

Royce patted his vest. "I almost forgot. The answer to your missive arrived from the king." He pulled it from his bodice.

The seal on the parchment was unbroken. Payne split the wax and unfolded the sheet. He stared at the words on the paper. When he finished, he let out a low laugh.

"What does it say?" asked Royce.

"Edward has given me permission to attack Brookstone. He wishes me luck with the endeavor, and should I kill

Coxesbury, he would forgive my trespass. If however I capture him alive, the king would like to see Coxesbury, and would I be so good as to send him to Windsor in chains."

"No," wailed Coxesbury from the ground, where ropes banned his movements.

"I think the king wants to discuss your hunger for power." Payne turned to Royce. "Would your men bring Coxesbury to Candlewood for me?"

"They'd be happy to." Royce gave the order.

"I believe *his lordship* is ready to travel," said Nigel, testing the ropes that bound Coxesbury.

"Good. Gather the horses." Payne gave a sharp whistle. Elf watched Merlin trot to him from the woods. Payne turned to her. "Let's go home, my lady."

Margaret rode bouncing up as they prepared to leave. She grabbed the reins as if she were choking them, and indeed the horse tossed its head in discomfort more than once.

"Damn it, woman, do you want to strangle that animal?" Nigel ran to her and took the reins from her.

"You're hurt." Margaret jumped from the horse and ran to Nigel. She lifted his arm.

"And now you're hurting me," said Nigel.

"Hush, you old fool. I need to see what must be done." She untied some of the dressings and grew pale. "How could you let yourself get hurt?"

"They didn't ask my permission," grumbled Nigel.

Margaret nodded. "A few stitches, and your arm will mend like new. Good thing I'm a weaver's daughter."

Nigel jerked his arm from her. "Go see to your mistress and master. They are injured as well."

"Why didn't you say so sooner?" Margaret glared at him for a moment then ran to Elf. "My lady, your arm. Let me see it."

"No, Margaret. Payne first, then Nigel. My injury is small. We must get the men home."

Margaret glanced at her horse and groaned. "I suppose I shall have to climb aboard that beast again."

"Yes, but this time you'll just have to hang on. I'll lead the animal." Nigel still held the reins.

Margaret shook her head. "But your arm isn't strong enough. You'll just hurt yourself more."

"Do I have to prove my strength to you?" Nigel dropped the reins and grabbed Margaret with his good arm. He held her to his chest, then kissed her squarely on the lips. When he released her, Margaret stepped back with a dazed look on her face.

"Now I suppose I have to marry you," said Nigel.

"Humph. As if I would put up with a man like you." Margaret placed her fist on her hips.

"Oh do, please, Margaret," Payne said. "Nigel can be rather churlish if he doesn't get his way."

Margaret sighed. "I suppose I can marry the man for your sake, my lord."

Elf stared in surprise. She turned to Payne. "Did you know about this?"

"I had an idea." He looked entirely too pleased with himself. "Let's go home."

Chapter Thirty

They reached Candlewood while the sun still shone. The stones had just begun to glow as they rode in. Margaret ordered candles to the solar and a fire laid. Elf had no more than a fleeting glimpse at the servants who cheered her return, for Margaret impelled her and Payne upstairs. Margaret saw to the tending of their wounds, each in turn—Payne, then Nigel, then Elf, as her lady ordered. Then Elf and Payne fell asleep without the need of any coaxing or scolding from Margaret.

The following morning Elf woke early. She stirred in bed, not knowing for an instant where she was. Then she smiled. Payne was still asleep. She touched his brow. It was cool and dry, no sign of fever.

When she looked down, his eyes were open.

"Good morning, my love."

"My love?" Elf gazed into the golden depths of his eyes.

"Aye, my love, my life, my wife. I love you."

Elf's eyes welled up. "Do you?"

"Why do you doubt me?"

"I forced you to marry me."

"And as I told you, no one could force me to do anything I don't want to."

"And you got Candlewood in exchange—"

"Candlewood means nothing to me if you are not within its walls." Payne stroked her cheek. "I think I fell in love with you the night I kidnapped you, but I didn't know until you were gone."

"I think I fell in love with you the moment you rolled me in that stupid tapestry."

Payne raised his eyebrows.

"Perhaps after that."

Payne laughed. "I didn't think you were that forgiving."

"I was horrible to you." Elf hid her face in her hands.

"And I attacked you once."

Elf opened her mouth to protest, but Payne put his fingers over her lips. "Shh. It doesn't matter now. I love you." He placed his arms about her with care. "If we weren't so injured, I would show you just how much."

She giggled. "I do know you are not to move much until the wound has healed."

He lay back as if in pain. "I cannot tell which aches more, my heart or my stomach."

"Your stomach?"

"Aye. We ate nothing last eve, and I fear my stomach grieves for food."

Elf laughed and rose from the bed. "I'll fetch you something."

"What of your arm?" he asked with concern.

"It does no more than twinge." Elf threw on a robe and went to the door. She paused and walked back to the bed. She touched him as though to make sure he was real. "So much has happened in the past day. It's hard to fathom it all."

"Such is the aftermath of battle."

"Well, no more battles."

Payne raised an eyebrow. "With your nature and mine in the same house, battles are unavoidable."

Elf glared at him in mock outrage.

"And I look forward to every one." Despite his injury, he sat up and kissed her until she was breathless.

In the next week, Royce and his men accompanied Coxesbury to the king. A few weeks after that, the first snow fell. They celebrated Christmas and the Epiphany and the wedding of Nigel and Margaret. Margaret's two daughters came to live at the castle and the halls rang with their laughter and playing. The snow lay deep around the castle, but Candlewood wrapped its protective walls around them and the winter had no power in the comfort of the restored keep. And spring would come in a few weeks.

Elf had never spent a happier time in her life. Her arm had a thin red scar to remind her of the ordeal with Coxesbury, but she seldom thought about those disturbing days. She rubbed her belly, which now rounded to the smallest of mounds. In fact, she had little to complain about.

"Is our child kicking?" Payne stepped up behind her and wrapped his arms around her waist.

"No, not yet. It must be a wondrous feeling." Elf sighed.

"Don't fret. It will happen soon enough. I've even heard tell that women complain that a babe kicks too much and they cannot sleep." Payne smoothed her hair.

A knock at the door kept her from answering him.

"Yes?" said Payne.

Margaret entered the room. "You have a visitor."

They descended to the great hall.

"Royce." Payne crossed the hall and embraced his

brother. "It's good to see you."

Elf smiled to herself. Payne had become accustomed to having family in a short time. He wasn't ready to forgive his eldest brother, but he welcomed Royce with honest affection.

"What news of Coxesbury?" asked Payne.

"The king has stripped him of his lands and titles. Coxesbury won't trouble anyone for a long time." Royce reached into his pouch and retrieved a scroll of parchment. "Edward sent this to you."

Payne looked at the scroll. He broke the seal and read the words. For a moment he didn't move.

"Payne?" Elf touched his arm.

"The king has granted me Brookstone." Payne looked at her. "He has named me the Earl of Renfrey and asked that I swear allegiance to him. He shall come to visit in May."

Royce let out a whoop. "My brother, the earl. Do you mind if I tell William? I may be his brother and vassal, but I do like to goad him at times."

Nigel grinned. "Serves that overbearing, pompous—"

Payne just smiled as Royce jumped to his liege lord's defense.

Elf slid up beside her husband. "Are you sure you want a liege lord, even if it is the king?"

"Aye. It comes with holding land and having a home. Besides, I wouldn't have my son think me a mercenary without roots."

"Son? What if she's a daughter?"

"Then she'll be as beautiful as her mother."

"And as tall." Elf frowned.

"Tall?" Payne looked down at her with a grin. "You're not tall. Why do you think I call you Elf?"

Elf laughed. "Now that Brookstone is yours, I suppose the Black Knight need never ride again."

"She had better not. The Black Knight belongs to legends now. I expect the people will talk of the Black Knight for many years to come, embellishing the tale over the years."

"No doubt they'll believe the Black Knight was a man. Perhaps I should instruct our child—"

"You will not. No one would believe such tales of the wife of an earl, in any case."

Elf laughed again, then she gasped. Payne looked at her in concern. "Are you ill?"

"No." She felt the tiny little flutter in her belly again and knew this time it wasn't her hunger speaking. "I think the baby agrees with you."

About the Author

Gabriella Anderson lives in New Mexico with her husband, three daughters, two dogs, and assorted pets. When she's not writing romance, she teaches language arts and literature, plays volleyball, and tries to avoid cooking and cleaning. She holds a master's degree in teaching German and German Literature, and a bachelor's degree in Literature with a minor in European History. She's even appeared on *Jeopardy!* and *The Family Feud.* Fluent in English, German, and Hungarian, as well as knowing Latin, Gabriella loves the way language works, especially when she can use it to put a story on paper.

You can reach her at P.O. Box 20958, Albuquerque, NM, 87154-0958, or through her web site at www.gabianderson.com.

About the Author

MASHPEE PUBLIC LIBRARY
0 2000 0065749 0